1

And I knew when we kissed, I had found the love of my life.
And it wasn't a happy ending after all.
It was just the beginning for us.

I closed the book with a contented sigh as the Tube train pulled into my station. I hastily stuffed *When I Met You* by Jake Richards into my bag, jumped up and alighted, following the throng of my fellow commuters onto the long escalator, tapping my card at the barrier at the top, and walking out into the fresh air. I left Oxford Circus station and passed by the shops that were a dangerous temptation every day and headed down a side street towards my place of work.

It was a bright June morning and the sign of sunshine, coupled with the warm, fuzzy feeling I always got at the end of reading a romance novel, left me beaming as I walked to the office. My smile broadened further when my phone buzzed in my bag and I saw that it was my cousin Liv calling me.

'Morning, Liv,' I greeted her as I slowed my pace to chat. I

pushed back my wavy, auburn hair off my face, wishing I had
tied it up.

'Hey Freya, where are you?'

'Walking to work... I just finished the new Jake Richards book
on my way in.'

'Oh my God, how was it?' Liv asked eagerly. She not only was
a huge romance reader like me but we also made our living from
romance books. Liv was an author, and I worked for a literary
agent specialising in the genre.

My chunky ankle boots clip-clopped along the cobbles on
the road where the tall, white building that housed the Hayley
Harper Literary Agency stood. 'It was so swoony, Liv. When the
couple finally kiss and declare they love each other at the end, I
had tears in my eyes. It's gorgeous. I think it might be his best
book but who knows if it will ever see the light of day?'

'Hmm. I still can't believe he said what he said,' she agreed,
darkly.

I nodded even though she couldn't see me. 'It kind of broke
my heart a little bit,' I confessed. Jake Richards wrote the most
romantic stories and he had always been one of my favourite
authors.

But now, I wasn't so sure.

'His readers are all heartbroken; I wonder if Hayley can get
this book published,' Liv mused.

'Time will tell,' I said, pushing open the door to my office
building and heading towards the lifts that would take me up to
the fifth floor. I had been assistant to Hayley Harper for six
months after Liv recommended me for the position. Liv was one
of Hayley's clients, and her romance-writing career was off to a
great start, although she had a long way to go to reach Jake
Richards' heights. I was confident she would one day, though. I
loved her writing, and was so grateful that after trying to get a job

LONG STORY SHORT

VICTORIA WALTERS

Boldwood

First published in Great Britain in 2025 by Boldwood Books Ltd.

Cover Design by Alexandra Allden

Cover Images: Shutterstock

A CIP catalogue record for this book is available from the British Library.

Paperback ISBN 978-1-83518-980-1

Large Print ISBN 978-1-83518-979-5

Hardback ISBN 978-1-83518-978-8

Ebook ISBN 978-1-83518-981-8

Kindle ISBN 978-1-83518-982-5

Audio CD ISBN 978-1-83518-973-3

MP3 CD ISBN 978-1-83518-974-0

Digital audio download ISBN 978-1-83518-975-7

This book is printed on certified sustainable paper. Boldwood Books is dedicated to putting sustainability at the heart of our business. For more information please visit https://www.boldwoodbooks.com/about-us/sustainability/

Boldwood Books Ltd, 23 Bowerdean Street, London, SW6 3TN

www.boldwoodbooks.com

To my editor Emily Yau – thank you for all your support on this book!

in the publishing world for a year, she helped me get this one. And I was determined to become a literary agent myself one day.

'I just don't understand how someone who can write a story like this one seems to hate romance. This book is so full of heart.' I sighed wistfully. 'God, I love reading romance but sometimes, it does make me hate being single.'

'I'm sorry, Freya. But look, I felt the same way and then I got together with Aiden. It will happen for you too. You're too lovely not to find someone special.'

I smiled as I pushed the call lift button. 'You're biased as you're family but thank you. I can't help but wish it would happen sooner than later. This dry spell is going on a long time.'

'Dry spell?'

'I haven't had sex for three years.'

'Three years! But I thought you were on the dating apps?'

'I am but seriously, Liv, none of the men on there appear to have even heard the word "romance". They all want to start sexting or sending nudes or meeting up for "Netflix and chill" straight away. What happened to going on a date first? Buying a girl dinner? Or even giving a compliment that isn't "you look like someone I want to fuck"?' I continued ranting down the phone, the passion in my voice making it increase in volume as I waited for the lift.

'Ugh. That does sound horrible. Men should definitely read romance novels...'

'They really should. I have to go; the lift is here. And I need to start work.'

'Okay. I was just checking we're still on for drinks tonight?'

'Definitely. See you at the bar at seven.' I hung up, stowed my phone in my bag and when the lift doors opened, I stepped in and turned around.

And froze.

Because I was now face to face with a familiar figure who I hadn't realised must have been standing behind me waiting for the lift too. Our eyes met, then he stepped in beside me.

'Morning,' he said with a curt nod.

I couldn't speak. My face flushed as he turned around, giving me his back and pushed the button for the fifth floor. Humiliation and horror washed over me like I'd just stepped into one of those ice baths that athletes use. I couldn't believe that not only someone could have overheard me telling Liv all about my dry spell and how men have lost the romance gene lately, but I knew this person.

And it wasn't just anyone.

It was Jake Richards. Bestselling romance author.

It was as if I'd manifested him by talking about the man with Liv on the phone. Jake Richards had made me fall in love with romance novels but then disgraced himself by slagging off the genre. He was also our biggest client. Hayley, my boss, was his agent.

Fuck!

Staring at the tall, imposing man in front of me, wearing an expensive-looking grey suit, I wished I had the superpower of invisibility. But no such luck. I was very visible and I knew I had been speaking really loudly to Liv. So now Jake Richards probably knew I hadn't had sex for three years.

'Uh, morning,' I said, finally, realising I still hadn't answered him yet. I was so mortified; my voice came out high-pitched enough that it resembled a chipmunk.

The lift arrived at the fifth floor then and the doors swung open to show a glass sign declaring we'd arrived at the Hayley Harper Literary Agency.

Jake strode out of the lift without a backward glance at me. I watched him go, his long legs striding confidently across the office, and I marvelled at how imposing this guy was. He was also handsome. His dark hair had a few grey streaks in it that somehow made him look even more distinguished and he had designer stubble across his chin that must have taken him ages to style so perfectly. The heady, spicy scent of his aftershave lingered in the lift right along with me. I didn't want to get out. I half-wondered if I could go back down, call in sick and hide for the rest of the day, but our receptionist, Ellen, saw me then and waved happily.

With a resigned sigh, I stepped out of the lift and attempted to make my face look somewhat normal.

'Hiya! Jake Richards looked particularly scary this morning; I didn't even get a formal nod,' Ellen hissed as I passed by her desk.

'I think Hayley has called an emergency meeting with him so he's probably even more tense than usual,' I said, thinking she was right about him seeming scary. I was nervous when I first met him because I was such a big fan of his books, but those nerves had never gone away because he was so cool and composed all the time.

And I was, well, rarely either, if I was being completely honest.

'Not surprised after what happened,' Ellen said, shaking her head.

'I know, right? I'll see you at lunch,' I told her, walking on into our open-plan office, looking over as Hayley stepped out of her private office to greet Jake. She gave me a quick wave before disappearing in there with him and closing her door.

I headed to my desk and hoped that Jake had more things to worry about than my lack of a love life and would forget everything he might have heard by the lifts. I wanted to be my most professional self when dealing with him, but my rant this morning had completely obliterated any success I might have had so far at doing that.

Smoothing down my summer dress, I sat down at my desk and thought about Jake's latest book. I had begged Hayley to let me read it. I had genuinely loved it but I wasn't sure if it would, or should, be published. Three months ago, an article had circulated like wildfire after Jake was overheard talking about the fact he hated writing romance. He was quoted by the journalist as saying, 'My readers are stupid for believing in happy ever afters. But I'm happy to take their money anyway.' His fanbase had rightly been furious and his publishers were now being cagey about offering him a new contract. I knew Hayley was meeting him this morning to discuss how they could fix the fallout and get him a new book deal.

But did he deserve a new deal?

His words had stuck a knife into my heart, confirming what I'd said to Liv about modern men having seemingly lost the romance gene. It was like Jake Richards had destroyed all the happy ever afters he had written in one fell swoop. It had made me question whether happy ever after could ever exist in real life. If my favourite romance writer didn't actually believe in love then maybe I needed to give up on finding it for myself. And that was an incredibly depressing thought.

Hayley's office door opened then and she leaned out and called my name. 'Freya, can you come in for a sec please?'

I turned around and swallowed hard. 'Uh okay,' I called back, wishing I could refuse. I really didn't think I could look Jake Richards in the eyes right now. I prayed he hadn't told Hayley about what I'd said in the office. Surely, he wouldn't do that? I

really didn't want to have to find out but Hayley was waiting for me so I stood up, took a deep breath, and walked into her office.

As I closed the door behind me, I hoped that I wasn't about to be sacked from my dream job.

2

In Hayley's office, I took in my boss where she was sitting behind her desk. She looked like the tough cookie she was with her short, blonde hair, bright-blue glasses that made her eyes look even more startling blue, and today, she wore a sharp, dark suit. Hayley was in her forties and I aspired to be as successful as she was one day. Opposite her in a chair sat Jake, whose eyes turned towards the door as I walked in. I was too nervous to look back at him and so I kept my gaze on Hayley instead. I did wonder though what Jake thought of my summer dress and boots combination. The two of them looked so smart and business-like in front of me; I suddenly felt even younger than my twenty-five years.

'Freya, I have good news...' Hayley began. 'I want you to go to New York.'

'New York?' I repeated in shock.

She nodded. 'Yes, next week. I realise it's short notice but I have my sister's wedding and I tried to tell her I couldn't come but she used the words "never speak to me again".' Hayley rolled her eyes. I wasn't sure if she was joking or not. 'So, I need you to go instead. And what did you think of Jake's new book?' Her eyes left me and fixed on Jake. 'Freya read it over the weekend.'

'Oh.' Jake turned in his chair and I felt his eyes on me. 'Is that so?'

It took my brain a second to take in everything Hayley had just said. I was still stunned about her telling me I needed to go to New York, let alone asking me to tell Jake what I thought about his book. I felt under pressure from their gazes.

I swallowed hard and forced myself to focus on Jake's question. 'Y... yes,' I stuttered a little before finding a stronger voice. 'I thought it was beautiful. I honestly had tears in my eyes at the end.'

'There. See?' Hayley thumped the desk and I jumped a little. 'I told you it's one of your best books, Jake.'

I risked a peek at Jake and he was still looking at me.

'I'm glad it won you two over but we have no idea if my publishers will ever agree to bring it out,' he said finally, moving his gaze from me and onto Hayley. 'But you think this will work?'

'I do,' she replied briskly. 'I pulled in all my favours to get you into the conference and your publishers will see the romance community still want, no they still *need*, Jake Richards' books in their lives. So...' She turned back to me. 'You'll go to New York, Freya? I remember you said you've always wanted to go. I'll need you there for five days.'

I nodded eagerly. New York was definitely a bucket list city for me. I was convinced I'd watched every film or TV show set there, and read every book that used it as a location, so it was somewhere I'd always wanted to see for myself. Excitement pumped through my blood at the thought of it. And not only would this be a trip that work would be paying for; it was for five whole days! 'I would love to go.'

'It's a very overrated city,' Jake said, leaning back in his chair and folding his arms across his chest like he was bored with our conversation.

I decided to ignore that comment and not let him dampen my good mood. 'What do you need me to do there?' I asked then, thrilled Hayley's sister was getting married so she had to send me instead of going herself. I couldn't believe she'd almost cancelled going to her sister's wedding but then again, she was a self-confessed workaholic so it wasn't a huge surprise.

'I've managed to get Jake onto the programme of the Romance Readers Club's international conference. It's a chance to show readers and Jake's publishers that he still loves romance, that he will always be one of the genre's biggest players, and that the *article*...' she said, her voice bitter on the word, 'was incorrect. So, I need you to go with Jake and help us to do just that.'

My mouth fell open but no words came out. I would be going to New York with Jake? Suddenly, the trip didn't seem like the dream come true it had a few moments ago.

'I have told Hayley I'm unconvinced this will work,' Jake said then.

'Nonsense,' Hayley said, waving her hand dismissively. 'Of course it will work. You will charm everyone there and they will forget all about the article.'

I couldn't stop the snort that left my mouth. I tried to turn it into a cough but I'm not sure I pulled it off.

'Look, yes, things have been difficult the past few months since that bloody article went viral,' Hayley said, throwing me a warning glare. I didn't dare look at Jake. 'But this is why this trip *has* to happen. It's an opportunity to repair the damage from it and build Jake's reputation back up to where it was before, and secure a new book contract. You need to convince everyone you're still the king of romance, Jake. And Freya, you'll be there to logistically make sure it all runs smoothly, but also offer any advice along the way to get Jake's fans and publishers back on board. You both have got this.' She sounded so confident while my brain started to get foggy. 'And you can use the company credit card for everything, first class all the way...' she added, giving me a smile. 'Okay, Freya?'

I couldn't smile back. I shifted uncomfortably. 'I guess, if you can't go...' I said, but the enthusiasm had left my voice.

'Great, start organising everything. Make sure you liaise with Jake,' Hayley said. 'Call me if you need anything, Jake.'

'I will.' He got up as I walked to the door, and we left one after the other. As we walked away from Hayley's office, I felt my nerves increase and I turned towards my desk, Jake moving past me towards the exit.

'Freya.'

I paused in surprise at him addressing me directly, and looked back at him.

He looked down at me, our height difference almost as large as the ten-year age gap between us. 'You'll email me the details for the trip then?'

I was still a bit stunned about having to go on this trip.

'Yes?' Jake prodded when I stayed silent. He sighed in frustration, clearly indicating that I irritated him.

'Yes,' I said, nodding. 'I will organise it all, don't worry,' I added as confidently as I could manage.

'Hmm,' he replied. 'Well, at least the weather in New York looks good at the moment. It's supposed to be *dry* all week.'

Did I imagine that he emphasised the word 'dry'? Was it a warning he had overheard my conversation with Liv about my dry sex spell?

'See you,' he said before I could respond and carried on walking back towards the lifts.

A minute later, when Hayley came out of her office, I still hadn't moved from the spot where he left me.

'This has to go well, Freya. Jake's career is hanging in the balance. I hope you know how important this conference is to us all.'

I finally woke up from my shocked trance to frown at her. 'But does he even want a new contract?' I asked. 'That journalist heard him say that he hates writing romance books.' I couldn't even fathom why someone would hate writing them, especially someone who could write one as well as he could, but there we were.

Hayley shrugged. 'His books make us a lot of money. So, you need to do all you can to make sure we can keep that going, okay?'

'Okay,' I found myself saying because she was impossible to argue with. And what could I say anyway? *No, I can't go because Jake Richards knows how long it's been since I last had sex and how I think I'll never find anything close to the romance in the books he writes...*

Hayley eyed me. 'You want to be an agent yourself so why don't you view this trip as your audition, if you like?'

'What do you mean?'

'Prove to me you can handle more responsibility, make a success of this trip with Jake and we can talk when you get back about how we can move you from my assistant to being an agent,' Hayley said.

My heart leapt at the possibility of a promotion. I wasn't at all thrilled at having to work so closely on my own with Jake – I found it hard to communicate with him and I didn't understand why he had even said those things about romance books. But Hayley was offering me a chance to step up. A chance I was desperate for. 'Really?'

'Show me how much you want it, Freya.'

'You know I do. I will work really hard out there,' I said, determination to impress my boss setting in.

Hayley beamed at me. 'Right answer. And Jake is a pussycat. You tell him what to do and he will do it; he wants to fix this. He's fully on board. So, get everything booked and next week, you'll be on your way to New York. Kind of exciting, right?' She left me, sweeping back into her office, and I watched her go, wishing I could feel the excitement she was talking about.

Hayley thought that Jake was a pussycat?

If you could mistake a tiger for a pussycat.

I had no idea how I was going to even talk to Jake, let alone tell him what to do. Even though I had a big reason to try to do it now.

My dream trip felt like it had the potential to be more of a nightmare instead.

3

I was relieved that I'd already organised after-work drinks with Liv so I headed straight from the office to one of our favourite bars and after we'd grabbed a bottle of wine to share, we found a table by the window and I filled her in on Hayley's New York bombshell. As well as the fact Jake had been behind me when I had talked to her about my love life earlier.

Liv took a long gulp of wine before responding. 'Well, we don't for sure know that Jake overheard you...'

'He made a comment about the weather being dry in New York!'

She tried not to smile. 'If that was intentional, maybe he has more of a sense of humour than we thought.' She saw my glare. 'Sorry! But even if he did overhear, he's not going to tell Hayley. Your love life isn't any of their business. It has nothing to do with how well you do your job. Which is pretty damn well,' she added, confidently, tossing back her dark, shoulder-length hair.

'I hope you're right,' I said uneasily.

'And besides, he has more important things to worry about

than what you say in the office. He has to try to save his career, right?'

'That's a good point,' I agreed, feeling a tiny bit better. But then I sighed. 'I just wish it wasn't me that has to help him do it, you know?'

'There is one bit of good news, though: I'll be in New York too, remember?'

I looked across at her, my heart lifting. 'Oh, I forgot! Yes! You'll be at the conference too.' Liv's publisher had organised for her to be on a panel and meet readers there. It was a huge relief that there would be a friendly face around. 'That helps but seriously...' I leaned forward and eyed my cousin. 'How can I be with Jake Richards for five whole days on my own? He intimidates the hell out of me. I mean, why does he intimidate me so much?!'

'Because you love his books and he's easy on the eyes. Also, he has that whole moody creative guy thing going on... Don't tell Aiden I said that,' she said.

'Plus, he's ten years older than me and is so blooming confident,' I grumbled. I didn't feel anywhere near enough like a fully-fledged adult yet.

'I don't know,' Liv said. 'Maybe he's not as confident now as he used to be – these past few months can't have been easy. He might lose everything he's spent ten years building after what he was caught saying.'

'Maybe. I still wonder why he said those things. Just to look good in front of those crime authors?'

'Maybe you'll find out on this trip.'

I took a sip of wine. 'And then there's the question of why should I help save the career of a man who is completely ungrateful about it? If he hates romance, then readers should bloody hate him.'

'I'm as passionate about romance as you but I think Hayley is right. You need to think about yourself and your career. If she's seeing this trip as a chance for you to prove to her you can be an agent yourself one day, then you should go ahead and prove it to her,' Liv replied.

Worry hit me instantly. Could I prove it to her? 'What if I can't, though? Jake Richards not only broke my heart when he slagged off romance books, but half the romance community is boycotting his books now.'

'Well, that should make you feel far less intimidated by him,' Liv said firmly.

'What do you mean?'

'It's last chance saloon for his writing career so he should be on his knees begging you to help him. He should be intimidated by *you*. You are there to help him. You have the control here; he doesn't.'

'Wow. Maybe I should see it like that,' I mused. 'But I bet he can't believe Hayley has asked me to go with him. I'm ten years younger, inexperienced at this job, a nobody...'

'Then you'll just have to show him you are a somebody. Which you are! Like me.' She winked.

'So humble,' I told her but I smiled. Liv's cheerleading of me was helping to raise my confidence ever so slightly. 'You're right, though; this is for my career so I need to focus on that and how I can somehow turn the tide from everyone being against Jake Richards to being for him again – and not about what he thinks of me.'

'We do not care what he thinks of you,' Liv agreed, raising her wine glass. I clinked mine against hers in agreement. 'And to think we'll be going to New York finally, after all the times we've watched *Serendipity*.'

I smiled; it was one of our favourite Christmas films and was set in New York. We were a family who watched the same festive movies every year.

'And I'm staying in the hotel from it!'

'Oh my God, I need to book me and Jake in there too,' I said, my eyes lighting up.

Liv clapped her hands. 'Yes! It will be so much fun.'

'I've always wanted to see the city; I can't let being there with Jake take all the excitement away for me.'

'You can make this trip what you want, Freya; you always find the light in whatever you do.'

'Aw, Liv, that's so sweet.'

I was happy to be finally seeing the city I'd always wanted to visit – plus, the opportunity it could present for my career. I just wished it wasn't something I had to do with Jake Richards. Someone it felt like would just ignore all light instead of trying to find it.

After we'd finished the wine, I headed home to Clapham. I shared a tiny, messy flat with three people I'd found online and whom I rarely saw or interacted with. It was all I could afford right now and it made me want to stay out as much as possible or hide in my room. So, I headed straight there once I got in. I changed into my pjs and curled up on my bed, pulling my laptop open in front of me. Then I googled the article that had put Jake's career into crisis mode.

Readers are stupid for believing in happy ever afters. But I'm happy to take their money anyway.

His words still were a gut punch to my romantic heart.

There were thousands of angry comments on the page from fans of his books, shocked that he didn't believe in the romance he wrote about. I searched the other articles about it and looked at the various headlines.

Has Jake Richards Destroyed His Bestselling Writing Career?
  Why Write Romance If You Look Down On It?
  Romance Books Are So Unrealistic, Even Authors Writing Them Don't Believe In Them Any More.

I sighed when I saw that headline. Romance books were often treated like second-class citizens when it came to books being talked about in the press, Jake saying what he had about them had stoked that fire even more.

Then I went on Jake's Instagram account and found the apology post that Hayley had helped him to draft after the article caused such a furore.

I was misquoted in that article and have contacted my lawyers about it. I'm sorry if any reader of my books has been hurt by the comments in it. I will always love being part of the romance book community.

Scoffing out loud, I put my phone down and laid back against my pillows. I knew that statement was bullshit. Jake had admitted to Hayley that what the journalist had overheard had been correct so they couldn't contact lawyers but Hayley told him to lie. I hated that they had done that. It hadn't helped much, though. Readers had still unfollowed his social media accounts in droves and his publisher was so far refusing to commit to a new contract. Somehow, Hayley had got him into this romance conference and this trip was clearly make or break.

As I rolled over and got ready for sleep, I wondered what the real truth was. Why had Jake said those things? If he believed them, why did he even want to carry on writing romance books? Just for more money? There was a bitter taste in my mouth about having to help him pull the wool over romance readers' eyes, readers who somehow all felt like friends to me – and all to help my own career. It kind of felt like I was being just like Jake and Hayley. But it also seemed like I had no choice.

I had agreed to go to New York with Jake Richards. Talk about something I would have never believed while I was at university reading his books and dreaming of finding the kind of the love he wrote about. The way he had poured scorn on all of that had really hurt but if he and my boss could be selfish and only care about making more money out of romance readers, I needed to push that hurt away. I needed to be as cold about my own career.

Even if I had never been cold about anything or anyone in my life before. My mum had once told me she was worried that the world might chew me up and spit me out, and as I'd grown up, I'd tried to become tougher. Moving to London and getting this job had helped me stand firmer on my own two feet.

So, I just needed to push my feelings aside and not think about the fact that the person who had been my instruction manual for romance didn't believe in any of it. Otherwise, I was never going to get through this trip in one piece.

And if Hayley was using this trip to assess my future at the company and my ability to be an agent myself, I had to not wear my heart on my sleeve but be like Hayley and Jake and treat it all as business.

But when my eyes fell on my shelf of romance books, I knew that wasn't going to be at all easy to do.

4

The following week was spent frantically preparing for New York. With butterflies swirling in my stomach, I booked first-class plane tickets. I hadn't even travelled first class on a train before. When it came to a hotel, I copied Liv and booked us into The Waldorf Astoria, which had been used as a filming location in *Serendipity*. Why not tick off one of my life goals? I was trying to hold on to as much positivity about the trip as possible and staying there would surely make any difficult moments with Jake worth it. I booked two deluxe rooms next to one another with a view of the city and then arranged for a car to collect us from the airport. I then took myself to the shops and spent some of my pretty meagre salary on two new dresses. New York would be warm and after a few rubbish summers in London, I was missing a plentiful summer wardrobe. I made sure I didn't spend much though by getting them in Primark, along with a new pair of boots, a straw hat in case I left the conference centre, and a pair of heart-framed sunglasses.

Then my last day at work before we headed for New York

arrived, and Hayley called me into her office first thing so we could strategise for my five days in the city.

'Your main goal on this trip,' Hayley said as she paced around her office while I sat with a notebook on my lap to jot down her instructions, 'is to remind everyone that Jake Richards is the king of romance books. To make them forget that article ever came out. That readers love his books and are desperate for more. Our success metric is, of course, getting him a new book deal with his publishers,' she said, barking at me like she was an army sergeant.

I nodded along as that seemed to be all she required.

'Jake will be on two panels at the conference, plus he's doing a book reading and signing, and an interview with a romance book podcast,' Hayley continued. 'I'm most concerned about the signing and reader session as it's allotted just to him.'

'You're not sure if readers will turn up?'

Hayley sighed. 'Exactly. Will they boycott it or will they show up so they can accuse him about what he said? Or will his diehard fans still support him? It could go a number of ways. So, you'll need to really be ready for anything.'

I wrote down in the notebook, *be ready for anything* and tried not to panic about failing spectacularly, with Jake Richards sinking without a trace along with my career dreams.

'As you know, Liv is also there and her publisher will be looking after her, but make sure to check in with her just in case.' Hayley looked at me. 'Any questions?'

I bit back the urge to tell her I had nothing but questions. 'I have one...'

I wondered whether she would tell me the truth. I knew that logically, it shouldn't matter; this was my job and I needed to do it. But the word 'why' just kept on floating into my mind.

'If Jake truly hates romance and pities the people who love

them, then why has he agreed to this trip? It can't just be about money. I mean, he must be a millionaire...'

Hayley barked out a laugh. 'Not quite: I don't make *that* much commission out of him. But yes, he's had a lucrative career... and it's one that I want to keep on managing. All I know is, he's asked me to get him another book deal and that's what I'm going to do. Anything else, you'll have to ask him.'

I stared at her, knowing that would be impossible. There was no way we could have that kind of tête-à-tête on this trip.

As Hayley went on again about saving his reputation, I zoned out a little bit and drew a heart in the margin of my notebook. I wondered if what Jake cared more about than money was his reputation. He had gone from being the number-one romance author in the UK, maybe even the world, and that kind of fall from grace must have been hard to take. He had always seemed super confident to me, a man with a large ego, so maybe he wanted to get his power and status back.

'The only thing Jake has refused to do at the conference,' Hayley said, drawing me back from my thoughts, 'is to have his own stand on the final day. He said he didn't want to be in the room with everyone in the industry and all the conference attendees because he might be murdered.'

I snorted. 'He has a point, to be fair.'

Hayley gave me a warning look again. 'Perhaps, but I told him the welcome drinks on the evening you arrive are non-negotiable. Everyone at the conference will be there so I suggest you both go, take a tour of the room, make sure he's seen and is polite to anyone who matters then get him the hell out of there before there is a hint of murder.' She said this so matter-of-factly, I had no idea if she was joking or not. I didn't want to find out though so I underlined the note I had jotted down about leaving the welcome drinks ASAP.

The meeting with Hayley lasted most of the morning but thankfully, she then told me to go home so I could pack and get a good night's sleep ahead of my flight to New York in the morning.

When I got back to the flat, I opened up my suitcase on my bed and started to put my clothes into it. Nerves swirled around with excitement about the trip ahead. I grabbed toiletries from the bathroom and stared at what I had packed so far, hoping I wasn't forgetting anything important like my passport or something equally embarrassing. I needed to get off on the right foot with Jake Richards, so instead of letting him see how ruffled I was, I needed to act calm, cool and collected. I thought that maybe a mantra could help so I repeated those words over and over in my mind as I packed and hoped they would become true.

* * *

Spoiler alert: the mantra failed.

Calm, cool and collected. My arse.

First, the car I had ordered was half an hour late to pick me up. I made frantic phone calls and checked my emails with them and finally, the car company admitted my driver had set off late and was now stuck in traffic. Jake consequently arrived at the airport before me and sailed through check-in, sending me a curt message saying he'd meet me in the first-class lounge. So, we didn't get off to the best start there. When I finally got to Heathrow, there was a long check-in queue and then, of course, they wanted to look through my suitcase because I clearly looked so nervous and frantic, they thought I might be planning to do something dodgy.

When I finally got all checked in, I hurried to the lounge with my carry-on bag, red-faced, heart racing with a bead of sweat dripping down my back. As I walked through the lounge entrance, I missed the yellow 'caution wet floor' sign and hurried across the shiny floor in my three-inch boots, and slipped instantly. I let out a strangled yell akin to a cat if you stood on their tail then promptly fell down. My bag collapsed open beside me, its contents flying everywhere.

I lay on my back in a heap on the floor, wondering if I had died and gone to hell, when someone cleared their throat. I looked up in confusion into a pair of hazel-coloured eyes. 'Am I alive?' I asked, clutching my chest with my hand.

'You're talking so I would say yes,' the man replied, dryly. 'How about I help you up to make sure?'

'Oh, okay, yes, good idea,' I said, nodding. My whole body hurt along with the stabbing pain of intense humiliation. I was certain my face was the same shade as a lobster. A hand stretched out for mine and I grabbed it, clammy and sweaty, and let the man pull me up from the floor with easy strength.

Once I was back on my feet, I swayed for a moment but the hand holding mine steadied me. I shook my head to clear my confusion and then the man in front of me became clear. I dropped his hand instantly. 'Oh, it's you,' I said stupidly, as I realised it had been Jake Richards who had not only witnessed my epic fall, but who had had to help me get back up.

Awesome start to our trip.

'It's me,' he confirmed. I was unable to read his expression but he must have been pissed off. 'Shall we pick up your things?' He was wearing a suit, which felt kind of crazy for a long-haul flight, and his hair was as immaculate as ever along with his perfectly styled stubble. I must have looked completely chaotic to him in my knee-length, polka dot dress and cowboy boots, my auburn hair wild after leaving it to dry naturally. I felt it too.

'Oh.' I looked around at my belongings strewn across the floor and could only hope the pencil topped with a rubber penis that I had kept from a friend's hen do last year was not in Jake's eyeline.

'Here.' He held out my notebook with Hayley's instructions in and the aforementioned pen. 'Your favourite?' he asked, his mouth pursed as he handed them over.

'No! Oh my God...' I yelped and snatched the items from him then grabbed my bag, hastily stuffing them in. Jake edged backwards from me and I couldn't blame him wanting to make a swift escape if he could. Grumpily, I bent down and hurriedly collected my other things before he could see anything else embarrassing. Once the floor was clear, I turned around. 'I think I'll just go to the ladies,' I said, trying to sound dignified when I had proved I was anything but.

'I'll be over there with coffee,' Jake said, striding away with his usual confidence. I watched him go with dismay. My plan to start off with him having everything in hand had failed completely.

'Why am I incapable of not embarrassing myself in front of this man?' I muttered aloud as I shuffled off to the bathroom to try to compose myself. I had no idea how I'd ever turn around his opinion of me now. But I supposed when you hit rock bottom, the only way is up. So, maybe by the end of this trip, I could convince him that I was an actual functioning adult.

I walked into the loos and looked at my reflection, my hair standing in all directions, my face still red, my make-up sliding off it, my dress strap hanging down on one side, and the penis-shaped pencil sticking out of my bag, and decided that I had my work very much cut out for me.

5

When I returned from the bathroom mildly fresher looking after fixing my hair and make-up and blotting the sweat off my body, Jake was at a table in the corner. He looked the epitome of calm, sipping black coffee and reading a newspaper.

I took a deep breath and walked over to the refreshment area, and grabbed myself a coffee and a sandwich and then reluctantly went to join him. 'That could have been a meet-cute,' I blurted out as I slid into the chair opposite him.

His eyes left the newspaper and slid to me. 'I'm sorry?'

'Like in one of your books,' I said, inwardly telling myself to stop talking but I was somehow unable to. 'You know, a woman falls to the floor in front of you, then you help her up and then the two of you fall in...' I stumbled under his piercing gaze. I let out a nervous laugh when he said nothing, further mortification rolling over me. I waved my hand. 'Never mind. Let's just hope the rest of this trip is uneventful,' I said, hoping he couldn't see how red my face was again. I grabbed the coffee cup and took a long gulp even though it was too hot to enjoy doing so.

'Quite,' he replied coolly, going back to his newspaper like I was an irritating fly.

I leaned back in the chair and pulled out my phone, cringing at myself. So much for being less intimidated by Jake. Now I was back in front of him, I was worse than ever. It was like the more embarrassing I was, the more composed he became. It was bloody annoying. I kind of longed to see what would happen if that coolness cracked for a minute. I wondered if I would ever be able to witness it.

I sent Liv a panicked message, knowing her flight was a couple of hours later than ours.

> Yet again, I have made a fool of myself in front of Jake. How do I salvage the situation?

Liv replied instantly.

> Focus on the fact you are there to help save his career. He needs you. You have the upper hand! Enjoy first class, future literary agent...

I read her message twice then put my phone away, and cleared my throat. She was right. The key was focusing on the reason why we were here together and heading to New York, and not how much I had made a fool of myself in front of this man. I tried to adjust my face into an expression that would show how capable I was. Fake it until you make it and all that. 'So, should we discuss our strategy for this week?' I asked, straightening in a vain attempt to look as tall as him.

Jake sighed but put the newspaper down. 'Hayley sent me a long email yesterday all about it.'

I nodded. 'She copied me in. Our main goal is to get as much good publicity for you as possible. So, you need to be the perfect author for the next five days. Engaged, open, chatty and polite and above all, enthusiastic about not only your books but the other authors at the conference, and love stories in general. Also, do not mention *that* article. If anyone asks about it, Hayley advised—'

'To say I legally cannot discuss it,' Jake cut in. He looked at me. 'She told me you disapproved of our statement when the article came out.'

'She did?' I replied, startled. I had tried not to let her see how upset I had been about it all, but clearly she'd realised anyway. Jake was giving me a scrutinising gaze across the table and my nerves dialled up again. My mind went fuzzy as I looked back into his eyes. I had never met a man who could make you feel like he was looking into your soul like that before. It made me feel like I couldn't lie to him. I blinked but he was still watching me and the truth came tumbling out. 'Well...' I shifted uncomfortably in my chair. 'I supposed I would have handled it differently. I don't believe in lying like that and I think readers probably found your statement... impersonal.'

'So, how would you have handled it then?' he asked, raising an eyebrow. I couldn't tell if he was pissed off by what I had said or not. I knew that he was our client and I should be professional, but I also wanted to be honest like I always was. I had no idea if Jake would respect me more if I was, or even less than he did already.

'I think I would have accepted what I had said and been honest and admitted in the statement that I had said it. I would have asked my readers for their forgiveness, if that was what I wanted. I would maybe have explained why I had said those things in the first place.' Curiosity sat deeply in me about why someone who had a career in writing romance had suddenly slagged it off like he had done. Was he really so materialistic that he had written all his lovely books just for the money? Did he really not believe in love and romance at all?

After meeting Jake Richards, I had found it hard to believe he had written things that had made my heart swell, my knees weak and my cheeks blush. That he believed in happy ever afters. But I assumed that was because I was nothing to him. A lowly assistant he only saw in a business setting. That underneath the stone-cold exterior, he did have a romantic heart like mine. Then he made those comments and I thought maybe the exterior he showed was actually the real man after all, and that made me feel betrayed like his other readers. I wondered if he realised how personally we had all taken his comments.

Jake sat silently for a moment and I wasn't sure he was going to answer me then he opened his mouth to speak. He was cut off though as an announcement came on over the speaker, and we heard that our flight was now open for boarding.

'Shall we?' Jake said, getting up and gathering his things in one smooth motion. He started for the door and I was left scrambling to hurry after him, grabbing my croissant to eat on the way, feeling like he had been saved by the bell.

I followed Jake to the boarding queue and when our passes were checked, we walked onto the plane and headed for the front. I tried not to let my eyes widen too much when I saw first class for the first time in my life but it was really hard not to. Excitement replaced the earlier stress of the day. I couldn't believe I was travelling this way. I took in the separate pods and the amount of space, the leg room I'd have, the fancy TV screens and the freebies they had left out for everyone. My eyes fell on a pair of silky pyjamas folded ready for me in my pod. 'Oh my God, this is amazing,' I said breathily in wonder.

'Your first time?'

I jumped and turned to see Jake beside me, watching intently.

He hovered by the pod opposite mine. I had forgotten for a moment we would be side by side for the flight.

I flushed as I nodded. 'Yes,' I said, thinking he must have flown first class hundreds of times. But it wasn't like many people could afford it so I knew I shouldn't let his scrutiny embarrass me. This wasn't something to be nonchalant about. I had dreamed of being able to travel in style like this. 'And I'm going to enjoy the hell out of it,' I told both Jake and myself with a shrug. Then, I pulled out my phone to take a photo of my pod, ignoring the fact he was still watching me.

Afterwards, I sat down with a contented sigh. 'Oh yes,' I said, leaning back in the seat, which was approximately ten times more comfortable than economy ones.

'A drink to settle in?'

I jumped as a flight attendant peered around the pod at me, smiling widely. 'Oh, um...'

'How about champagne?'

'This is a work trip, though,' I confessed, biting my lip.

'What would your boss do?' he asked me.

'She'd order champagne,' a voice sailed over from across the aisle.

I jumped again and looked over at Jake, who had sat down in his pod opposite but was still watching me with interest. I raised an eyebrow at his encouragement, which was surprising, but I also knew he was right. Hayley Harper was the champagne queen so I nodded at the flight attendant. 'Yes, please, a glass of fizz would be lovely.'

'You too, sir?' he asked Jake, who thought about it for a moment.

'Why not? We need to mark Freya's first time here.'

'I am a first-class virgin,' I agreed as the flight attendant left to get our drinks.

I caught a small smile on Jake's lips while my hand flew to my mouth that I'd made another sex comment in front of him.

'Why do I keep embarrassing myself in front of you?' I groaned, then my cheeks began to turn pink again. I wouldn't need to use blusher at all when I was around Jake at this rate.

Jake looked at me for a moment then he ran a hand through his dark hair. My eyes tracked the motion involuntarily. 'I don't know, Freya, but if it makes you feel better, I embarrassed myself in front of thousands of people. I need this trip to work out because of it. So, don't worry about embarrassing yourself in front of me. You don't care what I think about you, do you?'

I stared at him. There he was, finally admitting to the fact that the article calling him out for slagging off romance books had been humiliating and damaging. And telling me that it didn't matter I had embarrassed myself in front of him. His last words echoed though my brain as the flight attendant returned with our glasses. Did I care what he thought about me? I wanted to say no. He had gone down in my estimation after finding out he might not care about the books he'd written that had made me so happy to read, and he was so much more reserved than I was but... I wanted to impress him still. It was annoying but I couldn't help it.

I liked that he had acknowledged he needed this trip to work out. That he needed my help. Finally, we were on a more level footing. If I ignored him being ten years older, a rich and famous author, and handsome as hell... Still, it was something and I grasped at it eagerly.

'Here's to making this trip the most successful one we possibly can,' I said, leaning across the aisle so he could hear me. I lifted up my glass of champagne.

Jake raised his glass too. 'Cheers to that.' He kept his eyes on mine as we both took a sip.

6

Once we took off towards New York, I was able to relax and enjoy first class as much as I wanted to because Jake put in ear buds and closed his pod curtain. I didn't have to worry about being cool any more or not embarrassing myself; I could do exactly what I wanted to. So, I had another glass of champagne, put on the sheet face mask I'd brought and changed into the pyjamas they'd given me, even though it was daytime. Then I feasted on fancy food they brought around and watched old episodes of *Sex and the City* to put myself fully in a NYC mood.

Halfway through the journey, I turned my seat into the bed and for the first time in my life, had a great sleep on a flight. When I woke up, more food came, including a slice of chocolate cake, and I watched a romcom while I ate it. When I changed back into clothes, excitement began to build again for my first sight of New York.

As the approach to the city began, Jake opened up his pod and gave me a nod as we all fastened our seatbelts. He looked remarkably refreshed, whereas my hair and make-up had definitely taken a turn for the worse but my worry about that completely disappeared as the plane began to descend. I looked out of my window and let out a gasp when I caught sight of New York below stretched out like an urban blanket, fluffy clouds like candyfloss breaking up the view. A thrill ran through my veins at the thought of finally being able to walk around the city I had been fascinated by in films, books and TV shows. I knew I wouldn't have as much time as I would like to explore as I needed to be focused on the conference, but I would make use of it as much as possible.

My gaze drifted over to Jake, who was scrolling on his phone, uninterested by the view, and our descent into New York. I supposed he had seen it many times before. I hoped that he wouldn't make me feel bad for being so excited to be here for the first time. I was determined to not let him. This was a dream come true for me and even if I was with someone who appeared to be world-weary, I sure as hell wasn't going to be like that.

* * *

Getting off the plane and through security and immigration was an *experience*.

The officer who spoke to me made me feel flustered and I stuttered through his questions about why I was in New York, my cheeks hot with a pool of sweat settling at the bottom of my back. When I finally made it through, I found Jake waiting for me, unruffled naturally by the process. I tried to not let him see how unsettling I had found it.

We walked through to collect our luggage. I always watched the conveyor belt nervously in case my suitcase had disappeared but thank God, mine was through quickly. It was, of course, me though, and I struggled to grab the handle and lift it off.

'Here.' Jake leaned around me and pulled it off easily, then grabbed his. 'You have a car waiting for us?'

I bristled as I pulled out my suitcase handle, tilted it and began walking. 'Of course I do,' I muttered, annoyed he was questioning my capabilities. I knew I had been functioning even less like a grown-up than usual in front of him but it was bloody annoying that he was worried I hadn't organised our trip properly. Then I remembered my car in London had arrived late despite all my double-checking and I crossed my fingers that wouldn't happen at this end too.

We weaved our way through the airport and finally breathed in New York air. I scanned the area nervously but with relief, I saw a man holding up a sign with my name on and headed towards him, Jake following behind me. It was a sleek, black car and the driver stowed our luggage while we climbed into the back. Then finally, we set off for the city itself.

'First time in New York too?' Jake asked after a few minutes of silent travel. I studied the view out of the window, angling myself away from him, and I didn't turn around to answer.

'Yes.'

'I thought so.'

I glanced over but he was looking out of the other window. I shook my head but didn't respond. So what if I hadn't travelled by first class or hadn't been to New York before? Did that make me even more inferior to him? I wasn't going to let his indifference bother me. I couldn't wait to see the city for myself even if he was immune to the delight of it all. I needed to make sure that Jake Richards didn't stop me from enjoying myself.

'I suppose you've been to New York loads?' I asked him.

He turned to look at me briefly. 'Many times.'

I shrugged. 'Well, maybe you can remember your first time and understand why I'm glad I'm here.'

Our eyes locked. 'I do remember my first time,' he said.

Was it only me whose mind went in a very different direction to New York? I knew that my dry spell was probably to blame but I had to look away.

'Well, then,' I muttered. Mercifully, Jake didn't respond.

As we approached the bridge, I forgot all about the man beside me and watched as the famous skyline came into view and we drove over the water, yellow taxis on either side. I smiled to see them. A quintessential New York moment. The skyscrapers seemed so familiar as we drove closer, like they had been there waiting for me all along. Our car took us right into the heart of Manhattan towards the Waldorf Astoria and my heart leaped to see the sights I had always wanted to. Whatever happened at the romance conference and with Jake, I was finally getting to see NYC first-hand and that made the stressful past few days worth it.

I snapped a photo of Times Square as we paused in traffic. When I put my phone down, I turned from the window and saw Jake's eyes, which had been on me, swivel quickly to the front. I supposed he found it amusing that I wanted to take so many pictures of my first time here. But I wanted to document as much as I could. This wasn't what I'd planned for my first trip here but I needed to make the most of it.

Our hotel came into view then; the car dropped us off with our bags and we walked in to the grand and bustling lobby.

'Why did you choose this hotel?' Jake asked as I turned towards the check-in desk.

'It's in one of my favourite films.'

'There are better hotels in the city,' he commented from behind me.

I rolled my eyes. Of course my choice of hotel wasn't good enough for him. I forced on a smile for the woman at the check-in desk and ignored him. We were given our room cards and directed to our floor, and when we stepped into a lift, we had to endure the excruciating silence as we rode up to where our rooms were.

When the doors finally opened and we stepped out, I turned to Jake. He had really got my back up with his comment in the lobby and if we were going to spend the next few days together, I knew I couldn't stay quiet about his attitude. I put a hand on my hip and looked up at him, wishing I was taller as it wasn't easy to give the man a dressing-down.

'The romance conference is in the hotel opposite so we have literally a few feet to go to get there,' I told him in the haughtiest tone I could manage. 'As you were a late addition to the line-up, there were no rooms left in that hotel so I thought it made the most sense to come here. And yes, I have always wanted to stay here after watching *Serendipity*. If it isn't up to your standards, maybe Hayley would be willing to let you move hotels but I think most people would be delighted to stay here.'

The air between us was thick as Jake stared back at me for a moment. Then he shrugged. 'It's fine, Freya; no need to put on your schoolteacher voice about it. Maybe you should lie down for a bit. It was a long journey. I'll see you at the welcome drinks.'

He strode off with his case, leaving me watching him go and wishing I'd been the one who had flounced off. With an irritated sigh, I followed at a slower pace, watching him go into his room and then I headed into mine, closing the door harder than was strictly necessary.

7

My hotel room was lovely with a huge, comfortable bed and a marbled bathroom. Best of all, I had a front-facing room so I could look down on the city below. The people and cars looked no bigger than ants from up here. I was surrounded by iconic buildings and my smile was wide at being able to see it all. I ignored Jake's patronising suggestion to lie down and hastily unpacked then had a shower and got changed, ready for the conference welcome drinks, which started at 7 p.m. I was tired from travelling but this was a mandatory event and I knew it was important for Jake to be seen there and to make the best first impression he possibly could.

I pulled on my long, silky, black dress that I kept for special occasions which I'd found at a designer outlet place and would never have been able to afford otherwise. It wasn't my typical style of short dresses and boots but it felt like this event called for something more elegant. The dress clung to my curves in the right places and when paired with my four-inch heels, I felt pretty good. I made my eyes look smoky and kept my hair down.

When I left my room, I hovered outside Jake's for a moment,

wishing we'd agreed to meet at the conference. Going to collect
him from his room gave the whole thing a slight date vibe even
though I knew it was ridiculous to think that. Jake was the last
man I'd ever go on a date with. But that thought made me feel
more nervous than I was already.

I finally summoned the courage to knock.

Seconds later, Jake opened up the door and we both took a
visible double take at one another.

Jake Richards in a dark suit was something to behold. My
eyes trailed against my will down from his dark hair, ever so
slightly still damp from his shower, to those hazel eyes you could
get lost in, down to his freshly styled facial hair. Then my gaze
travelled over his broad shoulders from which his dark jacket
hung perfectly, the top of his crisp white shirt, and down to his
long legs in his trousers and his polished shoes. He could have
played James Bond if I was being honest. I swallowed hard and
when I quickly moved my eyes back to his, his eyes were slightly
wide, as if I had just caught him doing the same trail down my
body. I highly doubted it but I was pleased he seemed momen-
tarily surprised to see me looking so dressed up.

'You look different,' he said then.

'Different?' I repeated. Not exactly a compliment and he still
looked a little bit shell-shocked. In a good or bad way? I couldn't
tell.

'It's not what you usually...' He cleared his throat. 'Never
mind. Shall we?'

I nodded vigorously because this moment had become really
awkward. 'Yes. Let's go.'

I turned towards the lifts and heard him close his room door
and follow me. 'So...' I said, switching my brain firmly away from
admiring his appearance to discussing why we were here. I tried
to ignore the smell of his aftershave as we stepped into the lift

together. It was sultry and appealing. 'I think the best plan of action is to say hello to the two women who have organised the conference, and thank them for including you when we get there. Then we should circle the room and have you talk to as many authors and industry people as possible so they all know you're here, and that you're excited and happy to be part of the conference. Be... charming,' I said, fixing him with a look.

'I can be charming,' he replied, looking down at me with a piercing gaze that caught me a little off guard. I quickly faced the front again. 'I can do that,' he added.

'Excellent,' I said brightly. 'And we should only stay for an hour and a half.'

'Okay. Why?'

'So you don't make any mistakes and so people can talk about you afterwards: about how you've changed, how good you look in that suit, blah blah blah...' I waved my hand as the lift reached the ground floor and the doors opened. I stepped out.

'You think I look good in this suit?'

I jumped a little bit as I felt how close Jake was to me, leaning down to ask me that in a low voice, his hand hovering just ever so slightly against the small of my back. And God, even though he barely touched me, I felt it like he had his whole palm on me. I strode ahead of him, unable to bear it, and hurried for the doors, hoping the noise in my throat came out as a dismissive snort and not an aroused moan because honestly, I was torn between both. 'You look smart, which is befitting the event,' I replied, reverting to my haughty voice again.

'Befitting? Are we back in the eighteenth century?'

A doorman opened the door and we stepped out into the early New York evening. I ignored the amusement in Jake's voice and glanced across the road at the tall hotel that we would spending a lot of time in this week. There was a lot of pressure on both of our shoulders and I wondered if it was making us interact in a way we never would have done ordinarily.

'We could just walk in the opposite direction,' Jake said then from beside me, his gaze fixed on the conference hotel too.

I glanced at him in surprise. 'Jake Richards is nervous? Is that even possible?'

He looked down at me. 'Don't you dare tell anyone,' he said, taking me by surprise yet again.

My brain felt kind of fuzzy, trying to work out his personality. One second, he was the cool, calm, all-business Jake, making me feel embarrassed for my excitement at being in New York, but the next, he was admitting he needed my help, telling me that he felt nervous and giving me a look that suggested he liked how I looked tonight.

Who was the real Jake and why did I so desperately want to figure him out?

I forced myself to focus on what we were here to do. 'We only need to stay for an hour and half. We can do it. You've got this,' I told him firmly. I took my phone out of my bag and set the timer, holding it up to show him before I stowed it away again. I nodded at the crossing telling us it was okay to 'walk'. 'Let's go.'

'Only an hour and a half. Okay then,' he agreed, stepping off the pavement too.

We walked across the road and through the door of the modern hotel, following the sign for the romance conference and heading towards the large banqueting room.

I glanced at Jake but suddenly, the shakiness he had displayed outside was gone as if it had never been there in the first place. I blinked as he strode into the room, transforming into the confident man I'd always seen in our encounters. I thought that I could learn something here, follow in his stride, so I pulled my shoulders back from their current tense position and walked in after Jake, hoping that we were capable of turning the opinion against him with only five days to do it.

Once inside the long, narrow room crowded with people, we were greeted by a long welcome table and we joined the queue there.

'Names,' a bored-sounding woman said without looking up from her clipboard.

'Freya Harrison and Jake Richards.'

There was a beat.

The woman looked up and her eyes narrowed as she took us in. I suddenly felt the gazes of the people around me. A conversation behind me ceased. Was it my imagination or did the air conditioning suddenly turn up, dropping the temperature in the room by a degree?

'Oh.' She paused. 'How... interesting,' she said, her voice dripping with sarcasm. 'Here.' She handed me two badges and looked down at her clipboard again dismissively.

'Come on,' I said to Jake, who was staring at the woman like he was desperate to say something, and based on our interactions so far, I knew that would turn out to be a very bad idea. 'Come on,' I said again, more firmly, putting my hand on his arm and steering him away from the queue and into the corner. 'We were prepared for this,' I hissed as quietly as I could manage, thrusting his name badge into his hand. I pinned mine on my dress, ruining the elegant vibes of the outfit instantly.

Jake looked around. 'Everyone is looking at me,' he hissed back as he pinned his badge on his jacket.

'So, let's give them something positive to talk about.' I peered behind him. 'I see the organisers. You ready to charm them?'

Jake met my gaze then and I was startled by the sudden eye contact. The room around us seemed to fade just a little bit like the blurring of a camera lens if you accidentally cover it with your fingertip.

'You're coming too?' he asked gruffly.

'I'm right by your side,' I said.

The corners of his lips turned upwards just ever so slightly for a second. If I had blinked, I would have missed it but I was unable to look away from him looking at me.

'Okay then.' His eyes left mine and I let out a puff of air as I followed him to find the Romance Readers Club organisers. The conference was run by two women – Nora Davis and Christine Adams – who had set up the online club ten years ago to unite romance lovers from around the world. This conference had become an annual event, which seemed to grow bigger and more popular each year.

'Nora, Christine, it's lovely to see you both again,' Jake said when we reached the two women. 'I'm delighted to be here.'

Nora, who I estimated to be in her fifties, was my height and wore a grey bob and a flattering trouser suit. She eyed Jake over her glass of champagne. 'Ah, Mr Richards, we were in two minds about having you here, but your agent is very persistent and to be honest, we knew it would generate publicity.' She flicked her hand and we both looked over to the side where a photographer was rapidly taking photos of this conversation. I tried to make sure I was smiling and didn't have a resting bitch face. 'Everyone is very interested to hear what *else* you have to say about romance books.'

The emphasis was clear. A prickle ran down my spine.

'I look forward to obliging you,' Jake replied in his politest voice. 'I think you'll be pleasantly surprised.' He turned to Christine, who was a blonde woman in her forties with funky, pink glasses framing her face. 'You two, Christine.'

'Well, we shall see, won't we?' Christine replied. She looked at me. 'Hayley was too nervous to come herself?'

'The opposite,' I replied, as calmly as I could manage. 'She has complete confidence in J— Mr Richards,' I said, correcting myself to copy how they had addressed him.

'And in Freya,' Jake added. 'Ladies, we mustn't keep you; I know you'll be in high demand this evening. I hope the conference will be as successful as it always is. Shall we get a glass of champagne ourselves, Freya?' He gestured and I shook off my rabbit-in-the-headlights expression and nodded. I quickly followed him and we headed straight to the refreshments table. I wondered how many glasses of champagne it would be polite to down because I felt like I needed several to get through the rest of the next hour and a half.

8

'There you are!'

Relief at seeing a friendly face flowed through me when an hour later, Liv burst through a group of people to pull me into a quick, tight hug. 'I've been looking for you for ages; this place is packed. You look stunning.'

I eyed her red dress. 'Right back at you!'

Liv leaned closer. 'How's it going so far with Jake?' she asked in a lower voice, glancing at Jake, who stood a couple of feet away talking to another author.

'A bumpy start, to be honest. He's had an icy reception,' I hissed back. 'But he's pretending not to notice and is ploughing on.' I checked my phone. 'It's actually time for us to head out. I didn't want him to be here for too long; we don't need people starting to talk about the article once they've had too much to drink. We need to build him back up slowly.'

'Well, if anyone can do it, you can,' Liv said. 'He's lucky to have you. I'll circulate for a bit. I need an early night after the journey, though, to be ready for the rest of the conference. Shall we have breakfast together tomorrow? I'll message you.'

'Let's do that,' I agreed, happy I wouldn't have to have an awkward breakfast with Jake. We had a quick goodbye hug then Liv faded back into the crowd and I tapped Jake on the shoulder. 'I'm sorry to interrupt but, Jake, you have that phone call to take...'

Jake's eyes found mine and he nodded. 'Oh yes, you're right, thank you for reminding me. If you'll excuse me,' he said to the author he had been speaking to then he followed me towards the exit. I felt eyes on us as we weaved through the room, as if we were a zoo exhibit or something, and I suddenly couldn't wait to escape the claustrophobic room and lie down on my hotel bed.

We had reached the door and my chest was sagging with relief when a man stepped smoothly in my path, forcing me to come to an abrupt halt. Jake paused beside me and out of the corner of my eye, I saw him tense.

'Fancy bumping into you here, Richards,' the man said, arching an eyebrow. His dark eyes swept over me then. 'And who is your lovely date?'

'This is Freya,' Jake said, sounding like he was speaking through gritted teeth. 'We work together.'

'How delightful.'

I regarded the man, who appeared to be Jake's age with fair hair, wearing a crisp, blue suit. I realised then he was familiar to me too. 'And you are?' I asked pointedly, even though I recognised him to be the very successful crime writer Davis Mulberry.

'I'm surprised to see you here,' Jake said then as Davis's eyes narrowed at me, clearly put out that I didn't know who he was. 'You know where you are, right?'

I was surprised he was here too. It was unusual for a romance conference to have authors who wrote other genres in attendance.

'I was invited to be on the panel discussing writing popular fiction; they thought they would experiment and have one panel that featured authors from all genres to get different perspectives, not just romance.' Davis shrugged 'Maybe they thought that would be beneficial for romance writers. You know, learn from the best and all that.'

I rolled my eyes as I saw Jake tense up further at Davis's very arrogant implication he was a better writer than Jake.

'I'm on that panel too,' Jake said with a panicked expression.

Davis grinned. 'Oh yes, I know, and that definitely was a big reason I agreed to do it. I'll see you there.' He grinned and swept past us like he'd just done a mic drop.

I raised my eyebrows, watching him go. Had he come all the way to this conference just because he knew it would piss Jake off? I looked back at him and saw that if that had been Davis's goal then it was definitely working.

'Fuck,' Jake said with a puff of exasperated air. 'I need to get out of here now.'

I nodded, sensing their interaction had caught people's attention and we definitely didn't want this to set us back so early on. 'Let's go.'

We hurried out of the door and out of the hotel, crossing the road to the Waldorf and walking towards the lifts, all in silence. Jake looked even more brooding than usual, his eyes smouldering, his shoulders stiff, his mouth set in a tight line. My heart was still racing from that encounter. It had been so awkward. Were Jake and Davis just author rivals? It had felt more personal than that somehow. I was so curious to know why they were such enemies and I was worried about how Davis being here might affect our plan to save Jake's career. That was going to be hard enough without someone trying to sabotage us.

The lift doors opened, we stepped in and then watched them close, side by side.

Finally, I couldn't take it any more. 'Davis Mulberry isn't one of your friends, then?' I enquired quietly.

'Definitely not,' he said firmly. 'I had no idea he was going to be on the same panel as me. Hayley didn't tell me.' His tone betrayed his anger.

'Why wouldn't she tell you?' I asked, surprised. Hayley was nothing if not a consummate professional.

'Because she knew I wouldn't have agreed to do it if she had,' he replied darkly.

'Oh.' I longed even more to know what was up between him and the crime author.

We reached our floor then and stepped out of the lift, walking to our neighbouring rooms.

'Do you want to back out of the panel?' I asked reluctantly as I paused by my door and watched him step past me towards his.

'Right now, I want to,' Jake said.

'Maybe that's why he's here, though: to wind you up,' I suggested, hoping he wasn't going to let Davis do just that.

'Oh, he lives for it,' Jake said bitterly. He turned and must have seen the anxious look on my face. He sighed. 'But no, I won't back out of the panel – I need to do it, I know that. And Davis has already almost ruined... everything. I can't let him ruin this too. Goodnight, Freya.' With those parting words, he let himself into his room, disappeared inside and shut the door.

I stood there for a second, confused, before walking into my own room. I discarded my bag and heels and flopped on the bed. What with the crazy journey here and that event, I was now exhausted. And more nervous than ever about the start of the conference in the morning. Because Jake was being watched by everyone, and now it seemed his rival could make things even more difficult. I grabbed my phone and sent an email to Hayley asking what was going on between Jake and Davis Mulberry because I needed to be prepared. Jake had two events tomorrow – the podcast interview and his panel with Davis. And I wasn't sure if we could make it through them in one piece.

After I sent the email, I got up to get ready for bed. I glanced at myself in the bathroom mirror as I went to take my make-up off and I couldn't help but allow myself a little smile as I remembered Jake taking in my dress, his eyes trailing down my body with a hint of approval in them. I bit my lip as I thought about how he looked in that suit. We had looked good walking in that room together. Not that we had been together, of course, but still.

My phone vibrated then and I checked the reply from Hayley, who kept her phone with her at all times and replied even from her bed.

Davis Mulberry was the author Jake was talking to when the journalist heard him slagging off romance books. They have been rivals for years, and I think Davis was winding him up about writing romance. I knew Jake would have turned down this trip knowing Davis was attending, so I kept it from him because this conference is his only shot at repairing the damage from that article. Just keep them at arm's length, Freya, and it'll be fine.

I read the email twice before sighing and putting my phone down. I had an uneasy feeling that Hayley had made a mistake in agreeing to Jake and Davis being on this panel together. And if it did end up going badly tomorrow, I'd have to pick up the pieces. I had no idea how to keep the two men at arm's length when they were due to spend an hour discussing books together.

Talk about being thrown in at the deep end.

* * *

After a restless sleep, I headed downstairs to meet Liv for breakfast. I messaged Jake and asked him to meet me before his podcast interview so we could strategise about what he was going to say. I was hoping that a strong coffee and some bacon would help fuel me for what was looking like a long and stressful day ahead.

I went to the buffet and filled up a plate then searched the room until I saw Liv, who waved. I smiled and went over, seeing that she wasn't alone but had been joined by fellow romance author Tessa Elliot.

'Hey, ladies,' I greeted, sitting down, feeling better for seeing the two friendly faces. Liv and Tessa had become friends through Liv's best friend Stevie, who was Tessa's publicist, and we had all hung out together a few times. Tessa was Liv's age, with high-lighted hair and while Liv and I both wore dresses this morning, she looked cool and comfy in jeans and a t-shirt.

'I went a bit crazy at the buffet,' I told them with a rueful smile.

'Is it even a hotel stay if you don't?' Liv quipped, gesturing to their similarly full plates.

'I think we'll need the energy,' Tessa said. 'It's a full-on itin-erary, isn't it? I always get nervous at things like this.'

Liv nodded. 'Me too but everyone here is on our side, right? We all love romance books.'

'They are definitely on your side,' I agreed as I took a long gulp of my coffee and then a big bite of toast. 'Unfortunately, I won't have the same luck. What with having to chaperone Jake Richards,' I said, unable to help myself from starting to go off on a rant again. 'I mean, I have no idea how anyone is going to react to him today; I've been running nightmarish scenarios through my head about it and Hayley just seems to think I'll be able to help him win everyone over but what if we're trying to do something that's impossible? And then yesterday, I found out he's on a panel with his author arch-enemy, which Hayley failed to mention in advance to either of us, and honestly, I have no idea if Jake can turn on enough charm to turn things around but both of our careers depend on it and...'

Liv cleared her throat loudly as Tessa waved her cutlery in the air and plastered on a bright smile. I looked confused at them, my words trailing off.

'Morning,' came a tight voice from behind my shoulder.

My cheeks immediately flushed as I looked up into Jake's eyes. There he was again, overhearing things that I really wished he wouldn't. When was I going to learn?

'I better go and get some coffee to help me turn on enough charm for today. Excuse me,' Jake said, looking away from me to Liv and Tessa, before striding off as quickly as he had appeared.

'Well, the day's got off to a great start,' I muttered when he'd left. 'Me and my big mouth.'

'You weren't saying anything that wasn't true,' Liv said consolingly. 'Your work is cut out for you.'

'I know but I was trying to make us into a team to get through this conference, and I think I've blown it,' I said, the hurt look on Jake's face haunting me.

'You can fix it,' Tessa said.

Liv nodded in agreement.

I picked up my coffee cup and drained it, hoping they were right.

9

I found Jake in the lounge area of the hotel, reading something on his phone. I paused before approaching, feeling nervous all over again to talk to him after what had happened at breakfast. I didn't think I'd ever had so many awkward interactions with a man before. To say I felt flustered was an understatement. If this was a man I was interested in, I would have run away by now as fast as my legs could carry me but Jake was stuck with me and I was stuck with him.

Pushing my shoulders back, I started off again and walked over, sitting down in the armchair opposite him, a small table dividing us. 'I'm sorry you overheard what I said,' I greeted without preamble. 'But you know this conference is make or break.'

Jake's eyes lifted from his phone to meet mine. 'You don't need to keep reminding me,' he said coolly.

I raised an eyebrow. 'Oh, so it's my fault that we are on damage control?' I snapped, my patience evaporating. What was it about this man that got my back up so much?

He slouched in his chair like he didn't have a care in the

world, which only annoyed me further. 'You've made it very clear, Freya: this is all my fault. So, instead of telling me again how useless I am, how about we go over what to say in this podcast so we can do "damage control" as you so eloquently put it?' He went heavy on the sarcasm, even going as far as to do air quotes around the words 'damage control'.

I exhaled long and hard then looked away from those piercing eyes of his. 'Yes, let's do that,' I replied finally, with false brightness. I pulled out my phone. 'They sent over the questions in advance so I'll ask, you answer and we can tweak as needed…'

We focused on the interview and avoided eye contact as we went through it and I made suggestions if I thought Jake could answer a question better. We were sticking to Hayley's lines about the unfortunate article and when Jake repeated the same answer about lawyers looking into it, I couldn't stop a small sigh from escaping my lips as I listened to him parroting what she had told him to say.

'What was that?'

'Huh?' I looked up from my phone in surprise at Jake's sudden, demanding tone. He was staring across at me again, and the eye contact was startling. 'What was what?'

'That sigh. You have something to say, Freya, so why not go ahead and say it?'

There he went again, making me want to say things I shouldn't. The challenge in his eyes was impossible to back down from, however. 'Fine. You know I think the statement you gave after the article first surfaced was a mistake, so yes, sticking to it now feels wrong. I think you could be more honest about it all and then maybe your readers would understand and your publisher would see that signing you again is a safe bet. Right now, I don't think they know what to do.'

'Hayley feels differently,' Jake replied.

I nodded. 'Yes. But Hayley is looking at it as your agent, not as a romance reader like me. I love romance; I was a huge fan of your books and it hurt to hear that you don't care about them, that you only write them to make money. Also, that you don't believe in the happy ever afters that you create,' I said, everything coming out in a rush.

Jake raised an eyebrow. 'Do you *really* believe in happy ever afters?'

'I hope they exist. I haven't had the kind of romance in my life like you write about, no,' I admitted. 'But I hope it is out there, and that I will find it one day. I know all your readers feel that way too. So, hearing that you don't believe in what you've written made us all not believe in it either,' I told him honestly.

He looked a little bit stunned and I saw a flicker of something behind his eyes – regret, or guilt maybe? Then he shook his head. 'I don't know if I believe in love either.'

'Then why are you here?' I asked, exasperated. I threw my hands up in the air. 'Why come all the way to New York to try to save your career if you don't believe in it? If you don't care? Why carry on writing romance? Even if you need the money, you could write something else. Crime like Davis Mulberry, for instance,' I said, unable to help myself from bringing up his arch-enemy.

I thought about younger me curled up in bed falling in love with one of Jake's stories and how heartbroken she would be to hear that author talking like he was right now. That girl longed for love and the woman I was now still longed for it. Jake was making me feel like I was right when I told Liv romance seemed to be dead. What if I never found it? My heart ached suddenly.

'I don't know, Freya. I really don't know.' He stood up abruptly. 'Thank you for going through the interview. I'll stick with what Hayley told me to say. Even if you don't agree with it, she's my agent and your boss, and I trust her opinion.'

I flinched at the implication my opinion was worth nothing. 'Because a romance reader doesn't know what they're talking about,' I said with a sigh. He had sneered at his readers and that article had shown us all what he really thought about us. I had clung to the hope that wasn't true but Jake was confirming it right now. He didn't think I was right because I loved romance, and he clearly hated it. Talk about confirming the idea you should never meet your idols. Disappointment flowed through my veins.

I stood up too. 'Okay, Jake, let's go to the meeting and then we'll do this interview the way that you and Hayley see fit. I just hope it works out for you.'

I got up and turned around, walking towards the exit.

* * *

'So, it's been six months since your last book was published and no one has heard anything about you releasing a new book. Do you have one on the way?'

I was relieved that the hotel meeting room had the air conditioning on an extra cold setting because the interview with Jake was not going well, and I would have been sweating from the pressure otherwise.

The interviewer, a woman around my age called Eva, had been batting questions at Jake for twenty minutes, all in a tone that suggested she really didn't like him, and she was continually veering away from the questions we had been sent in advance, but only slightly so we couldn't complain but the phrasing was much more negative. I wasn't sure what to do. Would Hayley have called a halt to the whole thing if she was here? Jake was steadfastly avoiding my eyes so I had no idea if he wanted me to do anything or not so I sat on the edge of my uncomfortably hard chair, across the room from them, my body torn between flight or fight.

'I have written a new book,' Jake replied carefully. 'And I can't wait to tell you all about it soon.'

'Okay,' Eva said doubtfully. She leaned forward and my panic dialled up a notch. 'We've reached my final question. I know my listeners are keen to understand what happened earlier this year. We all know the furore that followed the article that was published by Kelly Shepperd but in case anyone missed it, here are the highlights. Shepperd said she overheard you at a party talking with other authors saying, and I quote, that "readers are stupid for believing in happy ever afters. But I'm happy to take their money anyway." You then claimed this was a fabrication by the journalist and were taking legal action. However, nothing seems to have come of that. So, my question is: do you really expect us to believe that you didn't actually say that?'

I stood up immediately. 'That was not on your list of questions,' I called over. 'You said you were going to ask how Jake felt about the article, not questioning whether it was true or not,' I added desperately because I knew Jake had decided not to be honest about it all, and I didn't want him to have to tell more lies on top of lies.

'I stand by the statement I made,' Jake said, standing up. 'As that was your last question, I think we can call time on this interview now, yes?'

Eva sighed. 'Yes, fine, that's it.' She leaned forward to shut off her recording equipment. 'But honestly, the whole romance community doesn't believe that article was made up. Why would a respected journalist randomly do that? Kelly Shepperd hasn't retracted it and your lawyers haven't managed to prove it was a lie, right? I think you *did* say it. So, if you don't think writing or reading romance is worthwhile, I'm wondering why people should ever read one of your books again?'

Jake stared at her furiously. I hastily walked over, hoping I could steer him out of the room before he said anything to make this interview even worse than it already was. But he responded before I got a chance to. 'I don't care if they do or don't,' Jake flung at her. Then, he marched out.

My heart sunk.

Eva watched him go then looked at me, gesturing to her equipment. 'I hadn't turned it off. I recorded that. And I think his readers deserve to hear that's what Jake Richards really thinks about them.'

'Please don't include that!'

'I'm sorry, but Jake brought this all on himself.'

The problem was, I couldn't really argue with her.

10

Jake disappeared for two hours after the interview and didn't answer my calls, so I sent him a message to warn him the last part had been recorded. Hayley emailed me then to ask how the interview had gone but I was too nervous to tell her. I hoped I'd be able to temper sending news of that disaster with a good report from the author panel at least, so I held off replying to her for now.

I walked into the room the panel was going to be held in. There was a table set up with five spaces for the authors and the chair of the panel. The rest of the room had chairs placed in rows and people were starting to fill them, a buzz of chatter humming around me. I was relieved to see Liv and Tessa in the back row, waving at me to join them.

'I didn't think you'd come to this,' I said as I sat down next to Liv.

'We wanted to support you and see how Jake went down in the room,' Liv replied. 'Plus, we always need writing tips ourselves,' she added with a laugh.

I leaned in closer to them. 'The podcast interview didn't go very well so I'm worried...'

I trailed off as the panel host, the romance conference organiser Christine came in, followed by Davis Mulberry, two other authors I vaguely recognised, and then Jake. He strode in but I wondered if anyone else in the room could see the way his eyes roamed over the packed-out audience or the way he stumbled a little on the way to his seat, or if it was just me.

As Jake sat down, his gaze fell on me. I tried to give him a reassuring nod.

He kept his eyes on mine for a few seconds, his face expressionless. I longed to know what he was thinking. He had to be nervous especially after the difficult podcast interview. I was too. I really hoped this would go better otherwise I had no idea what Hayley was going to say. When Jake looked away from me, I felt strangely disappointed. I was intimidated by that piercing gaze of his but it also felt weirdly special to be on the receiving end of it.

'Welcome everyone,' Christine said then into the microphone in front of her and the room immediately hushed. 'Today's panel is going to discuss how to write popular fiction. This year, we thought we would try something new and see if it works. We wondered how writing differs between the genres and if authors from different genres might have ideas when it comes to writing that could help if you're trying to write a romance book. Do you approach writing popular fiction differently depending on the genre? Can we get any tips from other genres? Let's find out, shall we?' she asked enthusiastically. There was a scattering of applause and then Christine introduced the authors on the panel.

'So, I'm delighted that with us today we have: Davis Mulberry, who writes crime; Kate Asher, who writes historical fiction; Taylor Baker, who writes fantasy; and Jake Richards, who writes romance,' she continued, gesturing to each of the authors who nodded and waved to the room in turn. 'My first question for the panel is: how did you choose the genre you write in and how did you get started in it?'

The talk started off smoothly; Jake answered the questions well and the authors were in agreement about lots of things, but when Christine asked about how hard they found writing their books, things started to take a turn.

It began with Davis Mulberry taking the lead in answering the question. 'Well, I think when it comes to writing crime, plot is so key; you really do need to prepare and plan and come up with twists and turns... and in fantasy, you have all the world building, don't you? And historical novels need a lot of research, of course, for accuracy. I've always thought that romance...' he turned to look down at Jake pointedly, '...is probably the easiest of these genres to write, don't you think? Less focus on plot or setting or research, just two characters who you know are going to end up together from the start.' He leaned back in his chair with a definite sneer on his face.

'What a dick,' Liv said under her breath as Tessa beside her tutted. I gave them both a sympathetic look, knowing how much time and effort they put into their romance novels, then I looked back at Jake nervously to see how he was going to react. There was no doubt that Mulberry was deliberately trying to push Jake's buttons with that statement. I wondered again if the only reason he had agreed to be on this panel was to wind Jake up. He was doing a good job if so.

Jake shook his head. 'Romance, as everyone in this room probably knows, has often lacked the respect given to other genres, but I'm disappointed to hear it coming from a fellow writer. We should all support one another. And I can assure you, writing any book is difficult, no matter the genre. I'd argue romance is actually one of the hardest because you mainly have two characters who you are taking on a journey to a happy ending and you need to keep the reader hooked, desperate to know if they really will make it or not. Making a book easy to read is damn hard to write.'

Both Liv and Tessa cheered this sentiment and most of the room clapped and nodded in argument. I allowed myself a smile in Jake's direction. That was a really good answer, and the room was on his side.

Davis Mulberry leaned forward again to respond. 'And yet when we spoke last year, you seemed to agree with me that writing romance was easy. In fact, you indicated you felt writing it was beneath your talents. You dismissed the whole genre as being predictable. And told me that readers are ridiculous for believing in happy ever afters. Didn't you, Richards?'

You could have heard a pin drop then. The whole room went deadly silent as the two men locked eyes down the table at one another.

'Maybe we should—' Christine began, clearly sensing the panel was getting away from her.

Jake cut in, though. 'I did say that but...'

There were multiple gasps as Jake finally confessed that he had slagged off romance books. Jake stopped speaking as he turned to the room, realising what he'd just let slip.

'And yet you've been denying it for months,' Davis continued, looking triumphant. I longed to wipe that smug look off his face. 'So, there we go: your favourite romance author hates romance books,' he added to the room.

'Jesus, Davis,' Taylor said to him, shaking her head.

'I think we should...' Christine began again but Jake stood abruptly and left the room in two long strides, avoiding my eyes the whole way.

I sank back into my chair. 'Well, today just got worse, if that was even possible,' I said to Liv and Tessa as the room broke into outraged conversations about what had just happened, Christine failing to quieten everyone down again. 'How the hell is Jake going to save his career now? And what is Hayley going to say? I've completely failed.'

'This is on Jake, not you,' Liv hissed across at me.

Tessa nodded. 'Definitely, Freya, you're trying to help him.'

'Well, it's not working. I better try to find him and talk to Hayley...'

'Good luck,' Liv said as I got up and made my own hasty exit from the room.

I stepped out into the hotel corridor and looked both ways, catching sight of Jake heading for a side exit so I hurried after him. I went through the door, finding myself on the street. It was a hot day, I hadn't realised in the air-conditioned hotel, and the sun beat down on me as I walked over to where Jake stood on the corner, his hands in his pockets, pacing back and forth. Ahead of him, the city was in full flow and I could see yellow taxis and people in their work outfits walking with pace, but just a few feet away from it all, we stood in a quiet pocket together.

Jake glanced at me as I approached. He shook his head. 'I know I fucked up today.'

I paused two feet away from him. 'You got too angry in the interview earlier and made a rash comment.'

'You think?' he groaned.

'Then you let Mulberry goad you.'

'He was the reason I said all that about my books in the first place! He's always goading me. Always trying to find out shit about me, winding me up, making me feel less than because he writes crime and I write romance. He's been the same since we were at Cambridge together...'

'Why did you let him make you admit the article was true?' I was confused. Jake had been so adamant about sticking to the 'it was all a lie' line, and then in one second, he'd confessed all.

'Because I feel so crap about it, and he knows it. He was thrilled when we realised a journalist had overheard us. He has wanted to bring me down for years. Hated the fact I've sold more books than him. Well, he got his wish, right? I'll never have one published again now!'

My phone buzzed urgently in my bag. Reluctantly, I pulled my phone out. 'Hayley is calling me.'

We looked at one another.

'Put it on speakerphone,' he replied with a heavy sigh, as if realising there was no point in avoiding her. I nodded. I knew he was right.

'Hi, Hayley,' I answered.

'Social media is going crazy. Why the fuck did Jake just tell the world that journalist was right about what she overheard in his panel? And Eva posted online to say Jake acted like he doesn't care about readers during her interview. She's going to share the podcast episode soon. What did Jake say to her?' she ranted down the phone, making us both flinch. 'How could you let this happen, Freya? You think you could ever be an agent yourself now, after this? Jake will never be able to get another book deal. I knew I shouldn't have come to my sister's wedding instead of New York!'

I stared at Jake in panic, my eyes wide. Hayley was furious. I'd never heard her as bad as this. And I had nothing to say to her, no excuse to make. We had fucked it up.

Was my career over before it had even begun?

Jake reached out, took my phone out of my hand and deftly hit the end call button.

11

'What the hell, Jake?' I said, staring in horror as he handed my phone back to me. 'You just hung up on Hayley!' I wasn't sure anyone had ever done that before; she was too formidable to even consider it for most people surely.

'We'll say it was a bad connection,' he replied. 'You really wanted to stand and listen to more of that?'

'Well, no... but what do we do now?'

'I don't know but I appreciate you using "we".' Jake shifted his feet. 'Freya, I'm sorry. I didn't realise you wanted to be an agent, that this trip... that Hayley considered it some kind of test for you to prove yourself to her.' He sighed. 'I told her it was a long shot that we'd be able to get my career back on track. I've made people really angry, and now I've made it even worse. I'm sorry that will affect you. Hayley really shouldn't have put it all on you for it to work out.'

'I think that's the most you've ever said to me,' I blurted out, shocked by his gracious apology.

'Maybe you talk enough for us both,' he replied with a small smirk.

I sighed. 'I was always told off for being a chatterbox at school, that's true. And sometimes, I do say inappropriate things...' I trailed off, thinking how he overheard me telling Liv about my sex life. I wondered if he remembered that. I certainly was never going to ask. 'I embarrass myself a lot. Particularly in front of you.'

'This time, it was me who did that,' he replied ruefully. We actually smiled at one another. 'What now?'

'We have the evening party. Maybe we can use that to repair some of the damage, and tomorrow, there's your reader session... You know what I think, though? I think you need to be honest. And tell everyone why you said those things. I saw your face back in that room,' I said, looking up at him and returning his piercing gaze. 'You were nervous to start with. And when Davis Mulberry said what he said, you were angry and hurt. I don't believe you'd have spent years writing romance novels that have made me swoon if you didn't enjoy doing it.' I took a breath, talking so fast that even I needed to pause for a moment. 'So, why did you say those things about romance?' I continued as Jake watched me. 'It can't have been just to shut Davis up or you would admit that. There is another reason. And you don't have to tell me, but I think if you don't share it, then Hayley might be right about you not getting another book deal. And yes, you could self-publish but you've turned even your biggest fans against you now so would they even want to read it? The question then is – are you willing to tell the truth?'

Jake sighed. 'I don't think I can, Freya.'

Disappointment made my chest sag. 'Then I think it might all be over.'

And I knew it wouldn't just be over for him, but for me too. Hayley wasn't going to keep me on as her assistant after this and no one else would want me working with authors. My dream felt the furthest away it ever had done. 'Maybe I'll see you at the party. We might as well drown our sorrows while we're still here...' I left him then, walking away and feeling his eyes on my back.

I guessed my original impression of him had been right.

There wasn't any heart underneath that cool exterior of his after all.

* * *

I sent Hayley an email when I got back to my room to say our call had had a bad connection and I was sorry that I'd failed her. I said I would try to repair things but I knew it was unlikely that was possible. All I could do was hope for a miracle before I had to fly home and face her again. She didn't reply and I knew that was a sign that she had no faith the damage could be undone. I was in no mood to party but it would be a chance to see what the conference was saying about what happened during the panel and if I was honest, I badly needed some alcohol. So, I got ready for the evening drinks.

After throwing on one of my favourite summer dresses, I considered putting on my sandals but I just felt like being comfortable, so I reached for my cowboy boots and left my hair loose over my shoulders. I walked out of my hotel, went into the conference hotel and edged into the event suite.

It was packed out for the drinks' night. I had messaged Liv and she told me she was by the floor-to-ceiling windows so I picked up a glass of sparkling wine from a server and went to find her.

'There you are.' Liv moved away from the three women she was talking to who I didn't recognise, and gave me a quick hug. 'Are you okay?'

'Not really. Hayley is furious about what happened, and I think she might actually fire me over it.'

Liv grimaced. 'God, I hope not. Can I do anything?'

I shook my head. 'Unless Jake works out a way to fix what happened... no one can do anything.' I looked around the room nervously. 'I suppose everyone is talking about it?' I saw her hesitate. 'I need to know, Liv.'

She nodded. 'Yes. It's all anyone wants to talk about. We all thought it was unlikely that a journalist would make up that quote but him confirming it... I heard a group of readers talking about having a Jake Richards book-burning ceremony.'

'Blimey.' I shuddered at the thought.

'I definitely didn't make it up.'

Liv and I both turned in surprise to find a tall woman in a stunning green dress beside us. She smiled. 'I'm Kelly Shepperd.'

I eyed the journalist responsible for telling the world what Jake had said about writing romance books. Liv and I introduced ourselves to her, and we all shook hands.

'Ah yes, Hayley Harper, trying to make everyone believe I would fabricate an article. Every word I wrote was true.'

'We know,' I said with a sigh. 'And everyone knows it now too.'

'Everyone is talking about the panel he was on earlier with Davis Mulberry. He always let that guy wind him up.'

'I know, but why?' I wondered aloud, taking a long gulp of my drink.

'They went to university together. Always been rivals, so I gather. But I think there may be something more personal behind it all. After I overheard him talking to Davis, I told Jake I was going to publish an article about it. I asked if he wanted to put his side over in it, but he said no.'

I stared at her. 'Why not?'

Kelly shrugged. 'All I know is Jake didn't stop me writing that article. He didn't want to explain himself or refute it. I always felt like there was something else he didn't want the world to find out about so let me tell them what he'd said to Mulberry instead.'

'But what you overheard might have ruined his career for good,' Liv said, eyebrows raised. 'What could have been that important to keep hidden?'

I was just as surprised as Liv sounded. It seemed like Jake had let Kelly publish that article because he was trying to hide something else. He had risked everything to protect something, or someone.

But what?

12

An hour passed but there was still no sign of Jake at the party. I was on my third glass of sparkling wine, and feeling slightly light-headed. I went for a bathroom break and when I returned, I couldn't find Liv where I'd left her talking with Tessa.

As I searched the room for them, I was accosted by someone I really didn't want to have to talk to.

Davis Mulberry blocked my path. He wore an expensive-looking suit and held a glass of sparkling wine too. 'Looking for a new job after today, Freya?' He chuckled at what I assumed he thought was a good joke.

My eyes narrowed. No wonder Jake was wound up by this guy. He just oozed arrogance. 'Why are you so obsessed with Jake?' I fired back, the wine having loosened my tongue much more than it normally would. I knew I should just walk away but it had been a very long day.

Davis scoffed. 'I think it's the other way round. He's always felt embarrassed by the fact he writes romance books. As he should be. It's not very manly, is it? I mean, would you be impressed if you were chatted up by a man who admitted he writes soppy crap like that?'

'Soppy crap?' I repeated, anger rising inside me at his attitude. Over his shoulder, I caught sight of Jake then, walking through the room. His eyes met mine, then he saw Davis and he stopped walking. It took me a second to look back at Davis, Jake's gaze having the usual effect: like he was looking right into my soul or something. It almost made me forget what was happening for a moment. 'Romance books are not soppy crap. Jake's books are beautiful. I, however, have never read one of yours,' I told him shortly.

Davis moved a bit closer to me and leaned down. 'I can give you a signed copy of mine and convert you to the darker side of books and...' his eyes dropped to the neckline of my dress. 'The darker side of life,' he added, his tone suddenly low so only I could hear. 'I think you'd enjoy it. Don't you?'

'I don't think Freya would enjoy *anything* you have to offer.'

Turning, I saw Jake suddenly appear beside me, his tone sharp, stepping so close that Davis took an instinctive step away from me.

'Isn't that up to Freya to decide?' Davis pointed out, glaring at Jake.

I rolled my eyes. 'Looks like you two don't need me for this conversation,' I said, turning away and setting off again to find Liv and Tessa. The last thing I needed right now was to be stuck in between Jake and Davis, and their pistols at dawn or penis-measuring competition or whatever the hell it was they were doing.

'Freya!' A hand reached out and touched my arm.

With a sigh, I paused and looked at Jake, who had hurried after me. 'I don't want to be some pawn in your rivalry with Davis. Leave me out of it.'

I looked at his hand on my arm and he quickly dropped it. It was the second time he'd deliberately touched me after helping me up off the floor at the airport, and I hated that I was counting the times.

'You're not; I just didn't like how he was being with you,' Jake said, moving closer to let someone pass by him. The room was crowded but when I returned his gaze, I wasn't aware of anyone else but him.

'What do you mean?' I asked. He was looking at me like he wasn't taking notice of anyone else either. It was intimidating but in a different way to how he had intimidated me in the past. This was more... disconcerting. Because I liked being his sole focus right now. And that was a startling thought.

'He was coming on to you.'

'With a crap line about showing me the darker side of life. And after slagging off romance books! Not really the best chat-up line I've ever heard,' I scoffed.

'Have you had quite a few then?' Jake asked, one of his eyebrows raised.

'Not many good ones,' I admitted.

'So, Mulberry's charms weren't working on you then?'

'Why do you care?' I asked in surprise.

Jake leaned just a little bit closer. 'If you're still trying to find a romantic man, he isn't it. I'm looking out for you.'

'Well, I didn't ask you to,' I said shortly. 'I can handle myself. And why do you think I'm looking for a romantic man? Oh yeah, you heard me...' I trailed off as my conversation on the phone flashed back to me. I felt my cheeks heat up because I knew what else he had heard then – the fact I hadn't had sex for three years.

He shook his head. 'I wasn't trying to eavesdrop but you have a loud voice when you're passionate about something, and the fact that men had been disappointing you for years was clearly a

passionate topic for you. Davis Mulberry will use you. That's
what he does with women.'

'And what do you do with women?' I fired back, still annoyed
he felt he had to step in between me and that twat of a crime
author in the first place. As if I would be interested in Davis
Mulberry! And I was also annoyed with myself for talking about
my personal life somewhere it could be overheard. It was yet
another power imbalance between me and Jake, and I hated it. I
wished he would feel intimidated by me, just once.

'I'd treat you better than you'd ever been treated before.'

My breath caught in my throat as we stared at one another.
Was that a general or a specific promise from him? He used the
words 'I' and 'you'... I couldn't believe he was flirting with me
though so I stepped back in case I got carried away. 'I'll take your
word for it. No need to warn me off Davis Mulberry; he's the last
man I would want. Like you said, and overheard, I'm waiting for
something special.'

'Aren't we all?' he replied softly. 'I'm glad to hear you don't
need warning off Mulberry; he's not worth your time.'

'I wish you'd realised that before you let him rile you up at
the panel today,' I said, desperate to stop talking about romance
with Jake Richards. It was too crazy. We needed to focus on work.
Our relationship was strictly business only.

Jake sighed. 'I really am sorry about that, Freya. And I have
been thinking about what you said. But opening up isn't easy,
is it?'

'No, it isn't,' I agreed. 'You're not who I thought you were after
reading your books,' I blurted out.

'What do you mean?'

'I suppose I thought that a man who could write so beauti-
fully about love and romance and matters of the heart would be
someone who *could* open their own heart. When I first met you, I

thought maybe you were putting on a professional front, that there was more going on beneath this cool guy vibe...' I waved my hand in front of him, '...you have going on. But I think I was wrong all along.' I turned to go but then my loosened tongue just wouldn't stop. 'Oh, I met Kelly Shepperd. I think she's the only one pleased about the panel today: that you'd finally admitted she didn't make it all up. But she told me that maybe you let her publish that article because you didn't want something else to come out. So, I don't know now, Jake. Do you hate romance or not? Like who is Jake Richards really? And will I ever get to meet him?' My words hung in the air as we looked at one another.

'I don't know, Freya,' Jake said after a moment. 'Would you want to meet him?' he added hesitantly.

'I know you don't care about my opinion, but yes, I would like to meet him. Maybe I'd like him a whole lot more than the man you've shown me so far.'

Jake visibly flinched at my words but I couldn't believe he really cared what I thought. Perhaps he did still care about his career though and might listen to me for that reason. I caught sight of Liv then and was relieved I could escape from this intense conversation. 'I need to speak to my cousin; I'll see you later,' I told him in a rush.

I fled again, but I could feel Jake's eyes on my back the whole way. And I couldn't decide if I enjoyed his gaze or wanted to hide from it.

All I knew was, I was only able to finally relax again once he wasn't looking at me any more.

13

I woke up with a groan when the alarm on my phone went off the next morning. I'd had a restless night's sleep. I kept replaying my conversation with Jake at the party over and over again. Once the sparkling-wine buzz had subsided, I was embarrassed by how direct I'd been with Jake, and how the way he had looked at me had made me feel. Because I was sure he hadn't been trying to flirt; he'd only wanted to make sure I avoided his arch-enemy. Plus, I knew for certain now that Jake had overheard everything I said to Liv about my lack of both a romantic and sex life. *Ugh*.

It would have been a perfect morning-after moment to hide under the covers and wish that the rest of the world would disappear. But if I had any hope of working in publishing again, I couldn't do that. I needed to try to stop Hayley from sacking me and the only way to do that was to face Jake again. We had his reader event later in the day and I had no idea if we'd be able to turn the tide against him.

So, I crawled out of my hotel bed and shuffled into the bathroom, wincing when I caught sight of myself in the row of mirrors above the sink. My skin was pale, my under-eyes puffy, and my hair was wild from my tossing and turning during the night. I also hadn't taken last night's make-up off properly so eyeliner was smudged across my face.

I supposed that at least I wouldn't need to fend off any more bad chat-up lines looking like this. Pulling off my pjs, I turned the shower onto the hottest setting and stepped under the water, hoping it would turn me from a zombie back into something resembling a human being. I stayed in there until my skin pruned, then I got ready for the day, pulling on a knee-length, floral dress with tan ankle boots. I tied my hair up into a ponytail and did my make-up then headed downstairs for breakfast. I knew Liv and Tessa had had breakfast really early as they had events of their own to do so after hitting the buffet, I carried my plate and coffee and looked for a free table.

'Freya.'

I turned to see Jake at a table for two having his breakfast. He gestured to the empty chair. I knew this could be awkward but we still had to get through the rest of the conference together so I nodded, took a breath and went over to sit opposite him.

'Morning,' I said as I put my plate and coffee down, and sank into the spare chair.

'Sleep at all?' he asked, watching as I took a long sip of my coffee, hoping it would give me some much-needed energy. Jake looked a little bit tired too, but his hair and stubble were perfect as usual. He wore a crisp, blue shirt and a pair of navy trousers. It was a pleasant view across the table, that was for sure.

'Not great, no.'

'Same. Listen, we have a few hours before the reader session; why don't we leave this hotel and see a bit of New York? I feel like we both could do with it.'

I raised an eyebrow. 'You want to hang out with me?'

'You haven't seen anything of the city yet and I know how

excited you were to be in New York; it doesn't feel right. Let's get out of here.'

I hesitated. 'But I thought you were over New York...' I remembered Jake's reaction to me looking out of the yellow cab from the airport. I was desperate to get out of hotels and see New York but not with someone who wasn't interested in enjoying it with me. Plus, things felt so awkward between us after him warning me about Davis last night and me questioning who Jake was as a person. And whether I would like him or not.

'Well, seeing it through your eyes might change my mind. I know the place like the back of my hand; I'm happy to take you anywhere you want to go.' He saw me still hesitating. 'Come on, what have you got to lose?' he challenged me, a twinkle in his eyes that surprised me.

I couldn't deny the fact that I liked it when I saw a different side of Jake than I had the past six months before this trip. A side that wasn't the cold, reserved, business-like author but a glimpse of who he was as a man. A side that I wondered whether I could really like. A side that was at odds with him lying about Kelly Shepperd's article. Which side was the true Jake? Maybe getting out of a work setting with him might help me to find out. So, I nodded finally.

'Well, okay then, if you're sure.'

He smiled. 'Where in New York have you most wanted to go?'

A thrill ran through me at being able to go somewhere that I had wanted to see. 'I'd love to go to the library,' I said eagerly. I remembered seeing it in *Sex and the City*, and I had vowed to see it for myself one day.

'Of course. Finished your breakfast?'

I drained the remaining drops of my coffee. 'All done.'

'Need to get anything from your room or to get changed?'

'You think I need to change?' I looked down at my dress and boots, knowing Jake was dressed far smarter than me.

'Of course not. That outfit is... you,' Jake replied. 'Let's go.'

It took me a second to get up and follow him after he said that. I thought about how startled he was when I was dressed up on the first night here. I assumed it was because he didn't think I was capable of looking elegant but he had just been surprised because it hadn't seemed like... me.

Which was exactly the way I had felt.

* * *

Stepping out of the hotel lobby, we both blinked as the New York morning sunshine beamed down upon us. The quiet, air-conditioned, dimly lit hotel was replaced by cars honking, people walking past with iced coffees, a bright-blue sky and warmth on our skin.

'Let's walk so you can see as much as possible on the way,' Jake suggested, setting off at a brisk pace. He soon slowed down when he realised I was struggling to keep up with his much longer limbs, though. 'When I first came here, I was overwhelmed,' he said as I glanced around, drinking the energy all around me in. I looked up at the skyscrapers leaning in on us, the sun sparkling off the shiny glass, feeling incredibly insignificant in comparison. 'It's so frantic and so big but once you adjust, you fit right in.'

'But you didn't seem happy to be back here,' I pointed out.

Jake shook his head. 'I'm sorry. I could see how excited you were. And on the plane.'

'You found it irritating,' I said with a shrug because I wasn't bothered, I was excited and didn't want to have to pretend otherwise.

'No,' he snapped at me. I raised an eyebrow and he spoke again in a calmer tone. 'It just made me realise how I've changed these past few months.' He coughed and ran a hand through his hair. 'It's been a difficult time.'

'Because of the article?' I asked curiously.

'Because of what led up to me telling Davis those things.' He looked across at me. 'I suppose I've always kept business apart from my personal life, but you met me at a very low point. I was angry and bitter and hurt. I guess I leaned even more into shutting everyone and everything out.'

Curiosity flooded through my veins again. What had happened in his personal life that lead to Kelly publishing that article? Why was it better for the world to believe that he hated romance books? 'Why do you find it so hard to open up?' I asked him.

'Maybe no one has encouraged me to do so before. You find it easy to open up, don't you?'

I was startled by the direct question. I looked over at him and our eyes met. He asked the question confidently, like he already knew me. I half liked it, and was half annoyed that I didn't feel the same about him. 'I suppose I have always worn my heart on my sleeve. But I'm trying harder not to... Since I moved to London and got this job with Hayley, I want to be more professional, less honest and stop saying exactly what I think.'

'Why would you want to do that?'

'Shouldn't I be more professional?'

'Well, maybe talking about your romantic life in the office isn't always the best idea.' He grinned at me and I shook my head, my cheeks turning a little bit pink remembering what he had overheard that day. 'But you should be yourself, okay?'

Jake seemed sincere but it was strange that he was so keen for me to stay honest when he hadn't been. 'Maybe you should take your own advice,' I suggested.

'Maybe you'll rub off on me,' he replied, a smile playing on his lips.

I shook my head but I couldn't help smiling back. He was still infuriatingly silent on why he said those things about romance but he had admitted it all had made him different these past few months. And it made me want to find out who the true Jake was even more.

14

We passed by the edge of Central Park then, and I looked at the buildings towering above green trees. 'I've seen this city so much in films or read about it books; I've always wanted to be here. It feels somehow so familiar. Like I already know it,' I said as we walked side by side.

'I get that. I loved watching *Home Alone 2* growing up, and I did feel like a kid again when I saw all the locations they use,' Jake admitted.

'Woah,' I said, holding up a hand. 'Not only was Jake Richards a kid who enjoyed movies but you got excited as a grown-up seeing locations from your favourite scenes. I may need a moment to recover from the shock of this confession.'

Jake rolled his eyes but he did grin at me. 'Ha ha ha,' he replied sarcastically, making me laugh.

We carried on walking until Jake pointed ahead. 'Here we are.' He gestured to the New York Public Library so I followed him up the steps of the grand building and through the door framed by white pillars. Inside, there was an immediate hush and coolness accompanied by a feeling we were somewhere important.

Jake was surprisingly a great tour guide, showing me his favourite exhibits and not rushing me as we looked at everything, but when we walked into the Rose Main Reading Room, we both lapsed into silence. I looked up at the ceiling I had always wanted to see in awe. The sky murals surrounded by ornate gilding were beautiful. Books lined the walls and in the middle were reading benches. Chandeliers hung above them. It was stunning.

'Imagine being able to just come here and read all day,' I whispered to Jake, my eyes still above us.

'Is it as beautiful as you hoped?'

'It's incredible,' I replied, looking away to find him watching me. I smiled. 'I'm so happy I got to see it.'

'I'm happy I got to show it to you.'

'A book lover's dream, right?'

Jake smiled back. 'It really is. When I first came here, I wondered if anyone had sat here reading one of my books. I hoped so.'

'I bet they have.' I pulled out my phone to snap a few photos. I knew they were unlikely to do this stunning room justice but it would be nice to be able to look back and remember standing right here.

'I've been thinking about the reader session later, and what you said last night,' Jake said then.

'Was I terrible?' I asked nervously.

'You're never terrible, Freya. More honest than most of the people I know maybe. But that's a good thing.'

'Wow, is that a compliment?' I blurted out.

'I am capable of making them, sometimes.' Jake looked at me seriously. Once again, I couldn't take my eyes off his. 'What you said, it got to me. I have always believed in romance. When I started to write, it just was natural for me to write love stories. I loved it.'

'What changed then?' I asked, relieved to hear that it hadn't all been a lie. That he *had* believed in love. That his books weren't a cynical marketing ploy, but he was compelled to write them. God, the thought of a man loving love so much that he decided to write romance books... it was pretty hot.

I really needed to stop thinking impure thoughts!

'I found out something that made me wonder if it was all just... bullshit.'

'Oh?' I wondered what could change your opinion about love so dramatically. 'A bad date?' I asked flippantly, thinking about my own romance crisis.

'I wish,' he said, bitterness tingeing the words. He shook his head. 'No, it was something that I didn't want to share with... anyone. And so when I was at that event with Davis, and he sensed I was in a bad mood, he started to wind me up, digging, pushing my buttons, getting me to tell him what was going on. Well, you've seen what he's like.'

'Yes,' I said with a sigh. 'So, you told him a different story to the truth?' I asked him.

'Exactly. I threw him off, pretending the issue was work. And not anything personal. I said that I hated writing my books, that I thought my readers were pathetic. Like you said last night, Davis always riles me up no matter how hard I try to ignore him. I used to be able to shrug off what he said to me, but that night, I let him get to me. Because I felt pathetic for believing in love and happy ever afters, for writing love stories and perpetuating the myth to the world. I felt cynical and angry and... hurt. And I took it out on my readers.'

'That was honest,' I said when Jake finished his long explanation. He had actually opened up to me. It felt good that he trusted me to do that. But he was still keeping a lot to himself. 'But was that really preferable to telling him the actual truth?' I dared to ask, wishing Jake would be completely honest with me. And the world too. Right now though, I just wanted to hear the truth myself.

'I thought so at the time. And maybe I still do.' Jake checked the time on his phone. 'Fancy some fresh air? We could take the long way back to the hotel before the reader session. And I could use another coffee.'

'Sure,' I said, my mind whirring from what he had told me.

We left the library and emerged back into sunshine. We started walking, stopping off at a coffee shop to pick up a take-away coffee each. I drank in the sights and sounds of the city, feeling it humming through my body, enjoying being here. Jake was quiet on the way back and our earlier conversation looped in my head like a song you can't stop listening to.

As we walked down Fifth Avenue, I checked my phone. Eva had shared the podcast episode featuring her interview with Jake. I told Jake who sighed but didn't say anything. Looking online, I could see people noting how he didn't seem to care about his books or readers anymore. It was hard to read so I put my phone away. I had to ask Jake the question that was burning inside of me. 'Is it really that bad? What happened that made you feel like romance is bullshit?' I asked.

Jake let out a sigh. He took a while to respond, and I wondered if he wasn't going to, but then he sipped his coffee and started to speak. 'It's private. But it's also almost... humiliating. *Because* I write romance. And the reason why I was inspired to start writing it in the first place.' He reached out and touched my arm. Like his few touches since we left London, I felt it every-where. I hastily sucked in a steadying breath. He let go and I felt a twinge of disappointment. 'I have never been good at sharing myself. That's why I like writing novels. I can hide behind my characters and their stories, and keep my own story to myself. And the people I'm close to.'

I nodded. 'I can see that.' His cool, reserved personality made more sense to me now. He had been keeping part of himself hidden at work. Knowing that made him far less intimidating. Like when you pull back the curtain and see the wizard. 'Sometimes though, you need to let people in, and allow them to see the real you. If you ever were going to do it, now is the time. If you want to keep writing romance. But I suppose if you've stopped believing in it then maybe you don't.'

'Do you think I should keep writing it?' Jake asked.

'Of course I do! Your books make me happy, and I'm far from the only one. There is so much darkness in the world, we need all the light we can get. If I had a bad day, curling up with one of your stories instantly made it better. Made me feel better. And after what you overheard me saying to Liv, you know that I'm not sure if I'll ever find love like it exists in romance stories but they make me want to, they give me hope that it is out there, and it makes me not want to settle for anything that's less than that.'

'You should never settle,' Jake said fiercely.

We looked at one another. I was surprised, he looked serious.

'I still want to hope that it does exist. And help others hope it does too, but I don't know if I can,' he added.

The conference hotel appeared in our eyeline then. It was almost time for Jake to face his readers. I had no idea how this was going to go.

'Everyone knows you did say those things about romance,' I reminded him. 'So, if you want to save your career, you need to acknowledge it, to say something to help readers believe that you don't look down on them for enjoying your books.'

'I do want to save it.'

'Just for the money?' I asked, really hoping that wasn't the case.

'No. For the reasons you said you enjoyed reading them. I like making people happy, I like giving them hope, I like that reading my books might make them feel better about life and love, that they can escape it all in one of my stories...' He trailed off as we reached the door of the hotel.

I smiled. 'I like that you like that. You've been more honest with me today then you ever have; why not continue with that?' I asked as we walked inside the hotel together.

Jake didn't answer and I had no idea if I had convinced him.

15

Jake's reader session was taking place in a meeting room. One of the conference administrators welcomed Jake and me into the large space, which was set up with two chairs behind a table, a poster behind with a picture of Jake and his books. The plan was for Jake to read from his last published book then meet readers.

The last time Jake had done an event like this, there had been over a hundred people who had turned up but, after the panel incident, and the fact social media and the conference were abuzz with Jake admitting that the article about him had been true all along, neither of us were sure what the turnout would be.

The admin person left us alone in the room, the only sound coming from the air conditioning as we sat behind the desk to wait for readers to come in. I could smell Jake's spicy aftershave, and it was a little bit distracting.

'What's the time?' Jake asked, thankfully shaking me out of my trance.

'Fifteen minutes until it's supposed to start,' I replied after checking my phone to find no reply from Hayley yet. I had no doubt she was still furious with us both. It felt like my future in publishing hung in the balance, along with Jake's career. But I felt powerless. Jake was unsure about whether he wanted to tell the truth about why he said what he had about romance books, and I certainly couldn't force him to. I was annoyed but when I glanced across at Jake, his worried look told me he did really care. It was so confusing.

Jake looked at the open door. 'I would have thought people would be coming in by now.'

'They will,' I said, but my eyes followed his to the door, a heavy feeling growing in the pit of my stomach. I had been so focused on how we could salvage Jake's good name, I hadn't thought about a scenario when we wouldn't be given the opportunity to actually do so.

'I don't know, Freya. I think I might have ruined it all. Now they know that article was true, would anyone want to read a romance book from me again?'

I bit my lip, hating that things were going so badly. Was it really all lost? Then an idea popped into my head. 'You could do a shout-out on social media? Ask your readers to come here today so you can explain why you said what you did about romance books. Ask them to give you a second chance. If that's what you want.'

'I don't know,' Jake said, shifting in his chair nervously.

'As you say, you've confessed that article was true. You need to say something at this point. You can't keep saying what Hayley told you to. If you want readers to want to read any more books from you,' I said, as encouragingly as possible. 'We could film a quick video and then post it online. See if we can get readers in here to listen to you.'

Jake thought for a moment. Then he nodded. 'Okay, I'll make a video and see if we can get some people in here.'

Hope lifted my heart that he was finally going to take my

advice and be honest with everyone. I pulled out my phone. 'Right then.' I opened up the camera, training it onto to Jake beside me. 'Tell everyone why they should come in here. Let's get you an audience.'

Jake took a deep breath then gestured for me to go ahead.

I counted him in and then he took a breath and faced the camera. 'Hi, everyone. I am about to start my reader session in room 10B. I understand that after the panel I took part in yesterday, there will be a lot of you who may have come to this session that have changed your minds. I can't blame you but I'm asking you to please come and join me. I want to explain what happened with that article that I know you all are aware of. I respect my readers with all my heart, and I want to be honest with you all. I hope you will give me a second chance.'

I stopped filming once he had finished speaking. 'That was great.' I quickly uploaded the video to Jake's social media, tagging the conference and everyone I could think of who might share it, including Hayley. I hoped she would at least see how much we were trying to make things right.

'Let's hope it brings some people in. And I can work out the right thing to say.'

'Just be yourself,' I advised. 'Be honest.' I felt like a broken record telling him that but he seemed to be really struggling with it. I had no idea what had caused such a big issue in his personal life that it had led to him putting his career in jeopardy, but I could see he really did care and seemed to want to fix things. I hoped if he cared enough about his career then he would finally open up.

It seemed like a long time before anything happened. I began to wonder if anyone would show up despite Jake's video. But then, I heard a noise from outside. We both turned to the door to see a group of four women come in, chatting excitedly, holding their phones. I breathed a sigh of relief.

More people followed then, the room filling up as everyone, curious to hear what he was going to say, sat down expectantly.

Jake turned to me. 'Thank you,' he mouthed.

My whole body lit up.

By the time the session was due to start, the room was about three-quarters full, which I knew was the best we could have hoped for giving how shaky Jake's reputation currently was in the romance-book community.

The conference administrator came back in and announced we were now starting. I held up my phone again to film what Jake said, hoping that readers who hadn't come in would then watch it later on.

Jake stood up, and everyone fell silent. I could see that his legs trembled slightly but to the room, Jake appeared confident as he smiled and ran a hand through his hair. I liked that only I knew how much this meant to him. And I willed the universe to make this go well as I started recording.

Jake cleared his throat. 'Thank you all for coming today. I know most of you probably felt like this was the last session you wanted to attend.'

There was scattered nervous titters at that.

'But I'm glad you're here. I want to start off by saying I'm sorry. Not only for saying that anyone reading my books is stupid for believing in happy ever afters, and implying that I only write romance books to make money...' He took a pause when there was an annoyed murmur around the room. 'But I'm also sorry for pretending that I hadn't said it in the first place. For blaming the journalist involved, Kelly Shepperd, and talking about taking legal action.'

Jake glanced in my direction then. He knew I had always

thought that had been a bad decision. I smiled from behind my phone, and he looked away and continued. Everyone was watching him with their full attention now; he had the room in the palm of his hand.

'I should have been honest and admitted what I had said,' Jake continued. 'But I was too scared to. Not only because I was trying to frantically save my career in any way that I could, but because if I accepted what I had said, I either needed to pretend that I didn't enjoy writing romance, and never do it again, or tell the truth. And I wasn't ready to do that. But the truth is...'

16

Jake trailed off and cleared his throat. He suddenly seemed to hesitate. He looked over at me again so I gave him an encouraging nod. 'The truth is...' he began again but his confidence seemed to be definitely failing him. He cleared his throat again then finally continued speaking. 'I wasn't sure that I wanted to write more love stories because of something that happened in my personal life. So, when I was with an author who kept trying to find out why I was in such a bad mood, I just snapped. I didn't want to tell him... You can guess from the panel that I'm talking about Davis Mulberry here,' Jake said, shaking his head when he said his name. 'I was desperate to get him to stop digging, he is the last person I would ever want to know what happened, so to throw him off, I started slagging off romance books and it worked, but as you all know, we were overheard. I didn't want him to know what was going on in my private life. And I can't share what was going on. I just can't. But long story short, I didn't mean what I said about romance books. I respect the hell out of romance books, and everyone who reads them,' Jake added.

After he paused, there were murmurings again around the

room, and some people who spoke loud enough for me and Jake to hear as well. I listened to the chatter with concern.

'Is that it? I thought we were going to hear the truth!'

'He's only telling us half the story.'

'Sounds like bullshit to me.'

'How can we believe him?'

'He thinks he's so charming that we will just accept what he says.'

'I thought there was one man in the world who believed in love like we do but now I'm not so sure.'

'Why would slagging off romance books be better than sharing what's going on in your personal life?'

'He's such a ladies' man; I think he writes romance just to get women into bed.'

When I heard that comment, my cheeks turned pink remembering how Jake said he would treat me well if I was his.

'How can anyone believe that you don't hate romance books after what you said?' someone called out to Jake.

Jake sighed and held up a hand, slowly quietening the room back down again. 'I love writing romance. I chose to write love stories. And I want to continue to do so. What I said was in the heat of the moment after a terrible few weeks. I know that shouldn't excuse what I did but maybe it might help you to forgive me,' he said pleadingly to everyone.

Again, there were murmurings. I was unsure, along with his readers. Jake had ended up telling half the truth. He had explained he was trying to distract Davis from his secret and I did believe that he had been going through a hard time and didn't actually look down on romance readers, but I still longed to know what he was trying to hide from everyone.

And I felt disappointed that I hadn't managed to persuade him to be completely honest today. I kind of wanted to have him respect my opinion like he had always respected Hayley's when it came to his career. But maybe he did still just think of me as young and inexperienced, especially after making a fool of myself in his presence as many times as I had done. If Jake didn't think he should be honest to save his career, it made me wonder if I was capable of advising authors, full stop. Hayley had given me hope if this conference went well, I could be an agent myself but it felt like I was failing on all fronts.

'I get why you are sceptical,' Jake called out above the noise in the room. 'But that conversation with Davis Mulberry happened at my lowest point. I did almost want to give my career up. After the article came out, I realised that I really could lose it all, and that made me see that I didn't want to. That there is still hope and love in the world, and I do want to write about it. Now though, I'm not sure I'll ever be able to. And that makes me feel really sad. It's up to you all to decide.'

There were a few scoffs around the room.

'I don't know what to think,' I heard a reader say loudly to the person beside them.

'It feels like his books are tainted now,' their neighbour agreed.

Jake sighed and walked down the room towards the door before he faced everyone again. 'I'm sorry I can't share the full story with you all. But I do mean what I say here today and I hope you will all give me that second chance. I don't suppose anyone wants me to sign a book but if you change your mind over the rest of the conference, just come and find me.' He walked out of the room then and I stopped filming.

I posted the video online and then I got up and hurried after Jake. He had looked so downhearted that even though I was upset he hadn't come completely clean, I had to check on him. I told myself that was because for all intents and purposes here, I was looking after his career like his agent would, but my heart ached for him in a way that I wasn't entirely sure was professional only.

Turning when I left the room, I caught a glimpse of Jake as he walked through the lobby of the hotel so I followed him outside, breathing in the fresh air with relief.

'Jake,' I called and he stopped, sinking down onto a concrete bench nearby. I walked over slowly and sat down next to him.

'I'm sorry,' he said after a moment. 'I was going to explain everything but, in the moment, I just couldn't. It's too personal and raw for me to do that. I felt like everyone in that room would be judging me, and people close to me, and I couldn't handle it. I thought telling them that I was trying to avoid Davis Mulberry finding out something personal would have been enough. Do they really expect me to be even more honest?'

'I suppose only getting half the story means your imagination wants to fill in the gaps,' I said, knowing that's exactly how I felt about it. 'It makes it harder for them to trust what you told them.'

'Maybe this is worse, them thinking I'm a liar, but I still wasn't able to say the full story, Freya.'

I sighed. 'I don't know if what you said was enough or not. It's best I tell you that.'

He nodded. 'I know. I'm not getting my hopes up. But worse than the reaction in there was the look on your face.' Jake turned to me and I looked at him in surprise. 'I felt like you were disappointed, and I hated that. I don't want to let you down. I know you believe I should be honest, and I trust you. It was nothing to do with me not respecting your opinion or anything. I'm just not used to being... vulnerable, I guess. And what's happened the past few months has made me even more reticent to open up.'

'It is nice to hear you respect my opinion,' I admitted. 'I was doubting my advice to you. I still am. I don't know where we go from here.'

'Let's get out of the hotel again. This conference feels like it's not the real world. When we went out earlier, that felt real.' He looked at me with those piercing eyes again. 'I'll take you anywhere you want to go.'

I hesitated, unsure if I should be spending more time with him not in a work situation. This was supposed to be a trip to help our careers, and it wasn't going the way we had hoped. This felt like we were running away from the problem almost. Plus, although I was drawn to this man, I wasn't sure if I could trust him.

'Freya, will you have faith in me, please? I promise you there is a good reason for all of this and in time, I hope I can share it with you. Out of anyone here, it's you who I want to share it with,' Jake said then, surprising me again. 'I need time, though.' He stood up. 'Come on, let's have some fun. All this will be waiting for us later, right?' His lips curved into a mischievous smile and I couldn't resist smiling back.

With an exhale, I pushed myself up from the bench. 'This feels like a bad idea but I would like to see more of the city,' I said. I also hoped that spending more time with Jake might let me see more of who he really was and allow me to have faith in him. Because right now, I really wasn't sure if I could.

'You won't regret it,' he promised, leading the way.

I followed, really hoping that I wouldn't.

17

Jake continued being a good tour guide like he had been when he took me to the library. He really knew the city and pointed things out to me if he thought I had missed them, asked me where I wanted to go next, and had no complaints when I suggested another tourist spot that I wanted to see.

'Are you sure you don't mind?' I asked as we headed for Grand Central Station after we had walked around Rockefeller Center.

'No, I told you I'm enjoying seeing the city through your eyes. Remembering what it was like to come here for the first time.'

'Who did you come here with?' I asked, wondering if he'd had a romantic break with an ex. I couldn't help but feel curious about his love life after he knew how crap mine had been.

'My parents,' he said, glancing at me before looking ahead again. 'I was a cynical teenager but this city won me over. It was bright and vivid and enthusiastic.' He looked at me again. 'How could I resist?'

I liked the smile that was playing on his face. 'That does sound like a good combination,' I said, smiling back.

'An irresistible one you could say. We're here.'

I swallowed and followed Jake inside, taken aback by that flirty exchange but enjoying more than I should have done.

Grand Central Station was stunning. I couldn't help but have a little fantasy while I was there about kissing someone right in the middle before they went off to do something heroic. When Jake asked what I thought of the station, I quickly pulled myself out of my reverie to tell him it was as impressive as it had always appeared to be on film.

When we left, I asked if we could take a proper look at Central Park. Jake suggested we headed for The Lake, so we walked there together. It was beautiful with the trees and bushes framing it and above were skyscrapers looking down on the clear water like they were keeping watch over it. It was such a gorgeous late afternoon, the light danced and sparkled on top of the water and it felt that not only was I seeing something I had seen in so many movies, but like I was in one myself.

'This is my favourite part of the day,' I declared when we paused in our walk. My feet ached despite my comfy cowboy boots. We must have done thousands of steps. But I was a happy kind of tired. I knew I would feel achy tomorrow but it was worth it. I was here in New York and the stress of what we'd been through at the conference melted away with my happiness at drinking in this magical and vibrant city. And I was surprised by how at ease I now felt with Jake.

'This has always been one of my favourite New York spots,' Jake agreed. 'You feel so removed from the city. And yet it's right there above and around us. This park is a little oasis in the middle of such urban sprawl. I know we have beautiful parks in London and I love walking through them, but this is special. I love looking at the skyscrapers reflected on the water. Nature reminding us it's here for us to appreciate and look after.'

'You can tell you're a writer,' I joked. I liked it when he talked poetically. 'I could never write anything. I don't have an imagination. That's why I want to help books get into the world instead.'

'I think that's the perfect goal for an agent; plenty of them don't have the same passion for stories.'

I glanced at him. 'Like Hayley?'

'She is great at the business side of things, as I'm sure you know, but I never get the impression she loves books like I can tell you do,' Jake said. We faced each other. Central Park was busy but I found myself only focused on him. 'When you talked about reading *When I Met You*, your whole face lit up.'

I smiled, a little bit embarrassed at how I had fangirled over his latest book. 'Well, it's a really great book, Jake.'

'That means a lot to me that you think so,' he said softly.

'I only wish loving books was enough for this job. This conference is showing me that maybe Hayley has the right idea in treating it just as a business. Maybe I listen to my heart too much,' I said, biting my lip.

Jake's eyes narrowed in on my lip before moving back to meet my gaze again. 'I wish you wouldn't put yourself down,' Jake told me. 'I like that you listen to your heart.'

'You do?' I felt a sudden spark of electricity from his eye contact. It travelled down my spine right down to my toes.

'I wish I could do the same.'

I wished he could too but I was too scared to say it. Instead, I exhaled shakily and cleared my throat. 'What now?'

'Can I show you a place here that I love?' Jake asked.

I nodded. 'I'd love to see it.' We broke our eye contact and started to walk out of the park but I couldn't stop myself from wondering if Jake had felt the same spark I had. It was too crazy to think he would have done though so I tried to push it to the back of my mind, but my body felt its effects the whole way.

* * *

'Wow, this place is amazing...' I said, walking across the rooftop in shock. Not only was the bar and pool area of the members' club Jake had taken me to cool, but the view beyond it was incredible. I stepped towards the glass wall that encircled the rooftop and came up to my waist. Beyond it, New York was laid out in front of me, sparkling with light and life.

'This view,' I gasped. The cool breeze ruffled my hair as I looked down at the city. The sun was starting to dip now, making me realise we'd spent a lot of time together today. Soon, we'd see a beautiful sunset; I could feel it in the air.

Today hadn't started out well with the tricky reader session and I still had no idea if we could do enough at this conference to help change opinions on Jake but I had enjoyed spending time with him in the city more than I thought I would. When we were alone, it felt like less and less like we were just colleagues. And that both scared and thrilled me.

'I'm glad you like it,' Jake murmured, close to my shoulder. 'Being an author has some perks,' he added with a wry smile.

I glanced at him. 'I'll say. You're one hell of a tour guide, Jake.'

'You've enjoyed the day?'

'I've loved it.'

Jake smiled. 'I'm glad, Freya. You deserve it after what's happened at the conference. I am sorry that I fucked things up for us.'

The word 'us' hovered in the air. I kind of liked it. Jake seemed so sincere; I really wanted to have the faith in him that he wanted me to have.

'How about a drink?'

'Sounds good,' I replied, and Jake disappeared to the bar. I watched him go, marvelling that someone who had seemed so intimidating to me just a couple of days ago had become someone I was enjoying hanging out with.

I looked out at the view again. It was incredible. I would never have thought I would see all this with Jake Richards but now I couldn't imagine having seen it with anyone else.

'What's your name, beautiful?'

I jumped as a man appeared on the other side of me, close to my elbow. I glanced at him. He looked about my age and wore jeans and a tight t-shirt, flashing muscles at me. He held a bottle of beer and gave me a long look up and down.

'That's not your boyfriend, is it? He looks too old for you.'

That surprised me. Obviously, I was well aware Jake was ten years older than me and that had always made me nervous of him but today, the age gap hadn't seemed an issue. As I grew more comfortable with Jake, we felt closer to equals. This guy though was reminding me that we weren't.

I looked behind us to where Jake was getting us drinks. This place screamed money and being out of my league. And Jake in his immaculate outfit, looking like a movie star, screamed the same. I felt my chest sag and I wasn't sure why. Maybe it was because being up here with him hadn't felt like a continuation of our city tour but a little bit like a... date.

18

'No, he's not my boyfriend,' I admitted to the New York stranger when I realised I hadn't responded to his original question.

'Come and have a drink with me then.'

'Thank you but no,' I said, politely but firmly. If romance in the UK had been difficult for me, I couldn't see how starting something with someone who lived thousands of miles away would be a good idea.

I glanced back and saw Jake coming over with two drinks but hesitating when he saw the man with me.

'Your loss,' the man tutted, stalking away, annoyed.

'I wasn't interrupting anything, was I?' Jake asked when he reached me. He held out a glass of wine to me.

'Definitely not. Thank you.' I took a long sip.

'Every time I leave you, the wolves descend,' Jake said quietly. He took a sip of his wine and our eyes met over the rims of our glasses.

'Another bad chat-up line,' I said with a laugh, remembering Davis Mulberry's failed flirting attempt with me.

'What kind of line would work on you, I wonder?'

My eyes widened a little bit that he would wonder about that. 'Maybe that's the point. I don't want a line at all. I want someone genuine. Who likes me for me. Who wants a relationship, not a disappointingly quick fumble in bed followed by ghosting.' I was a bit embarrassed by my outburst but then I remembered he had heard me be even more frank to Liv so I might as well be honest with him.

'You deserve someone genuine,' Jake replied firmly. 'I like how you see the world. Full of optimism and excitement. Like today. Seeing New York through your eyes felt like I was seeing it for the first time. You've made me smile a lot since we set off on this trip.'

I shook my head. 'Yeah, laughing at me...'

'No, Freya, never at... always with,' Jake said softly. 'You know I let myself get a little bit cynical and bitter, I kept myself aloof, afraid to open up and let people in but you make me want to change. To get back to the man I was.'

'I told you – I would like to get to know that man,' I said, wishing he would open up to me fully. 'I was so intimidated by you when we first met, and for a long time. I was so nervous about this trip,' I admitted. 'But I want to succeed in this career so I knew I had to get past it. And the more I got to know you, the more I saw that we needed each other. That made me less nervous of you.'

Jake raised an eyebrow. 'You were intimidated by me? Well then, the feeling was mutual.'

I choked on a sip of wine. 'Are you joking? There was no way you've ever felt that way about me.' I gestured to myself, thinking I must be the least intimidating person on the planet. Especially to someone like Jake Richards.

'I was nervous for this trip too,' Jake said. 'Everything felt like it was slipping away, and I saw on your face how disappointed you were in me. I knew you loved my books and I hated letting you down. I wanted this trip to go well. Needed it to. And when I found out that your career was dependent on it as well... I felt terrible when both the interview and the panel went so badly. I tried to fix it earlier.' He shook his head. 'I bet you want to just give up on me now, and I wouldn't blame you.'

'I do find you frustrating,' I said, the wine loosening my tongue.

'I want to make it up to you so bad,' he said gruffly.

'Hayley won't want to promote me after this trip; I've accepted that. Maybe I am not agent material after all,' I said, thinking about how Jake hadn't followed my advice. It hurt more than I cared to admit to him. More than it should for a work situation.

'I'll tell her that you are,' he said fiercely. 'I can't let this trip mess things up for you as well. I'll do whatever I can.'

'I don't know, maybe my advice hasn't been right...' I wondered.

'Don't doubt yourself because of me.' He took a gulp from his drink. 'You will go far, I know it. You're tenacious. And ambitious. And great with people.'

'Ha. Not great with men, though...' I trailed off, wishing sometimes, I could go back in time and not blurt things out.

'You're doing pretty good with me,' he replied. 'Or is that because this is just professional?'

'Are you asking me or telling me?' I asked, once again wishing I had a better filter between my brain and my mouth, but I couldn't help myself. I was suddenly desperate to know if this was still just professional for him.

I had definitely shocked him. Jake stared at me for a moment and I was sure his eyes flicked over me in a way that was definitely not professional. But then he stepped back with a sigh, breaking our eye contact. 'It has to be, right? I know I'm not technically your client, but we are working here together. I'm ten years older, Freya, and you want romance, which is something I'm not sure I can give anyone right now.' He shook his head, his expression dark.

This man had secrets that I wanted to unlock but I didn't know how. 'I thought you weren't like other men,' I said, thinking back to him telling me he'd treat me better than anyone ever had. At the time, I wasn't sure if he meant women in general or me specifically but now I found myself hoping it was the former.

'Freya.' He said my name like it was precious to him. Then he broke our eye contact, looking out at the view instead of me. 'Romance isn't like it is in books.'

'I keep feeling like that but I don't want to give up hope that there is a love like that out there for me. And I think there is for you too. One day, we'll find it.'

'You think?' Jake glanced at me again.

'If we want it enough.' I really hoped that was true. Then I decided it was best to move the subject on. 'The sun is about to set,' I said, turning to watch, needing to stop looking into Jake's eyes.

I felt the sting of his rejection mixing with the alcohol in my bloodstream. I knew he was out of my league. I didn't know if he could give me love like the kind he wrote about, but it was clear he didn't want to try. Today might have felt far removed from it, but this was a work trip. I needed to remind myself quickly of not only that but also the fact that Jake was keeping something from me. I had to stop myself from feeling any more drawn to him.

We lapsed into silence as the sun started to set on the horizon. Everyone on the rooftop watched the sky turning orange around us. It was beautiful, and a reminder that whatever happens in a day, it ends, and you get a chance to try again tomorrow.

'Freya.'

I raised an eyebrow when Jake spoke my name after a few moments. My name had come out as a wistful sigh on his lips.

'What I said earlier about things having to be professional between us. I want you to know: just because it has to, doesn't mean I haven't been thinking all day about it *not* being professional.'

19

The walk back to the Waldorf Astoria was a quiet one. The sun continued to set as we finished our drinks on the rooftop in stunned silence. I had no idea what to say in response to Jake's admission, and he seemed to regret his words, turning away and not saying anything else either. We then headed back towards our hotel as night time rolled over New York, the city lighting up around us.

My heart was beating faster and harder inside my chest as my mind replayed his words in time with our brisk steps. It was like we suddenly both just wanted to be in our hotel rooms alone to think about the day, so I hurried to keep up with his long strides, and wondered how awkward things would be between us now. His words made me nervous because of how pumped up I felt after hearing them, like I'd just drunk an energy drink or something. To know he had felt the same spark that I had was both a relief and a terrifying thought. Jake had always seemed completely out of my reach but suddenly, he was saying that he wasn't.

I couldn't make sense of it. I had no idea if I could trust it. Or him.

We walked into our hotel and to the lifts, waiting in silence and getting in one. The journey up to the floor where our rooms were seemed excruciatingly slow. I had no idea what to say to break the tension, and Jake seemed at just as much of a loss as me.

Finally, the lifts reached our floor and we stepped out and walked to our neighbouring hotel rooms.

'Jake...'

'Freya...'

We said each other's name in unison as we approached the doors. Then we both smiled, the tension easing a little bit between us.

'I shouldn't have said what I said,' Jake said, running a hand through his hair as we hovered outside our rooms in the empty, quiet hotel corridor.

'You took me by surprise,' I admitted. 'But I kind of liked knowing you'd been thinking about me.'

'It's hard not to,' he said gruffly. 'I shouldn't, though.'

'Why not?' I asked boldly.

'There is a long list of reasons...' Jake shook his head. 'I'm trying to remember them but you're giving me the kind of look that's making it very difficult.'

I let out a breath. 'What kind of look?' I wondered if my attraction to him was showing on my face. By the darkening of his eyes, it definitely was. But seeing his made me feel less worried about him seeing mine.

Jake moved towards me. I moved so my back touched my hotel room door. He stopped instantly. 'No closer?' he asked, watching me carefully.

'No, it's just, I felt like I needed to lean...' I was feeling distinctly unsteady.

'Okay.' He moved closer. 'Me too.' He propped an arm up against my hotel door so he was slightly leaning towards me but he didn't touch me. There were inches of air between us even though suddenly, it felt like there was no air in this whole hotel. My eyes locked onto his. 'Have you ever thought about me?' he asked then, so quietly, I had to strain to hear the question. It was as though he didn't want to admit he was asking me it.

I nodded slowly, keeping my eyes on his. 'Yeah, I have,' I admitted, keeping my voice as soft as his.

Jake exhaled audibly. 'I like knowing that,' he said, repeating what I had told him.

'But I don't know if I can trust this... feeling,' I confessed. 'You asked me to have faith in you but it's hard.'

Jake sighed. 'I know, I'm sorry. But now you're getting to know me, do you believe that there is a good reason behind all of this?' he asked, gesturing into the air.

'Why you said those things, you mean?' I checked.

He nodded.

It was hard – I had read his books for years and the way he wrote about love made me think he did believe in it, that he had enjoyed writing love stories, and maybe he might be a true romantic in his heart. But I knew I was led by my heart and sometimes, I should let my head take over. Jake was keeping something from me, something he didn't want to share with me yet, so letting him in and sharing myself with him made me feel uneasy. But I fancied him a lot. I couldn't deny that.

'I want to believe it,' I said breathily.

'I want you to. I know there is a list of reasons why we should keep things professional but there is a spark here, though, isn't there?' Jake asked me, hope evident in his voice.

'There does seem to be,' I said softly back, unable to tear my eyes off him.

'Hmm,' he murmured. He reached out and gently touched a strand of my hair. 'I can't believe you'd even look twice at me, though.'

My eyebrows shot up. 'I feel that way about you,' I admitted before I could stop myself. This seemed so surreal. Jake Richards. Bestselling author. Telling me there was a spark between us and he couldn't believe I might want him.

'Are you serious?' he asked me.

'Are you?'

His fingertips moved to touch my cheek. I felt my pulse speed up instantly. I was sure he would be able to see my chest starting to rise and fall rapidly. He was so close but was still keeping the space between us. I wondered if he was considering kissing me. Then I realised a man had never considered it before. Never taken the time to do so. I replayed previous kisses in my life. Drunken ones, awkward ones, all hurried and sudden... This was so far removed from any of them.

Jake trailed his fingertips down to my chin then to my neck, cupping me there under my ear. 'I would love to kiss you,' he said, his eyes moving from mine to my lips. Then he moved them straight back again. 'But I want you to know I would understand if you said you didn't want me to. I'd like you to decide, Freya. Tell me yes... or no. Okay?'

A man had never asked me if I wanted to kiss him before. It shouldn't have felt like a big decision but somehow, it did. I could look back and wonder 'what if' and regret not diving in, or I could dive right in and then regret that. Was it better to regret what you did or didn't do in life?

'Yes,' I said. 'I want to kiss you.'

Better to regret what I had done, I knew that. My heart was

thumping in my chest, my pulse pounding in my wrist and behind my ear, and Jake's hand was on my neck, making me lean heavily on the door in case my knees gave out. He smiled at my answer, and closed the space between us.

Even though I had said yes, my body still startled when his lips found mine. It had been a long time since I'd been kissed. And this was Jake Richards!

But a second later, I was kissing him back. His mouth was firm and confident on mine. His stubble brushed against my chin slightly roughly but I didn't mind it. The kiss deepened and his tongue found mine, and his hand on me tightened ever so slightly. I couldn't stop a moan from escaping my mouth into his as I arched towards him, wanting to be even nearer. He took the hint immediately. His arm came down from the door to hold me around my waist, drawing me into his chest as our kiss turned even more passionate. I lifted my hands from the door and wrapped my arms around his neck, standing on tiptoe to reach him, our mouths never parting as we moved closer.

Jake made a contented noise and then finally tore his lips from mine. I took in a breath. I felt dizzy. My eyes opened to watch as he leaned down to kiss the corner of my mouth then press small kisses on my chin, along my jaw, then down the side of my neck. I gasped. He moved to the other side, letting go of his hold there as he kissed me where his hand had been. His kisses were soft but accompanied by the roughness of his facial hair. His arm around my waist held me firmly. Everything about the way he was handling me felt just right. When he lifted his head back up, our eyes met. He touched my lips, which were tingling. 'When you anticipate a kiss for a while, your expectations can be too high. But that exceeded all of mine.'

Fuck. I quickly pressed myself back against the door because that kiss followed by such a romantic sentiment threatened to send my trembling knees over the edge. And I really didn't want to fall over in front of him again.

'You've anticipated kissing me?' I asked when I was able to form a coherent thought again.

Jake grinned. 'Ever since I found you sprawled on the floor at Heathrow airport with a penis pencil in your handbag.'

I burst out laughing. 'You did not want to kiss me then!'

'I have never met a girl like you, Freya. Seriously, I have never wanted to laugh so hard but also help someone so badly as I did in that moment. Since then, you've occupied my thoughts quite a bit. And God, when I saw Mulberry flirting with you, I realised how badly I wanted you for myself. Even though I knew I shouldn't want you...'

I looked at him. 'Are you sure it wasn't because you heard me say I haven't had sex for three years so you thought I'd be easy?' I asked archly.

We stared at one another.

Then Jake started laughing. 'This is what I mean. You're not like anyone else. Jesus, Freya.'

I smiled. 'Well, just so you know, even though that was an epic kiss, I'm not easy.' I stepped away from the door and pulled out my key card to open it up.

'I meant what I said about treating you better than you've ever been treated if you were mine...' Jake's voice turned even rougher when he said the word 'mine'.

Suddenly, I wanted to be his. And I've never wanted to be anyone's before. But I knew I needed to be careful. I knew I had to tear myself away otherwise I never would. 'I should go to bed.'

Jake smiled. 'You should. Goodnight, Freya.' He leaned in and gave me a soft kiss on the mouth. 'I'll try to sleep but I know I'll be thinking about that kiss.'

'Me too,' I admitted. I giggled, then rolled my eyes. 'Goodnight,' I said firmly to both him and myself then I walked into my room and closed the door behind me. I ran to the bed and dived on it, laying on my back and staring at the ceiling.

I giggled in the darkness, reaching up with my finger to touch my lips. I could feel Jake's on mine still. The roughness of his facial hair. The way he'd held me with delicious pressure. The way I had longed to be even closer to him. My body had wanted more. So much more. And it had been a long time since I'd felt that way. That craving, that ache, that need for someone. It was almost unbelievable I was feeling it for Jake.

But if I was honest with myself, I had fantasied about Jake long before we'd even met. Reading his books had made me wonder about the man who could write such romantic stories. And that man himself had not only kissed me but told me the kiss had exceeded all his expectations, and then told me that if I was his, he'd treat me better than I'd ever been treated.

Did I want to be his?

Was that even possible?

Had he meant all of that?

Or had we been swept up after our New York date?

I had no idea what the morning would bring but I knew that I would be thinking about his kiss most of the night. Jake's kiss was unlike anything I'd had before. That made me think his kisses could quite easily become addictive. But I couldn't lose my head. He had been right when he said there were a ton of reasons why we shouldn't think about kissing again, let alone anything more. This was a work trip. Jake had always intimidated me. We were leagues apart. There was a big age gap...

...and he was keeping something from me.

But my body and my heart didn't care here, in this moment.

They wanted Jake to call me 'mine'.

I was definitely in trouble.

20

A stream of sunlight poured through a crack in the curtains pooling on the bed. The sheets were bundled up around me after my restless night. I turned over with a groan to look at the time. It was eight o'clock. I had no idea when I had finally drifted off to sleep but it had definitely not been until the early hours. I had replayed my day with Jake over and over again in my mind, spending a lot of time reliving our kiss against my hotel room door. It felt somewhat like a dream and I hadn't wanted to wake up from it.

But now I had to.

With a sigh, I sat up and stretched, letting out a loud yawn. I touched my hair. It was tangled from my tossing and turning, and I hadn't bothered to remove my make-up so there was mascara imprinted on my pillow.

On the bedside table, my phone lit up with a message. I saw Jake's name flash up on my screen and my heart quickened instantly. I took a breath and read it.

> Morning, Freya. Would you like to have breakfast together?

I exhaled. No immediate calling our kiss a mistake. I was relieved about that. No declarations about it being the best kiss ever again, but maybe he was unsure how I would feel when I woke up. And my mind was all over the place. Still processing the fact that Jake Richards had kissed me. How good it had felt. How I wanted more.

I realised I hadn't responded to his text. I was nervous to see him but I wanted to see him too. And it wasn't like I could hide in this hotel room. We were still at the conference together. It was better to see him sooner rather than later before I could over-think too much about the situation.

> Sounds good. When shall we meet?

He replied quickly.

> Can you be ready in 45 minutes? Meet you outside our rooms...

I jumped out of bed and sent a message back as I hurried into the bathroom to get ready.

> See you then!

Diving into the shower, I made myself look as good as I could in the forty-five minutes I had. Remembering what he had said about liking my outfits, I pulled on my favourite dress – it was short and white with tiny sunflowers on it – along with my favourite boots. I left my hair loose, did quick, basic make-up and was spritzing myself with my floral perfume when there was a knock on the door. I took a final look in the full-length mirror. I still looked a bit tired from lack of sleep but much more like myself again.

I opened up the door. Jake stood there wearing light-coloured trousers and a white shirt, looking extremely handsome. His hair was ever so slightly damp from the shower I assumed he'd not long had, which then led my thoughts astray and I had to try to stop myself thinking about him in there. He smiled warmly, oblivious to my naughty thoughts, thank God.

'Morning.'

'Morning,' I replied.

'Are you ready?'

'Sure.' I stepped out, closed the door and then we headed for the lifts together. I could smell Jake's familiar aftershave as we got in one.

'How did you sleep? I was a little bit distracted to get much,' Jake said as the doors closed. He turned to look down at me and when our eyes met, my breath hitched as the memory of the way he had held me and kissed me flooded back.

'I didn't get much sleep either,' I admitted.

'You were on my mind,' he said.

I smiled. 'Yeah? You were on my mind too.'

'I was really hoping you didn't regret our kiss. Because I didn't.'

Happiness washed over me that he felt the same way about it. 'Nor did I,' I said, my cheeks heating up a little bit at both my confession and remembering his lips on mine.

'Good.' Jake smiled at me as the lift reached the ground floor and the doors opened up. No longer alone, we stepped out and made our way to the breakfast room without any more talk of kissing. I wondered though if he was still thinking about it like I was. We were shown to a table for two at the back of the room. I looked around but couldn't see Liv or Tessa, which was a relief as I would have been hopeless at pretending this breakfast was normal. I recognised some people also attending the conference but thankfully, no one spoke to us.

Over at the buffet section, I tried not to glance at Jake too much as I got myself a large coffee and a plate of scrambled eggs, toast, bacon and a side of fruit and yoghurt, but it was hard. Twice, our eyes caught, and we smiled at each other. It was nice knowing he was looking over at me too. I went to our table and Jake joined me with his coffee, and a full plate too. It seemed we both needed lots of fuel after our lack of sleep.

I took a gulp of my coffee while Jake cleared his throat. 'So, we had a kiss that we don't regret but we are here working together,' he said quietly so no one could overhear us.

I nodded. 'You have your second author panel later this morning,' I said, trying to focus on said work and not how hand-some he looked across the table.

'I'll do better this time,' Jake replied with a wry smile.

'When I couldn't sleep,' I said, keeping my eyes on my plate as I felt shy admitting how much that kiss had played on my mind, 'I checked social media and everyone is talking about what you said at the reader session yesterday. I did see some people praising you for trying to make it right but just as many are on the fence about what you said yesterday. We have a lot of work to do to convince them that you can be their favourite romance author again.'

Jake nodded. 'I know. I will do all I can to win everyone round.' Then he gave me a small smile. 'But I have to admit right now, I'm mainly thinking about winning you round. Am I still *your* favourite romance author?'

I shook my head but I had to smile. 'You need to focus on what we're doing here.'

He raised an eyebrow.

'I mean work wise! God.' I put a hand to my face, flustered, feeling my cheeks heat up. I looked away from his gaze because it felt like he was peeling away layers off me with it. 'But you've always been my favourite romance author,' I admitted quietly.

'Even though I let you down yesterday,' he said. 'I am sorry about that, Freya. I want to be more like you.'

'If that's a good thing,' I said. 'Hayley definitely doesn't think so. I suppose you and me are very different.' I wondered if that was something that should be making me even more wary of this spark between us. 'Although they do say that opposites attract,' I added absentmindedly.

'So, if opposites attract then we're agreed we're attracted to one another?' he asked, his eyes twinkling with amusement.

'I suppose I didn't mind kissing you...' I said, teasing him right back.

'Oh, it was just an okay kiss for you?' Jake leaned on the table and lowered his voice. 'Am I going to have to try harder next time?'

'Next time?' I questioned, my heart thumping faster at the thought of him doing that.

'There you are!'

Before Jake could answer me, Liv was suddenly standing by our table. I jumped when she appeared, my cheeks flushing further. 'Morning,' I said to her, in a high-pitched voice, tearing my eyes from Jake's.

Liv frowned a little bit and looked from me to Jake as if wondering what was going on between us. 'So, are you ready for the panel later? I was going to come and listen with you as I'm free until lunch.'

'I can't promise it will be as entertaining as the last one,' Jake said.

Liv stared at him for a bit as if confused by him making a joke. I had to admit I was still getting used to him loosening up a little bit too. 'A lot of people will be there wondering what confessions you'll make this time.'

'What are people saying after the reader session?' I asked her, pushing our kiss as firmly as I could to the back of my mind. 'Can we still salvage the conference?' I knew that Hayley had decided we couldn't and I hated that I was losing hope.

'Of course we can,' Jake replied instead. 'I told you, I'm sorry I let you down; I will do better today. Have faith in me.'

Our eyes met again and I really was desperate to trust him.

'I think the problem is by giving them just a little bit yesterday, they want more,' Liv said. 'I've heard some wild theories going around about what the secret you wanted to hide from Davis Mulberry was. Like you have your wife hidden in your attic.'

Jake chuckled. '*Jane Eyre* is one of my favourites but there is no wife. I've never been married. Anything else?'

'That all your books have been written by someone else,' Liv said, smiling at his response like I was.

'That's definitely something Mulberry would be very gleeful about.' Jake said. 'But sadly, I have the neck pain to show for being hunched over my laptop for hours on end.'

Liv grimaced. 'Mine gets sore by the end of a writing day too. Well, just be warned: things are getting pretty crazy out there.' She gestured into the air. 'I think your panel today will be packed in case you share any more secrets.'

'I don't think I have any more secrets, do I, Freya?' Jake asked me, his expression innocent.

My face heated up again. 'Um...'

'I had an email from Hayley this morning,' Liv said to me.

'She told me I wasn't posting enough on social media. Sometimes, she scares me a little bit.'

'She was terrifying when she phoned me after Jake revealed that article was true. If I don't do better, there won't be a job for me when I get back home.'

'Oh, Freya.' Liv shook her head then gave Jake a glare. 'Freya would make a brilliant agent. She has great instincts and as her client; you should be listening to her more.'

'Jake isn't my client,' I said quickly.

'While you're here, he kind of is,' she replied with a shrug.

'I'm sorry, Liv,' Jake said. 'I'm doing my best. I just can't say any more about it.'

I couldn't look at Jake after Liv's comment about Jake being like my client while we were here. It made our kiss feel inappropriate.

'Well, anyway, we should probably prepare for the panel.'

'Sure. I'm looking forward to it. Writing meet-cutes are my favourite part. I'll save you a seat,' Liv said. She turned to Jake. 'Good luck!' Then she faded away to the breakfast buffet.

I sagged in my chair. 'Is it me or did that make you feel worried about what happened with us last night?' I was nervous to ask, afraid he would say that we couldn't kiss again, but also because that seemed like the right thing to do.

'You're not my agent but yeah, we are working together. I don't want to hurt your career, Freya. I feel really bad that Hayley is so pissed off.' Jake sighed. 'But I can't deny that I would like to kiss you again.'

'Shh,' I hushed him, looking around anxiously in case someone had heard him. 'This is too public. And we should prepare for the meet-cute talk.'

'Didn't you say that your arrival at Heathrow would have made a good meet-cute?' he asked. His eyes were twinkling again. I liked seeing this other side to Jake Richards. Although it was making me more attracted to him, which felt dangerous.

'What when I was sprawled on the floor in front of you?' I shook my head. 'I can't believe that didn't put you off for life.'

'It was the penis pencil that got me,' he said, chuckling.

'Yeah, my humiliation is hilarious,' I said with an eye roll. But I couldn't not smile back. 'I'm glad it didn't put you off.'

'I told you – I've never met anyone quite like you.' He looked at our empty plates; breakfast had passed by in a flash. 'Come on, let's plan this panel and then we can talk more about us.'

The word 'us' lingered in my brain.

21

The 'From Meet-Cute to Happy Ever After' panel was in an even larger conference room to Jake's first panel. The conference administrator said a lot of people had expressed interest in coming along so they had moved it to a larger room. I wished it was because Jake had won people over but after what Liv said, I was betting it was so they could watch it first-hand in case Jake made another shocking confession or revealed what he was hiding about that conversation with Davis. I felt nervous about that. Jake seemed determined to make this panel go smoothly but I had no idea if that would be enough. There had still been no more contact from Hayley so Jake's publishers can't have said anything about a new book deal. Everyone, it felt, was still on the fence about Jake.

And I supposed I was too.

We had half an hour to wait before it was due to start so we sat in the empty room and went over the questions, and what Jake was going to say. Talking about writing romances was easy for him.

'It all sounds great,' I reassured him once we'd gone over it all. We sat side by side at the table the panel would sit at. I looked out at the empty room full of chairs and thought about how they would all be filled with people shortly. 'As long as you don't get wound up by another author again,' I added.

'I will stay calm, I promise,' Jake said.

'I could never do something like this,' I admitted, gesturing to the room.

'Of course you could; you're really confident.'

'No, not for public speaking, and not really at work... yet. I am trying. But I really admire the fact you can do this.'

'I do get nervous, though. I mean, I bottled it yesterday, didn't I? Talking about personal things is hard for me.'

'It's hard for everyone,' I told him. 'Opening up and being vulnerable is difficult.' I longed to feel that comfortable with a romantic partner that I could share secrets with them.

'It is. Talking about my work is far easier because I am passionate about it.' Jake looked at me. 'I feel like you could open up easily, though. With the right person.'

'Maybe,' I whispered. I let myself have a quick fantasy that I could open up to Jake, and that he would open up to me.

We couldn't say any more as people then started coming in. I got up and found a seat, leaving Jake at the table to greet his fellow panellists and the chair.

Liv found me five minutes later and sat down next to me while the room filled up. 'Uh-oh,' she said in a low voice. I followed her gaze and my heart sunk to see Davis Mulberry slink into the room. Then he spotted us and came over.

'Mind if I join you?' he asked, gesturing to the empty seat beside me and then promptly sat in it without waiting for me to respond. 'I couldn't miss witnessing another car crash by Jake Richards.'

I rolled my eyes. 'The only car crash here is you.'

Davis turned and raised an eyebrow at me. 'Don't tell me, he's worked his charm on you, Freya? Aren't you fifteen years younger than him?'

'Ten,' I snapped back.

I felt Liv lean over to listen to us.

'And you work together.'

I really hoped I wasn't blushing. 'What's your point?'

'I can see the way you look at Jake,' he said so astutely, I was stunned. Davis sighed. 'I need to warn you, Freya. He's always been a ladies' man. Likes to break hearts wherever he goes. Women seem to get very excited by the idea of him writing romance novels, he uses that, pretends he's all about romance and love and finding that happy ever after when he just wants to get them into bed.'

My eyes drifted to Jake, who was talking to the authors beside him as everyone got ready to start the panel. The doubts I had niggled more. He was charming and he knew I loved his books. I'd even admitted earlier that he was my favourite romance author. Was he using my longing for a happy ever after to get me into bed? He knew it had been years since I'd had sex as well. I tried to remember the way he looked at me and how that kiss between us had felt. That had been real, hadn't it?

'It's pretty heartless,' Davis added. 'I'd never lie to a woman like that.'

I tore my gaze from Jake to give Davis a disparaging look. 'No, you just give them a cheesy chat-up line.'

He shrugged. 'At least I don't pretend I'm after something special like Jake does just to use women. You don't deserve to be treated like that.'

The panel chair called for quiet then so Davis had to shut up. I crossed my arms and exhaled slowly to try to calm down. The problem was, I wasn't sure if I was more pissed off with Davis

Mulberry or Jake or myself for kissing Jake last night. It had been an electric kiss. And I wanted to believe that Jake was a hopeless romantic like me. But all I really knew was that he claimed to love romance but was keeping a secret about why he allowed the world to think he didn't.

'Jake, why don't you start?' The panel chair pulled me out of my thoughts. 'What is a meet-cute for you and how can people wanting to write a romance novel create a good one?'

'Well, meet-cutes are basically the inciting incident in a romcom. A meeting between who will be the two love interests, setting the tone and course of their journey to a happy ending,' Jake said. He looked over at me. 'I think if you want to write a good one, you need to make it memorable, make it funny or cute, and establish some conflict so readers want to see what happens to the couple who have just met.'

I tried not to let his words affect me, remembering what Davis had just said, but it was hard when they were accompanied by such a smouldering stare in my direction. I had joked we had a meet-cute when I was sprawled on the floor in front of him at Heathrow but I realised our meet-cute was Jake overhearing me talking about my love life to Liv at work, and getting into the lift with me afterwards.

Meet-cutes could lead to a happy ever after or they could lead to heartbreak.

And I had no idea which one I might get if I kissed Jake again.

22

Jake's second panel thankfully went smoothly. The conversation was good and when it came to questions at the end, most focused on actually asking for writing tips. But there were a couple directed at Jake that made me shift uncomfortably in my seat.

'What do you think about people who say romances are too predictable, that once you have the meet-cute, it's too obvious there will be a happy ending?' one woman asked. 'I mean, we know you haven't exactly been complimentary about writing love stories so you must have a view on that?'

Davis chuckled beside me. 'They are completely predictable.'

'Why are you here to listen to how to write one then?' I whispered back, annoyed at him.

'As if I would need any advice,' he hissed back.

I just rolled my eyes then leaned forward to listen to Jake's response to the question.

'You go into reading a romance knowing there will be a happy ever after, yes, but the journey to get there isn't predictable. You can relax reading it knowing you'll get the pay-off at the end but the drama, the conflict, the chemistry, the slow burn in the middle, that's the story. It's life itself, isn't it? It's about the journey, not the destination. That's why I haven't become tired of writing love stories,' Jake said with passion. Everyone was listening hard. He was so good at speaking. 'My latest one, that I hope I will be able to bring out soon if you would like to read it, is about two people who meet years previously with no clue that they will become special to one another. It's called *When I Met You* and it's a story of how you don't know when you meet someone how they will affect your life.'

Glancing around, I was relieved to see some of the readers in the room smiling. One in front of me whispered to her friend that she hoped they could read that book. I smiled. He had made people curious about his novel and that could only help in encouraging his publishers to offer him a new deal for it. I grabbed my phone and quickly typed out a post about what Jake had said and I shared it on the agency's social media, tagging him. I'd get him to share it afterwards so everyone following him online could read what he said.

The other question that made me nervous was: 'How do you think you can still give writing advice for romance writers if you don't respect the genre?'

Jake looked at the person asking the question. 'I said yesterday that what I said wasn't what I really think. I was trying to distract someone from something I didn't want them to know. I made a big, stupid mistake to say what I did. I have written ten romance books. Why would I do that if I didn't love reading and writing romance? It would be a pretty miserable way to have spent my working life. I know I upset a lot of you. I am so sorry about that. I want you to remember how you felt reading one of my books. If you enjoyed reading them then hopefully, you will realise that I enjoyed writing them.' He then turned to me and I gave him a nod. That had been a good answer.

'Jake gave me some great advice when I was starting out,' one of the other authors on the panel said then. 'And he read one of my early manuscripts. That meant a lot to me, and I believe the reason I got my first book deal was because of the feedback he gave me. You can't fake that kind of interest,' she added with a grateful smile at him.

'You're really talented,' Jake told her.

'Probably shagged her,' Davis whispered in my ear.

I refused to respond to that.

The panel chair ended the session then. I listened to readers as everyone shifted and got ready to leave, and the comments were definitely more positive about Jake.

'He answered those questions well.'

'I like that he has supported other authors.'

'God, now I really want to read the book he spoke about!'

'I wonder when it's out?'

When I heard that, I tapped the woman on her shoulder. 'You should ask his publishers that on social media.'

'Good idea,' she said.

I smiled with satisfaction.

'It's gone really well,' Liv said quietly to me.

'I think so too,' I said back. A little bit of hope returned to me that this trip wasn't going to be a complete failure after all. I quickly typed out another email to Hayley to say the panel had been a success and things were improving and to look on social media. I was praying she would see we were working hard to make it right.

Davis turned to me then. 'I can't believe Jake's managing to pull the wool over people's eyes like this,' he groaned.

'If you hadn't pushed him to say what he said, he wouldn't have to try to save his career,' I replied.

'Aren't you worried about what his big secret is?' Davis chal-

lenged me. 'How about we go for lunch and we can talk about it?'
He gave me a lewd grin.

'I'm busy, I'm afraid,' I replied shortly. I understood why he
had pushed Jake that night to slag off romance books – he had an
uncanny ability to piss people off.

'Outstaying your welcome again, Mulberry?'

We turned to see Jake standing beside us, eyebrow raised.

'Not at all – Freya and I have been having a delightful chat,
haven't we?' Davis said, turning to me with a smile.

'Yeah, right,' Liv said with a snort.

Davis ignored her and carried on. 'I've been explaining to her
that just because you write romance novels, ladies shouldn't
expect any romance in real life from you. What was your longest
relationship again – six weeks?' Davis cracked, looking up at Jake
smugly.

I shifted uncomfortably in my chair as Jake looked stonily
down at Davis. The air around them was thick with tension.

'Look, both of you, we're in public and the two of you
need to—'

'I find your obsession with me unsettling,' Jake interrupted
me. 'Freya is right, though; you're not worth interacting with.
Freya, Liv, let's head out and leave Mulberry to his own thoughts:
the only person who cares to listen to him.'

I noticed Davis's face turning red so I hastily jumped up
before things got any worse. 'Yes, we have work to do. Bye, Davis,'
I said quickly, before he could say anything else to Jake. The last
thing we needed was the two of them getting into a fight and
undoing the work we were doing to repair Jake's opinion in the
romance books community.

'I need to get going for sure,' Liv agreed, also getting up.

I took hold of Jake's arm and steered him out of the room
with Liv behind us, not hanging around to let Davis say anything

else. I kept my hand on Jake as we hurried through the hotel lobby and out into the midday New York sunshine. Once outside, I let go of Jake and could breathe again.

'I know, I know,' he said, running a hand through his hair. 'I need to stop letting Mulberry get to me.'

'He's a twat,' I agreed.

Liv chuckled. 'A very apt description, Freya. He enjoys getting a rise out of you, Jake. And seems to want to charm you, Freya.'

I grimaced. 'Well, I wish he wouldn't bother because I definitely don't find him charming.' I glanced at Jake, who was watching me intently. 'Anyway, we don't want anything to ruin our progress here. So, I suggest we all stay out of Davis Mulberry's way for the remainder of the conference. And yes, I'm aware I'm being very bossy right now.'

Liv grinned at me. 'Bossy women get stuff done as I'm always telling my boyfriend, Aiden.' She looked at her watch. 'Right, I need to meet my editor for lunch now so I'll see you two later.' She headed off with a cheerful wave.

'I hope you didn't take anything Mulberry said seriously back there,' Jake said as I watched Liv go. 'You know what he's like.'

I nodded. 'I do but what he said...' I trailed off, annoyed that I had let Davis get into my head about Jake's intentions.

Jake stepped closer, the noise and sights of New York fading away as I looked at him. 'Forget about him. Let's go somewhere now, just us. Where else do you want to see in the city?'

I hesitated for a moment. I wanted to see more of New York and Jake had proved himself to be a great tour guide but I was nervous to be alone with him again. 'I did want to walk along the Brooklyn Bridge...' I admitted.

'Then I'll take you. If you want me to. Do you?'

'Yes. I'm just wondering if it's a good idea or not.'

'Why don't we decide that afterwards?'

I let myself laugh. 'That is a dangerous suggestion surely.'

Jake grinned. 'I can't help myself. Please, Freya?'

I hesitated but I was too weak not to want to spend more time outside of work with him. And the panel had gone well so we could afford a couple of hours away from the conference. I wanted to get to know him more, to know if this could be something or not. So even though Davis's words echoed in my head, I agreed to a walk with Jake.

We jumped into a yellow cab as Jake suggested walking from Brooklyn to Manhattan would give me a great view of the city skyline and then we could head back to our hotel. I watched the views out of the taxi window, in awe again, as we drove to Brooklyn. It still felt surreal to be here in the flesh.

'You're quiet,' Jake said. 'Did Davis upset you?'

'I guess what he said made me think... I don't know you very well.'

'He doesn't know me at all,' Jake said firmly. 'And he can see I like you, and you already know he tries to ruin anything I like. Why don't we get to know each other better?'

I nodded. I did like the sound of that. I knew I couldn't ask him what I really wanted to so I went with something else I was curious to know. 'When did you first really think about writing a book?'

'I haven't thought about that for a while,' he said. 'When I was about nineteen, I went on holiday with my family and I had just finished reading *The Catcher in the Rye*. We were in this remote place in the Lake District, and it was raining, and I was bored. My mum had a copy of *Emma* and I reluctantly decided to read it.' He smiled at the memory. 'But I was captivated by it.'

I smiled too. 'I love her books so much.'

'I enjoyed it even more than *The Catcher in the Rye*. I liked the humour and the irony, the way Austen created these characters I could absolutely see in my mind, and the fact that they made mistakes but things worked out in the end. Which is something I think I use in my books.' He paused and glanced at me. I nodded because he absolutely wrote very human characters that you believed in and rooted for. 'When I told my mum I had loved it, she said it was her favourite book because she had been reading it when she met my father. Anyway, I was inspired and after that, I found myself choosing romantic stories over everything else. That summer was long and I ended up starting to write my own stories. It was ten years until I'd get a book published but that summer shaped me as a reader and a writer, and started me on that journey.' Jake looked a little bit startled then. 'Sorry for such a long speech.'

'No, I liked it.' I knew then he wasn't lying about enjoying love stories. I could see it in his smile, in his eyes, the wistful look as he thought back to that summer. Whatever happened to make him say those things about romance books, it wasn't because he didn't love them any more. 'I hope you get to carry on writing books, Jake. I think the world would be a worse place without them.'

'That means more to me than you could know.'

We smiled at one another, and Davis Mulberry's warnings about Jake faded to the back of my mind.

We reached Brooklyn then and the taxi dropped us off so we could walk up to the bridge and start crossing it. We started at the point where the suspension cables were anchored. I sucked in an awed breath to be walking above the traffic, feeling like I could almost touch the cloudless, bright blue sky. Ahead, I could see the Brooklyn Tower granite archway which I recognised from scenes of the bridge I had seen; it looked like a cathedral open-ing. Behind the arches and cables, in the distance, was the incredible Manhattan skyline. Below us, cars sped on by like they had no idea we were up here.

I felt all at once tiny and on top of the world too. It was overwhelming.

I had to stop walking then and lean against one side to take everything in.

'Are you okay?' Jake asked, coming to stand beside me.

'Yeah, it's just incredible. I honestly wasn't sure if I'd ever get here. And in the run-up to this trip, I was so focused on what Hayley needed me to do and having to work with you, I didn't fully grasp the fact I'd actually be here. Seeing New York below me like this just makes me realise I did something I've wanted to do for years.'

Jake smiled. 'I'm glad you got to see this city, Freya. And I'm sorry if I made you feel like you couldn't be excited about it with me. Being with you has made me see how far removed from myself I've been for the past few months. You seem like you always are just yourself.'

'I'm not sure if that's always a good thing, though,' I admitted. I thought about how my advice to Jake hadn't really panned out.

'I wish you'd be more confident in your abilities. What made you want to be an agent?'

'I've always wanted to work with books. I went to a book signing once and I met the author's agent and she told me all about the job. It seemed like something I would love. But it took a long time to get the job with Hayley, and Liv was the one who kind of connected us, so maybe I've been struggling with a bit of imposter syndrome.' I sighed. 'That's why I was so nervous for this trip and so desperate to prove myself, I suppose.'

'Listen, I'll talk to Hayley when we get back. Whatever happens for the rest of the conference, it's on me, not you, okay?'

Jake said fiercely. 'There should be no consequences for you. I promise, Freya.'

I could tell how much he cared. I had no idea if Hayley would listen to him, though. The six months I had worked with her had made me wonder if she listened to anyone but herself.

'I appreciate that.' I would have preferred the truth from him but he clearly wasn't ready. He was trying to make things right. I had to give him that.

Jake looked across at me. My hair blew in the breeze and he touched a strand with his fingertips. I looked back at him.

'I'd love to kiss you again.'

23

My breath hitched. I wanted to kiss him again even though I could list all the reasons why we shouldn't. There was also a list of reasons why I wanted to, though. Out on the Bridge on a New York summer's day, looking into a handsome man's eyes, I just went with the moment. My body was already leaning towards him like it couldn't help itself. So, I smiled. 'I'd love that too.'

He closed the distance between us, his fingers sliding properly into my hair, catching my lips with his like they were something precious. I found myself melting into him as he pulled me closer, his other hand on the small of my back. I hooked mine around his neck as we lost ourselves in the kiss despite the fact people were walking past us on the bridge. Everything faded into the background once again as our lips explored one another.

When his tongue touched mine, I murmured contentedly and Jake's hand on my hair slid down to cup my chin.

Our kiss deepened and I tried to get even closer to him. His facial hair brushed against my skin again. His hold on me grew tighter like he was claiming me somehow. And I was happy to let him. Fire burned in my lips from his warm, passionate touch. I wondered if his kiss felt this good, just how good other touches from him might feel.

Then Jake broke away from my lips. 'Freya,' he said in a gruff voice that sent pleasure travelling down my body. His eyes were dark as he looked at me, his breath as ragged as my own. He shook his head. 'You're making me forget where I am.'

I smiled. 'Me too,' I agreed, also breathless.

He leaned in again and touched my lips gently with his. 'Should we keep walking?'

'I suppose we should,' I said, thinking that I'd prefer to be alone with him but as we were on the very public Brooklyn Bridge, we should probably pull ourselves together. But God, kissing Jake was addictive.

Jake took my hand in his and we left the railing to carry on strolling across the bridge. The clear day allowed us to see the Manhattan skyline perfectly. We were silent as we walked, taking in the view, our hands entwined like we'd always walked that way.

I snuck a look at his profile. He was so handsome; it was crazy to think I had kissed this man. When he caught me looking, he glanced my way and gave me a smouldering smile like maybe he also couldn't believe his luck. I had always wondered what it was like to kiss someone who gave you butterflies and who you craved more from with each touch of their lips. I hadn't had that before.

As I had told Liv, and Jake had overheard, my love life had never quite lived up to my hopes. I had read romance books, like Jake's love stories, wondering why I always felt like something was missing when I was with a man. I didn't want to get carried away thinking that Jake might finally be different, but kissing him was certainly a revelation compared to previous kisses in my life. My lips still tingled from his touch and my body was still warm from being pressed against his. My mind was alive with thoughts of what might happen next.

'I wish I knew what you were thinking,' Jake suddenly said. He was looking across at me. 'You are usually so chatty, so easy to read, so open with me but that look on your face right now... I want to decipher it so badly.'

My skin flushed at the thought of him knowing how I was feeling. 'I never know what you're thinking, though...' I replied with a raised eyebrow. I felt like I had misunderstood Jake from the first moment we met.

'You have to know that all I'm thinking is, "that was an incredible kiss and I can't wait for more".'

I couldn't stop a smile from spreading across my face.

'And how gorgeous you look right now,' Jake added. He squeezed my hand wrapped in his.

'Thank you,' I said, flustered by the way he was looking at me. I was happy that he wanted more kisses just like I did. But it felt crazy when I was only now starting to get to know the real him. And I worried that he would never show me that man completely.

'You look concerned,' Jake suddenly said, studying my expression. 'Are you worried about Hayley?'

'Yes, and this,' I said, gesturing to our hands. 'Liv reminding us that you're basically my client while we're out here, and Davis Mulberry seemed to sense something...'

'And tried warning you off me?' Jake asked astutely.

'He did,' I admitted.

'You told me that we should ignore him,' Jake pointed out. 'He's trying to push our buttons. He enjoys winding people up.

He brings out the worst in me, I can admit that. Especially when I saw him trying to flirt with you during the panel, and asking you out.'

I glanced across at me. 'You didn't like that?'

'Definitely not,' he replied quickly. 'And not just because I wanted to be doing that myself, but he really isn't someone you want to get involved with.'

I nodded. Davis gave me the ick so Jake had nothing to worry about there. But that didn't mean that he wasn't right about Jake and how he was with women. Not to mention the fact we did work closely together. This burgeoning attraction between the two of us was complicated. 'I suppose he did make me curious about you and past relationships...'

'I'm curious about you and yours too,' he replied. 'We have so much time to talk about all that. Do we really want to talk about the past now? When we have all this...' He gestured with his free hand at the city around us.

I looked ahead at the skyscrapers glistening in the summer sun and knew that he was right. We had limited time here, after all. 'Okay then, what did you have in mind?'

We looked at one another and I realised that had come out far more suggestively than I had planned. We giggled like we were teenagers or something, no mean feat considering I was in my twenties and he was in his thirties, but there was something about us being hand in hand on the bridge after an incredible kiss that suddenly made me feel giddy.

'Race you to the next bit,' I said, pointing to the archway ahead. 'Winner chooses what we do next.'

Jake looked at me for a moment like I was crazy, and maybe I kind of was right now, but then he grinned. 'Deal.' He dropped my hand and took off unexpectedly.

'Cheater!' I yelled and tore after him.

People watched us with a mixture of amusement and annoyance as we raced together along the bridge. My hair swept out behind me in the breeze as I tried to catch up with Jake's long legs. We were both laughing as we ran towards the archway of the Manhattan Tower. I honestly couldn't remember the last time I had run for anything other than a Tube train. It was kind of exhilarating, even though I was even more breathless than I'd been when we kissed. Jake glanced back at me and grinned like he was having just as much fun. I knew I wouldn't catch him, but I didn't give up and kept running until I joined him by the archway.

Jake clutched the rail as I skidded to a halt in front of him and tried to inhale as much air into my lungs as possible. 'That probably wasn't a fair contest given our height difference.'

'And my lack of any exercise beside walking to work in the mornings.' I tilted my head and squinted through the sunshine at him. 'I suppose you have a personal trainer and go to the gym every day?'

He chuckled. 'I definitely don't. I'm a writer; I like staying at home and drink far too much coffee. But even if it wasn't fair, I won so I get to pick what we do next, yes?'

I put my hands on my hips. 'I'm afraid to even ask what you're going to pick...' I had a sudden thought he might suggest we go back to our hotel, and I wasn't sure whether I would want to agree to that.

'I don't know about you but now I've mentioned coffee, I think we need to grab some food and drink. Okay?'

I nodded in agreement.

'And I know the perfect place to take you after we get back to Manhattan. Come on.'

Jake held out his hand again and I took it, and we walked over the rest of the bridge. I looked behind me as we left, the bridge rising up behind us, and knew I'd never forget walking across it. I always knew it would be an incredible experience but having the best kiss of my life halfway across it had made it even sweeter.

24

We walked from the bridge to a quiet side street and a tiny coffee shop that had a long queue outside. As we waited, Jake told me that this was his favourite place to get a coffee the last time he'd come to the city. 'I came here on a research trip for my book *Meet Me in New York* and discovered this place.'

I knew that was about two years ago as I had read that book while I did the rounds of interviews for a book-related job. I'd been starting to get frustrated and down, wondering if I ever would be able to work with books like I had always wanted to. I had started reading *Meet Me in New York* after a particularly bad interview where I had arrived late thanks to a sudden Tube station closure, been directed to the wrong floor by an unhelpful receptionist, and then proceeded to knock a bookcase of books over. I had sunk into my bed that evening and opened up Jake's novel, grateful to escape into a life that wasn't my own. 'That book really cheered me up after a bad day,' I told him. 'I remember the characters have their first kiss over a cup of coffee.'

'This is the place that inspired that scene,' Jake said. He

smiled at me. 'It's kind of crazy to think of you reading my books.'

'Yeah I guess you can't feed me a romantic line from one of your characters because I will know it's not really you saying that.'

He laughed. 'I'll watch myself. But just because one of my character's might have said it, all those lines were written by me and I'd never say anything romantic to you that I didn't mean.'

'I think dating a romance author could be dangerous,' I replied. 'Oh, not saying we're dating but you know what I mean; if you tell me romantic lines, I might get carried away...' I said then cringed at myself. 'See? I always get carried away and say stupid things in front of you!'

'I told you – I like the fact you say what you're thinking. Back on the bridge, I was dying to know what you were thinking after we kissed,' Jake reassured me with a smile. 'And maybe I want you to get carried away, Freya.'

I was still staring at him as we reached the front of the queue and were asked for our order. He wanted me to get carried away? This man really was trouble...

I ordered an iced coffee as it was such a lovely day and Jake ordered a latte then we both got a cream cheese bagel. Jake led us to the Battery – a park where we found a bench overlooking the Hudson River. We sat down and as we started to eat and drink, Jake pointed out the Statue of Liberty in the distance.

'So surreal,' I admitted, shaking my head at the fact that I was looking at such an iconic landmark for real. We sat in silence for a minute, drinking and eating, as we took in another amazing view.

The silence was a contented one. Which for me was unusual. For maybe the first time in my life, I didn't feel the need to shatter the calm by talking or trying to find out what the person next to me was thinking, or believing that I needed to entertain them. It again felt so far out of my comfort zone; I wasn't sure what was happening when I was around Jake but I hadn't experienced anything quite like it before. I liked it, though.

After a minute, Jake turned to me. 'Are you okay?'

I met his gaze. 'Yes. Why?'

'I don't know; you're quiet so I was worried.'

That made me smile. 'I suppose I'm usually not great at letting silences drag on. But this was... nice.'

'It's nice being here with you,' Jake agreed. His words made my heart stutter a little bit that he felt the same way I did.

'You ever have a moment and wish you could just freeze it and let it exist for hours and hours?' I asked.

Jake thought about my question for a couple of seconds. 'Yeah, I do wish we could freeze moments sometimes but then if we could, would they stay special in our memories? Or are they special because they are fleeting and we never know when we're going to have one or how long the moment will last? Maybe that makes us hang on tightly and enjoy it for as long as we are in it, right?'

I nodded slowly. 'It's true. I thought I'd like to keep this moment going for a long time but you're right; it's special because I know it has to end soon. And I need to make sure I remember it.'

'I'm honoured this is a moment you want to remember.'

I tore my gaze from his eyes and looked back out at the Statue of Liberty. 'I don't often feel calm or at peace. I'm thinking at a hundred miles an hour most of the time. And talking at it too, as you know. But I felt it then. I feel it now.'

Jake exhaled loudly. 'The fact that you feel calm with me... God, I want to kiss you again.'

I turned back to him. 'Why don't you?' I challenged.

He smiled and leaned in to brush my lips with his. Then he kissed my cheek and slid down to my jaw, moving to kiss me under my ear and then down the side of my neck, making me sigh. He kissed back up my neck to my ear then leaned in to whisper, 'Do you have any idea the hold you have over me already?'

I shivered with pleasure. I wanted to believe every sweet thing he said. He sounded so sincere. He made me feel so good. I could feel myself wanting to get carried away too. I had been looking for kisses and touches and moments like I had read about in romance novels. And now finally, here they were. How could I stop myself now?

His lips found mine again and this time, this kiss was even more passionate than it had been on the Bridge. Our lips met in a frenzy and I didn't think I'd ever kissed a man with such abandon in public. But there was a magnetic pull between us and I was helpless to resist it. His lips pressed harder against me, his tongue searched for mine and his arms held me snug against him. I moved closer, wishing I could climb onto his lap and maybe I would have done if we had been in private. His tongue massaging mine turned me on more than I could have imagined.

When Jake broke from my lips, and moved back to kiss my neck, his hand reached for my hair, tugging it over to one side so it fell over my shoulder. The move surprised and thrilled me. I let out a soft moan.

'That sound,' Jake breathed into my ear, 'might be my downfall.'

'Jake,' I breathed as he pulled my earlobe into his mouth and gave it a little suck. 'Everyone can see us,' I said, even though I wasn't sure I actually minded one little bit.

'Sorry, you're right, I'll stop.' Jake pulled away and looked at me. 'Shall we go somewhere else?' He stroked my hair. 'Anywhere you like?'

'Anywhere?' I asked, trying to focus my thoughts on his question but it wasn't easy with my chest rising and falling with ragged breaths and my whole body humming with desire.

'Hmm. Anywhere you want,' he replied, giving me another soft kiss on my lips, staying close to me as his eyes searched mine. 'What do you want to do, Freya?'

I thought about earlier when I wondered if he was going to suggest our hotel as our next destination. The words bubbled up and I couldn't stop them. I craved Jake. My body was desperate for more of his kisses and touches. I mean, it had been a long time since it had had any and I needed more. 'Let's go back to our hotel,' I said in a rush. My cheeks turned pink but I held his gaze as confidently as I could. I didn't think I was at all seductive but I hoped Jake wanted this as much as I did.

Jake's eyes darkened as he looked back at me, his eyes dropping to my mouth then back up to my eyes again. 'That's what you really want?' he asked slowly.

I nodded.

'But I know you were worried about what I'd overheard in your office: that I thought you might be easy...'

'I'll never really know if that made you think of me in that way more than you ever would have otherwise,' I said. 'But these kisses aren't enough. I want more. I need more.'

'You know I feel the same,' he said in a low voice.

'We don't have long left in New York...' I had no idea if there was even a possibility that this sudden and unexpected fire between us could continue past this trip and if not, would I regret not doing more than just kissing Jake? The answer was a resounding yes. 'We should make the most of it.'

'I feel like I never know what you will say or do next,' Jake said, shaking his head. 'And it's addictive.'

'So, yes to going back to our hotel?' I bit my lip, hoping he wouldn't reject me.

'It was always a yes,' he said. 'I just wanted to be sure you were sure. We do whatever you want, okay? You just want a kiss and a cuddle, that's more than enough for me...' He held out his hand. I took it and he pulled me easily up off the bench with him. Then he put his fingers under my chin, tilting my face up towards his. 'Okay?'

I nodded. 'Anything I want.' My mind was alive with delicious possibilities. It had been a long time since I felt this kind of desire for a man. It was heady. Exhilarating and terrifying. But one that I knew I would be forever pissed at myself if I ignored. 'Maybe we should get a taxi,' I added impatiently.

Jake chuckled but his eyes flashed with equal desire. 'Hmm. I think that's a very good idea.'

25

I had an irrational feeling that everyone in the Waldorf lobby knew that Jake and I were planning some sort of afternoon delight as we climbed out of the taxi and walked through our hotel. Jake's hand brushed mine and I looked across at him, and we exchanged a shy smile. My heart thumped inside my chest. It had been three years since a man had seen me naked. Three years since I had done anything more than kiss a man. Three years since I had been touched...

'You seem to be thinking really hard,' Jake said as we waited for a lift to take us up to our floor.

'It's hard to switch my brain off sometimes,' I confessed.

'I have that problem too,' Jake replied as the lift doors opened and we stepped in there together, and were suddenly alone again. 'I always thought it was part of the reason I became a writer. I have a brain that loves to overthink, which is great for letting my imagination flow and come up with ideas for my books, but not so great when it comes to worrying about my own life.'

'That makes sense,' I said, liking the fact he had opened up about that. 'My overthinking has no creative benefit though. I think mine is mostly worrying what other people think of me, and being desperate to do my best. Maybe I'm a bit of a perfectionist, so I always end up feeling like I'm coming short in some way.'

'I hope you're not worrying about that right now,' he said, looking at me. 'Because kissing you has been incredible so whatever else we do, there is no chance it won't be just as good.'

I smiled. His words did relax me a little bit. 'It's just been a while for me, as you know...' I trailed off, biting my lip. The lift reached our floor and we stepped out and walked to our side-by-side rooms. Nerves swirled in my stomach as we hovered outside.

'I meant what I said: we do whatever you're comfortable with,' Jake reassured me. 'I just want to be close to you.'

'Me too.' I reached for my key card and opened up my room, feeling like I might be a tiny bit more comfortable surrounded by my things. It seemed naughty to be thinking of using a hotel bed for anything other than a nap in the afternoon. I didn't think I'd ever be what could be described as naughty before but then I looked at Jake as I held the door open for us and I knew I'd never been with anyone like him before. It made me want to be a little bit naughty.

I closed the door behind us and took a breath.

'I'm sorry, it's a bit messy,' I said as we moved through into the area where the bed was. My things were strewn everywhere. I'd never been particularity good at getting ready in an organised way. 'I bet you're a neat freak,' I added, knowing by the grin he flashed me that I was completely correct.

'Some of that is a procrastination thing, though – if I'm not motivated to write, I clean and if I'm stressed, I organise so...' He held out his hand to me. I stepped over to him and took it, entwining my fingers with his. He brought our hands up to his lips and kissed the back of mine. 'You don't need to apologise about the room; I'm only looking at you.'

'We are so different,' I said, my skin instantly warming at his touch.

'Not when it comes to important things.' Jake let go of my hand and slipped an arm around my waist. My body instantly curved itself around his like we were two connecting puzzle pieces. 'Trust, loyalty, love...'

'Work ethic.'

Jake grinned. 'When you told me off about that bloody article, I had never wanted a woman more.'

'Maybe I need to tell you off more then.' I was only half-joking.

'I hate letting you down. I'm sorry that I couldn't do what you wanted at the reader session.'

'I'd be lying if I didn't want to know everything about you,' I confessed, wishing he would unpeel his layers for me. But I also knew this was early days, and I was expecting a lot when all we had done was kiss.

'I want to know you too,' Jake whispered.

Lifting my face to meet his, our lips came together like they had always been meant to. Kissing Jake got better each time as we fell into a rhythm, learning the ways we both liked to kiss and touch as we got more relaxed with one another. When our tongues met, I hooked my arms around his neck and he pulled me towards him by the waist so our chests touched. I wondered if he could feel how fast my heart was beating through our clothes. Then he reached up and rested his hand on the side of my neck, applying that little bit of pressure to my throat that made my desire turn up several notches.

'Jake,' I pleaded with him then.

'Too much?' he asked, starting to remove his hand.

'No,' I said quickly. 'I want more.'

He flashed a smile at me before he kissed me again. Then he dropped his lips to kiss down my neck and to my collarbone. He traced the sweetheart neckline of my dress with his lips, kissing me on that delicate, bare skin there so gently, he left goose bumps in his wake. His hands moved to my shoulders, caressing me. 'I do love your dresses but...'

'But what?' I murmured as he spoke through kisses.

Jake stopped and met my eyes. 'I'd love to take this one off.'

I giggled. 'I'd love you to take it off.' I held my arms up and Jake's breathed hitched as he reached for the fabric and lifted it over my head. I was thankful I'd put on a matching set of under-wear today.

'Mmm,' Jake said, his eyes drinking me greedily as he tossed my dress onto the bed behind us. 'Remember what I said? We do whatever you want...' he said, not touching me yet.

I looked at him and even though I was still nervous, the pull I felt towards him overtook that. 'I want it all,' I confessed out loud. I moved towards him and his arms met me halfway. Our lips met again and this time, there was no holding back. Jake pulled me down with him onto the bed and we rolled together, our limbs tangling up with one another as we kissed, trying to get as close as we possibly could.

'Too many clothes,' I pulled away from his mouth to grumble.

I felt his chest move with a laugh but Jake sat up and unbuttoned his blue shirt, pulling it off and tossing it on top of my discarded dress. I looked up at him from the bed as he reached for his belt, undoing it and pulling it off. He paused on the fly of his trousers but I nodded furiously and he smiled, unzipping and sliding them off so he was also now only in his underwear. His tall body was lean, but despite him saying he didn't go to the gym, his chest was defined and I could see muscles in his arms that suggested he'd be strong enough to lift me. My eyes trailed down to notice that he was straining out of his boxers, just as excited as I felt.

He came back to lean over me, propping up on an elbow to look down at me on the bed. 'You are so beautiful. Inside and out.' He reached out to stroke my hair then touch my lips with his fingertips. Then he looked at me. 'You said it had been three years... Are you sure you want it to be me?'

I thought about how attractive I found him, but also how attractive he made me feel. There was crazy chemistry between us. But it felt like there could be more to it. Like when Jake told me he liked me the way I was. He didn't want me to change. He loved the clothes I wore. He thought I could do whatever I wanted. He didn't want to let me down. 'Yes, because you really see me.'

He smiled. 'I see you. And I want you so much.'

'I want you too.'

Jake's eyes lit up and he caught my lips with his. His free hand traced the outline of my bra, slipping over the cup. I arched my back towards him and he moved from my lips to kiss down my chest, pulling my bra down to keep going, kissing my breast and then running his tongue over my nipple, hardening it instantly. He gave a contented sigh as he reached behind me and unclipped the bra, again tossing it away. He moved back, cupping my breast as his mouth returned to my nipple, and I let out an encouraging moan. My body was so eager, I should have been embarrassed but I could see by the look on Jake's face that he was loving how responsive I was to him. He kissed down the centre of my chest then, trailing down towards my belly button. This time, my breath hitched. He carried on until he reached my underwear, kissing the fabric as I arched my back more to try to feel more pressure.

'What now, baby?' Jake said then. His voice gruff, his eyes black as he looked at me.

'Take them off,' I pleaded with him, glowing at him calling me 'baby'.

Jake did as he was told, slipping his fingers under the fabric and hitching my knickers down my leg and throwing them on the floor. 'Open your legs; I want to taste you,' he pleaded then.

I paused for a second. I'd never been with a man who commanded me like that or even used anything close to dirty words. In fact, sex had always been a rushed and hushed affair after dark. But I was lying naked and exposed in the afternoon with a man who had no qualms at being honest about what he wanted to do to me. If I had been turned on before, now I was lost in lust. I opened my legs and watched as he dipped his head in between them and touched me with his tongue.

'God,' I cried at the contact, pleasure shooting up through my body as he expertly tasted me. I reached out and ran my fingers through his hair as he hummed against me. 'Jake,' I said, my legs already starting to tremble; I'd been that horny. He moved a finger inside me then and I moaned louder than I probably ever had.

Jake lifted off me for a moment to look at me. 'Good girl,' he said before he carried on.

I had no idea I would enjoy those two words but I moaned again and then he added another finger inside me, bucking on the bed beneath him. His tongue did things that I had only fantasised about when I was touching myself before. 'Jesus Christ,' I breathed as the pleasure built, and my legs began to shake for real. I found myself giving his hair a tug as I cried out, trying to gulp in air as I lost control. I fell back against the bed then, my body throbbing as I tried to come down from that delicious high. 'That was...'

Jake chuckled as he laid down beside me and ran a hand down my arm then leg. 'I loved seeing you lose control.'

I turned to him and bit my lip.

'Look at you.' He touched where I had bit myself. 'Your hair has gone wild from your writhing. And your lips and chin are red from kissing and this...' He rubbed his facial hair. 'And your breathing... it's so hot.'

'That was so hot,' I confessed, my cheeks turning pink at the way he was watching me but I liked his attention so much. He looked like he'd never seen anything more enjoyable. 'I've never been called that before...'

Jake watched me for a moment then smiled. 'Good girl? You are a good girl, aren't you, Freya?' he murmured, his fingertip still on my mouth. He applied a little bit of pressure and I parted my lips. He slipped a finger into my mouth and watched as I sucked it.

'I want it all,' I repeated then, catching his dark eyes with my own.

'You can have it all,' he replied.

26

Jake's lips met mine again as he propped himself up and leaned over me. I reached out to touch him and he murmured happily as I smiled at how aroused he was. His mouth left my lips. 'Are you sure? You really want this?'

'Yes, I really do,' I said eagerly as I stroked him. I was nervous but I wanted this too much to let my three-year dry spell stop me.

Jake reached over the bed to find his trousers and pulled out a condom. 'Take control, baby. I want this to be good for you,' he said, lying on his back on the bed as he slid the condom on. 'We can stop any time, okay?' His ran his hand down my arm and entwined his fingers with mine. Our eyes met and sparks flew between us. I was certain I hadn't felt this connected to a man in bed before.

I pulled myself on top of him, straddling his body with mine. Jake's eyes slid over my body and the look on his face was just as thrilling as his touch had been. I felt beautiful and desired and maybe even a little bit sexy, which was something I would never have described myself as before.

When I smiled down at him, Jake shook his head. 'I think I might be the luckiest man in the world right now.'

I shifted forward and lifted myself up, easing down on him slowly, taking my time.

'No, definitely the luckiest...' Jake said then as I took him inside me with a gasp. 'Are you okay?'

'Yes,' I breathed as he filled me up and it was clear I had been missing out on some really good sex because this beat every other encounter I'd had hands down already. I moved on top of him and this time, we both murmured with pleasure. Jake kept hold of one of my hands in his and slid his other onto my waist. I put my palm on his chest to steady myself as we moved together, our eyes staying locked, connected in every way possible.

'God,' I sighed out then as I rocked on top of him faster, leaning back and causing us both to moan with pleasure.

'Better than you remember?' Jake asked with a sexy smile.

'I'm not sure it's ever been like this,' I managed to say in between gasps.

'It's never been like this for me. Come here.' Jake gave me a tug around the waist so I leaned forward and he lifted his head so he could touch my lips with his. The hand not linked with mine moved to my hair, wrapping around it and moving it to one side, giving it a little pull, bringing me closer.

I moaned at that action and moved faster on top of him. 'Say it again,' I gasped as pleasure built inside me. My body heated up and my heart was pounding in my chest. I was starting to lose control in the best way.

Jake didn't even have to ask. 'Are you going to come on top of me like a good girl, Freya?'

'God,' I said again. What was it with those two words? The praise was doing something to me that I hadn't expected. I was shocked as I hit a second peak then, crying out in surprise and delight as another delicious shudder ran through my body.

'That's it, baby,' Jake said, gasping beneath me. He moved his hands to my waist and rocked me a couple of times as I slowly came back down to earth. 'Fuck,' he cried then, shuddering beneath me as he reached his own peak.

'You said it,' I said. Our eyes met then and we both started to giggle. I pulled myself off him and flopped on the bed with a breathless sigh. Jake tossed his condom then laid down on his back, lifting his arm up. I shifted on top of his chest, curling myself around him as his arm pulled me closer into his nook.

My whole body was throbbing in the best way. 'I don't think that's ever happened before,' I admitted in a whisper. I tried to think about whether I'd ever come just through having sex in my life but I couldn't. It might have been because it had been so long for me, but I suspected it was more because I had felt so at ease with Jake and him letting me take control. Either way, I wasn't complaining one little bit.

'It was pretty amazing,' Jake said softly back, holding me tightly against him.

'So, it was... okay?' I asked quietly then, the smile fading from my face as I shifted nervously against Jake's strong, warm body.

'Are you serious?'

'I just wondered...'

Jake moved then, turning so he faced me, keeping his arms around me. Our bodies curled even closer like they had always meant to be tangled up with each other. 'I wish you could see what I see,' Jake said. 'I wish you were more confident. It wasn't just okay. It was incredible. You are gorgeous, Freya. And so sexy. And that was hot from start to finish. You are so hot. But watching you come on top of my cock, that was something I'll never forget.'

'Bloody hell,' I said, my cheeks turning pink instantly. I tried to duck and hide my face but Jake reached out and tilted my chin to hold our eye contact.

'Why are you embarrassed?' he asked, looking amused at my reaction.

'You're so... open and honest,' I said. 'That's new for me.'

'I meant every word,' he reassured me.

I wondered if he would ever be so open and honest with me outside of the bedroom. I really hoped so.

'How do you feel? Was it okay for you?' Jake asked me gently then.

'I think you could tell it was,' I said with a dismissive laugh. But I saw his serious expression and I tried to push away my embarrassment. I nodded. 'Yeah, it was the best ever,' I whispered.

Jake leaned in to brush his lips gently with mine. My body tingled instantly. 'I can't wait for more,' he said when he pulled back. 'Do you want more too?'

Warring emotions churned through me. I wanted more, of course I did. But I had no idea what this was, or would be. Was this just a New York fling? The last person I wanted to think about in bed popped up – Davis Mulberry and his warning about how Jake treated women. That seemed so at odds with the way Jake was looking at me now, but it made me hesitate. I didn't want to dare to hope this could be something special if he was going to let me down. Maybe I needed to just try to enjoy the moment and not get lost in thoughts of what happened next. How could I walk away from sex like that?

'I'd like that,' I said quietly.

'I want to spend the rest of today together. Can we?' He touched my cheek. 'We could go out for dinner and a drink then come back here; what do you think?'

'Sounds perfect.'

I thought about tomorrow. We were supposed to make an appearance at the conference in the stand hall then there was an end-of-conference party that would run from dinner until late, and our flight home was at 6 a.m. the following morning. So, these were potentially our last hours alone together. 'Let's get dressed up and go somewhere for a New York moment.'

'A New York moment?' Jake asked with a smile.

'Yeah, you know when we can look at each other and say, "This could only happen in New York".'

'A New York moment. Okay, let's do it.' Jake pulled away from me and my body immediately felt his absence. He rolled across the bed and swung his feet over. 'Let's get changed then I'll knock for you and take you somewhere.' He looked at the bedside table clock radio. 'Say seven?'

'Okay. Where are you going to take me?' I asked, watching as he climbed off the bed and started to get dressed. I admired his body shamelessly.

'It's a surprise.' When he'd got dressed, he came around the side of the bed closest to me, his eyes drinking in my still naked body. 'Although now I'm not sure I can leave...'

I smiled. 'I don't want you to but it's not for long. We'll be back here later, right?' I would normally feel embarrassed at him being clothed looking at me naked. I would normally have been covering myself up, listing my flaws silently in my mind, but Jake was admiring me so openly, I didn't feel the need. In fact, I even liked him looking.

'I can't wait,' Jake replied. He leaned down to kiss me. 'I don't want to leave you.'

'I don't want to let you go,' I said.

I watched him leave my hotel room then I turned over to lie

on my back and smile up at the ceiling because holy hell, the last few hours had felt like a dream.

The problem was, I had no idea how long I would get to dream for.

27

As I was getting ready, there was a knock on my hotel room door and when I opened it up, Liv and Tessa were there asking if I wanted to hang out. I had pulled on my favourite short, black dress and was holding my hair as I wanted to put it up. 'Um, well...' I hedged as they stared at me.

'Why do you look like you're dressed up for a date?' Liv demanded.

I looked down the corridor, relieved it was empty. I certainly didn't want to become the gossip of the conference. 'Come in you two,' I said, stepping aside. They walked in and I shut the door, resuming my seat on the bed in front of the mirror on the wall. Liv flopped down on the other side of the bed, curling her legs up to watch me while Tessa sat down in the chair by the window. I piled my hair up on top of my head and reached for my pot of bobby pins. 'I suppose it is kind of a date,' I admitted, avoiding their eyes in the mirror as I carried on doing my hair.

'God, how did you find a date in this conference? It's 99 per cent women,' Tessa joked.

'You don't mean...' Liv said. 'Freya, are you going out with Jake?'

'Jake Richards?' Tessa repeated, looking from Liv back to me. 'I did not see that coming!'

'I did,' Liv said to Tessa. 'But I hoped I was wrong when I sensed some... chemistry. The way he was looking at Davis Mulberry trying to chat Freya up at the panel earlier, we almost had to break up a fight between them.'

'I am here guys, just FYI,' I said, shaking my head.

'Oh, we know,' Liv said, turning back to me.

'We're just going out for dinner,' I said, hoping that didn't count as a lie exactly. I was merely failing to mention our earlier afternoon delight even though I kept getting delicious flashbacks of it.

'Seriously, Freya, what will Hayley say if she finds out? I thought you were focused on your career,' Liv continued. 'You shouldn't date Hayley's client when you want her to promote you to become an agent yourself! Especially not at a conference where everyone in publishing could find out and gossip about it! And he's so much older...'

I spun around. 'Your boyfriend is older than you!' I reminded Liv.

She shrugged. 'Not ten years older. Plus, Jake is like a grown-up.'

'And I'm not?' I demanded. Then I sighed. 'Actually, don't answer that. I never feel like one, to be honest.'

'Nor do I,' Tessa said with sympathy. 'I don't think anyone will find out; they are working closely together here, right? And you both have to eat...'

'Exactly,' I said, nodding as I turned back to carry on with my hair. 'It's just dinner, Liv, don't worry.'

'I can't help it. I know how much you want to be an agent one day; I don't want this to mess that up. I hope Jake isn't taking advantage of you. Didn't Davis Mulberry say he likes to pretend to women he's romantic like his books, but just uses them for sex then dumps them?'

'Freya won't let him do that,' Tessa said. 'They're just going out tonight; it doesn't have to lead to anything.'

I swallowed hard. 'We can't trust anything Davis Mulberry says,' I mumbled.

'I know you fancy him; I can see the lust in your eyes but...' Liv began. Then she leaned a little bit closer. 'You look flushed. You're not telling us something, I can tell.'

'God, are you a detective now?' I snapped as I slid pins into my hair, wishing that I didn't have a family member on this trip; Liv knew me far too well.

'Freya,' Liv said, giving me a look that told me to cut the BS.

I sighed. 'Fine, fine. We have slept together,' I admitted, turning from the mirror now my hair was finished, bracing myself for their disapproval.

There was a moment of shocked silence.

'How was it?' Liv and Tessa asked in unison.

I couldn't help but smile. 'Bloody brilliant, if I'm honest. What am I going to do?'

'It depends if this is just a New York thing,' Tessa said slowly. 'If it was, would you be okay with that? I don't want to see you getting hurt.'

Her question echoed my own thoughts and I had no idea how to answer her so I deflected. 'Your relationship started on holiday, didn't it?' I asked, suddenly remembering that Tessa met her boyfriend in Paris when they inadvertently ended up having to share an Airbnb together. Liv told me all about it because it sounded like a plot of romance novel.

'It did,' Tessa said with a shy but happy smile.

'But they didn't work together,' Liv pointed out. 'What happened to you not wanting to date men as they weren't romantic and just wanted sex? I thought you were looking for more than just a fling.'

'This could be more than a fling,' Tessa suggested.

I sighed. 'I don't know. I got swept up in it all maybe. But he's so...' I trailed off, finding it hard to explain. 'I suddenly am so attracted to him. God. I don't know what happened. One minute, we seemed like the least likely pairing ever to being unable to keep our hands off each other.'

'Freya, you don't do flings or holiday romances. You don't want casual sex. You want to fall in love. Just like us,' Liv said, gesturing to her and Tessa.

'No need to rub your fairytale romances in my face,' I grumbled.

'I'm just worried that you've thrown what you are looking for out of the window because this is Jake Richards.'

Liv and I stared at one another. We never fought but I could feel her concern along with a hint of disapproval. She was right, though. I had been waiting for real romance – was I hoping that sleeping with a romance author would make that happen? Jake had shown me the sights of New York and promised me a New York moment, but no more than that. I had slept with him anyway. After three years of not being with a man. The attraction, the desire had been too strong, being away with him had made it seem like not a big deal. But maybe I was just fooling myself about that. Maybe I was setting myself up to get hurt.

I slumped on the bed. 'I got carried away maybe,' I admitted.

'It's happened to all of us,' Tessa said. 'Just because it's moved quickly, and you're away, doesn't mean it can't turn into something more once you get back home, right?'

Her sentence hung in the room like a crescent moon that we looked up at in silence.

After a few seconds, it seemed like none of us wanted to answer her question.

'He's taking me out so we can have a New York moment,' I said then. I gestured to myself. 'Hence getting glammed up. Dinner and drinks somewhere.'

'Sounds romantic,' Liv said. 'And you look gorgeous. He will be lucky to have you on his arm. Just be careful. Don't let anyone from the conference see anything they shouldn't. Think of yourself, Freya. And don't give that good heart of yours away to anyone who doesn't deserve it.'

'God, Liv.' I reached up to touch the corner of my eye to stop a tear from destroying the perfect winged eyeliner I had just applied. 'You are going to ruin my make-up. I won't settle for anything less than the kind of romance we read, and you two write about, I promise.'

She nodded. 'Good girl.'

I choked a little bit, trying not to laugh.

'Are you okay?' Tessa asked, frowning at me as I tried to compose myself. But after Jake calling me that in bed, I wasn't sure I could hear those two words outside of the bedroom with a straight face again.

I nodded as I sucked in oxygen and forced 'good girl' out of my mind. 'Sure. I'll take your advice on board, guys. I am just going to have fun tonight. I'll be okay, I promise.'

I got up to go into the bathroom to spritz on some perfume but in the mirror, I caught Liv and Tessa exchange a worried look behind me.

28

When I next opened the hotel room door, Jake was on the other side. Liv and Tessa had left ten minutes before, telling me to have a good time but I knew that deep down, they didn't think this was a great idea. The problem was when my eyes met Jake's, any good sense seemed to fly out of the window. He broke into a sexy smile as he took in my appearance and I admired his right back. He was wearing dark trousers and a dark shirt that I imagined immediately unbuttoning. There was instant heat between us.

'You look stunning,' Jake said, leaning in to kiss me softly on the lips. 'Are you ready?'

'Yes,' I said, coming out of my room and taking hold of the hand he offered to me. We walked to the lifts and got in one to go down to the lobby. When the doors opened, Jake let go of my hand. I spotted a couple of people I recognised from the conference who were clearly staying in our hotel too. I wasn't sure whether to feel disappointed or relieved that Jake had stopped touching me. I thought about what Liv had said – I didn't want Hayley to find out about this – but my heart still sank anyway.

Maybe this thing between us was destined only to exist here in New York.

'I hired a car,' Jake said as we stepped across the lobby towards the revolving doors. 'And booked a table somewhere that I hope you will like.' He gestured to a sleek, black limo waiting outside the hotel.

I sucked in a breath as I looked at it. 'Am I dressed fancy enough?' I asked, worriedly. In bed together earlier, we had felt like equals but now suddenly, the differences between us seemed to loom large again.

'Perfect,' Jake assured me as the limo driver opened the car door for us. Jake gestured for me to go ahead so I slid across the leather seat and Jake climbed in next to me. When the limo door shut, Jake reached for my hand and rubbed his thumb across it. It helped a little bit. I looked out of the window at the city lights twinkling around us. I had asked for a New York moment but suddenly, it felt like a whole lot of pressure. As if we had to have a magical night together or we would fail. I shifted on the leather seat.

Jake looked across at me and frowned. Then he leaned in close to my ear to speak. 'What's wrong?'

'I don't know,' I admitted.

'Hmm. Would you prefer to do something else?'

I turned in surprise. 'But you said you've booked a table?'

'Yeah, but I'll cancel it. I just thought when you said you wanted tonight to be special, you meant this...' He tapped the leather seat with the hand that wasn't touching mine. 'A limo, a fancy dinner but...' Jake leaned forward and spoke to the driver. The car took a quick turn. 'I have a better idea.'

'You do?' I asked, intrigued. Jake threw me a wink and I chuckled, wondering what he was planning now. The limo soon pulled up and I looked out. We were just parked on the street; I couldn't see anything special around us. 'Where are we?'

'Come on, you'll see,' Jake said, jumping out as the driver came around to my side to open the door for me. I climbed out and Jake took my hand again. He led me to a tiny pizza place. 'This is the best pizza I've found in New York. Want to try it?'

I stared at the neon sign, thinking this was a long way from the fancy restaurant I had been picturing he was taking me to. I felt suddenly relieved, though. This was much less pressure. And much more me. 'Yes, please.'

Jake smiled. 'Great.'

We went inside and a delicious smell hit me along with the warmth. It was busy; people were waiting and the staff behind the counter were rushing around.

'What would you like?' Jake asked as I studied the menu.

'Surprise me.'

'Okay.' He joined the queue and I leaned against the wall. As I waited for him, I touched the up-do hairstyle I had done. It didn't feel right now. Maybe it hadn't ever felt right really. I pulled at the bobby pins and they fell out. I put them in my handbag and ran my fingers through my hair, letting it fall down over my shoulders. I breathed out, feeling more like myself instantly.

After Jake had given our order, he joined me and reached out to touch my hair. 'It's such a pretty colour.'

'I used to hate it when I was younger,' I admitted 'But now I like being unique.'

He smiled. 'You are definitely that, Freya. I like taking you to my favourite places in the city.'

I hesitated before asking the question that popped into my head. 'Have you shown New York to lots of women?'

He seemed surprised. 'No, only you.'

Our order was called then so he missed the smile on my lips.

'Right, time for another surprise,' Jake said as he returned with a pizza box and two cans of Coke. We left and walked down the small alley to the side of the pizza place. I gasped as we emerged in Times Square. I hadn't seen it on foot yet, only through the taxi window, and it was a heady sight. Flashing lights, buildings crowding in on me, people weaving around people, and so much noise. Jake led me through the chaos with purpose and to a quieter spot where a trio of musicians were setting up. There was a pillar and we leaned against it, and Jake opened up the box and gestured for me to take a slice.

'These guys are great. Nothing better than good pizza and good music in my opinion,' Jake said, watching as I picked up a slice and took a bite. 'I know some people think margherita is boring but this is the best I've ever tasted.' He gave me a suggestive smile.

I smiled back as I took a bite and then I moaned. 'Oh my God,' I said as the cheesy deliciousness hit. 'So good,' I said with my mouthful.

'Yeah,' Jake said, gruffly before taking a bite of his slice.

The musicians began then. The string trio started paying orchestral versions of pop songs, and they were brilliant. Our spot meant we could hear them really well and the crowd that formed around them to listen wasn't intrusive. Jake stood close to me, our arms brushing as we ate the pizza and drank our Cokes while listening to the music. Even though we were surrounded by skyscrapers and bright lights, it was like we were having a private concert.

When we had finished eating, Jake turned to me. 'Dance?' he asked.

'Here?' I checked. I looked around. No one else was dancing.

'Yes,' Jake said, holding out his hand.

Reluctantly, I let him pull me towards him. Even though we were apart from the crowd, they could all see us in the bright lights of Times Square. But when Jake wrapped his arms around me and I moved closer and looked up to meet his eyes, they did seem to fade away. The trio were playing a love song and we started to sway to it. I hooked my arms around Jake's neck and I relaxed into his embrace. With his arms around me, I let go of any embarrassment or awkwardness and the romance of the moment took over instead.

He looked down at me with a small smile on his lips and it felt like we were in a bubble alone like we had been back in my hotel room this afternoon.

'I like you in my arms,' Jake said softly into my ear then.

'I like being in your arms,' I replied.

Jake twirled me then and dipped me down, giving me a long, lingering kiss. The bubble faded as I heard people around us clapping and cheering. I smiled into Jake's lips as I kissed him back. When he pulled away, his eyes twinkled.

I looked up at him. 'You gave me a New York moment after all.'

Jake lifted me back upright and we both turned to smile at the crowd who had cheered us. The song ended and we joined in clapping the musicians, one of whom turned to drop us a wink having watched us too it seemed. 'That's all I wanted,' Jake said, wrapping an arm around my waist. 'Was this better than what I had originally planned?'

I didn't exactly know his plans but I guessed a fancy restaurant and maybe a pianist or something, us drinking champagne while we looked out at another incredible view of the city. But here on the street after eating pizza and dancing in front of people to a beautiful song, I was sure I would have chosen this over whatever he had arranged. This had been spontaneous and fun and romantic, and I had enjoyed every minute. 'Yes,' I said, leaning in and reaching up on my tiptoes to give him a kiss. 'The perfect New York moment. I'll never forget it.'

Jake's eyes lit up. 'I won't forget it either,' he promised me.

I longed to ask him what would happen when we left New York but I couldn't.

'What do you want to do next?' Jake asked.

I knew that if this was just a holiday thing then I would regret not going to bed with Jake at least one more time.

'Let's go back to our hotel,' I suggested. We wouldn't get much time together tomorrow with the conference ending and then having to catch an early flight. It would hurt when we said goodbye so I needed this New York moment to last as long as possible.

29

My heart beat in time with Jake's later that night. I was curled up against his chest, his arm strong and secure around me. We had ripped each other's clothes off when we got back to my hotel room after our date, tossing them onto the floor and collapsing on the bed together. The sex had been urgent and passionate and we were recovering in silence, breathless and slightly sweaty, small smiles on our faces.

'Why weren't we doing this the whole time?' Jake murmured into my hair then.

I chuckled softly against his chest. 'Probably because we were at loggerheads.'

Jake looked down at me and I tilted my head to meet his gaze. 'This is much better. Were you really intimidated by me?'

'Well, you know I was a fan of your books so I was nervous to meet you, and you were...' I trailed off, not wanting to be too harsh when we were naked and still in a delicious post-orgasm state together.

'A twat?' Jake supplied, making us both laugh. He pulled me closer. 'I'm sorry. You must have felt let down meeting me. I wish

I could go back to that first meeting six months ago and do it differently. I know it's not a decent excuse, but I wasn't myself. I am slowly getting back to him. You have no idea how much you are helping. But when we met, I was bitter and angry and hurt, and I was taking it out on the world. I'm sorry, Freya. I want to make it up to you.'

'Why were you like that? Because of what had happened in your personal life?' I asked, wishing that he would trust me with the story.

'Yes,' he whispered. He moved then, scooting down and rolling onto his side to face me on the bed. He reached out to stroke my arm as he held my gaze in the semi-darkness of the room. I hooked a leg over his and he smiled. 'You know when you asked me why I started writing, and why I started writing romance books when we were on the way to the Brooklyn Bridge?'

I nodded.

He reached down and took hold of my hand in his. I squeezed it reassuringly.

'I didn't tell you the full story. After I read *Emma*, I asked Mum why it was her favourite book, she said it was because the first time she read it, she had been at university. She said she was on a bench in the middle of the campus, and my father...' Jake trailed off for a minute, his jaw clenching. He took a breath and continued. 'He had come and sat beside her, and asked her what she thought of the book. They had ended up talking for hours. Mum said she had known he would be important to her from that day.'

'That's so romantic,' I swooned. 'Like something right out of one of your love stories.'

Jake sighed. 'Exactly. I thought that was so sweet too. Their story inspired me. I thought I would love to have that kind of romance one day. I looked at my parents and wanted what they had. That, along with reading romances, inspired me to write my own one.'

I leaned in to kiss him. 'That's so beautiful,' I said, feeling even more attracted to him if that was possible. 'I used to read your books and wonder if I'd ever find a love like the kind you wrote about. I guess that's why I stopped dating these past few years.'

Jake shook his head. 'I've spent a lot of the last six months wondering if love like that does exist too so I get it. I wondered whether I wanted to read or write romance again.'

'Yeah, I felt like I would never find it...' I trailed off, not wanting him to misinterpret my words. I knew this wasn't love but when we looked at one another in this hotel-room bubble, it felt like there was a possibility that one day, this could be more than a fling. I longed to know if he could feel it too or not. 'I had a series of relationships that went nowhere. And then bad dates that made me not want to bother even trying.' Then I frowned, thinking about what Jake had told me. 'But why did you change what you thought about love? I mean, your parents still inspire you with their love story, don't they?' I asked him curiously.

'I wish they did.' He shifted uncomfortably on the bed. 'I want to tell you...' he trailed off.

I let go of his hand and took his face in my hands. 'It's okay. You can tell me anything. If you want to. I won't tell anyone, Jake. It can just be between us. Like what we've been doing in here.' I gave him a small smile and leaned in to brush my lips against his.

Jake pulled me closer and gave me a soft, deep kiss. 'Thank you, Freya. That means a lot.' He took a deep breath. 'What I found out six months ago made me wonder if I ever wanted to write or read a love story ever again. I wasn't sure I believed in

love any more because the happy ever after that inspired me to
write books with similar happy endings, and made me want to
find my own one day, turned out to have been far from happy.'

'Your parents aren't as happy as you thought?'

'It was all a lie,' he said bitterly. 'My parents, who inspired my
love stories, who have been married for forty years and who I
thought were the ultimate happy ever after... are actually not.'
Jake's eyes locked with mine. 'I found out that my father has got a
second family that my mum and I knew nothing about.'

30

There was a short silence as I absorbed his words. 'What do you mean your dad has a second family?' I asked, my heart going out to him as I saw the pain in his eyes.

'My dad has been having an affair for decades. But it's worse than an affair. They have a home and children together. He basically lived for years juggling two families,' Jake said, holding on to me tightly. I held him close, feeling his need for comfort.

'Oh my God, Jake. I'm so sorry,' I said. 'How did you find out?'

'He sat us down and told us because he's decided now he's due for retirement that he wants to retire with *them*, not us,' Jake said, shaking his head. 'It all felt like my whole life has been a lie. That their love story and marriage was just all bullshit, you know?'

I couldn't even imagine how it would feel to have everything come crashing down around me like that. His parents' love story hadn't been the one he had thought it was. Now I understood why he had fought against romance after that. 'No wonder you haven't been yourself the past six months. What about your mum?'

'Devastated. After forty years of marriage, she's now living alone. He's broken her heart. He's living with his other family. She is so strong but it's changed everything. I still can't get my head around it all, to be honest. I admired him so much. Now I realise I never really knew my father at all.'

'I can't believe that he did what he did to the two of you. It's just... shit.'

He smiled faintly. 'Shit is right.'

We lapsed into silence for a moment, wrapped around each other still, the only sound the beating of our hearts and the noise of New York floors below us.

'Have I completely ruined the mood?' Jake said then.

I smiled. 'No. I'm glad you trusted me with your secret.'

Jake leaned in to kiss me. 'I'm glad I did too.'

'Why did you feel that telling Davis Mulberry you didn't like romance books was preferable to him finding out about your father?' I asked him then.

'God, you love to ask me difficult questions, don't you?'

I shrugged. 'I want to get to know the real you.'

'I want that too,' he replied softly. 'You've made me want to be honest.'

My heart soared at his words.

Jake thought for a moment about my question. 'Well, I suppose it felt like my romance writing career *had* all been a lie because it had been inspired by my own parents' love story. And that had been as fictional as romance novels. I wasn't sure if I believed in love any more, let alone want to write about it. But also because Mulberry is the biggest gossip and I didn't want to admit what my father had done; I was ashamed and angry and hurt. And I kind of felt stupid.'

'Stupid?' I asked, confused as to why he would think that.

'I had no idea he had another family. And I'm scared too...'

'Of what?'

'Of being like him.'

I shook my head. 'I don't think you are. You didn't give up on love. You started writing again; you gave Hayley a new book. And I've read it. *When I Met You* is your best book yet. That can't be written by a man who thinks love doesn't exist.'

'I started writing it before Dad told us. It took months for me to be able to even open up the document again.'

'But you did. And you're here trying to save your career because it means something to you.'

'Freya, you are...' Jake didn't finish that thought but kissed me, rolling me onto my back. He trailed kisses down my neck to my chest, moving his hand between my legs. I gasped as he touched me. He lifted off me and raised an eyebrow. 'How much sleep do you need tonight?' He grinned and I knew he was done talking. I was so happy he had opened up to me, though and had trusted me with his secret. I felt closer to him. This felt so different to anything I had ever had before. I wanted to keep it. But I knew that was a secret I wasn't able to trust him with yet.

So, instead, I giggled. 'Who needs sleep?'

* * *

Voices outside the room awoke me with a start the following morning. I opened my eyes and looked at Jake's sleeping profile. Our legs were tangled together and my palm rested on his bare chest. Images from last night replayed in my mind like a movie. It had been so romantic to dance with him in Times Square, and then when we came back to my room, that sweetness turned into something smoking hot. I bit my lip remembering how good Jake's kisses and touches had felt.

And then he had finally opened up to me. Hope sprung in

my heart that Jake might see this as something that could carry on once we went home to London. He'd told me about his father, and how it had affected him. Why he had lied to Davis but also almost gave up on writing about love. But he hadn't. He was here fighting for his career and he was finally being honest about the past six months. I loved the fact he had listened to me. That he respected me. And had wanted to tell me the truth. That meant more to me than he probably knew.

I looked at the clock on the bedside table and sighed. We couldn't stay much longer in this hotel room, unfortunately. After breakfast, the conference was having a final morning event to showcase all the authors and their books for the last time. Everyone apart from Jake pretty much had a stand in the room that readers could stop at to buy books or merch, have things signed, or just meet their favourite authors. Jake had refused to have a stand but we still needed to be seen there. It was our last opportunity for Jake to be around readers and the industry, the last chance to fix things. I had no idea if that was possible but we had to try.

And then there was going to be an end-of-conference dinner and party, before we had to pull ourselves together for an early flight home. We'd have to pack after breakfast and check out too. There seemed to be a long list of things to do today but snuggled next to Jake, I wished we could blow them all off.

'I can feel you thinking hard.' Jake's eyes opened. He pulled me closer. 'What's wrong?'

'Just thinking about what we need to do today and then we'll be leaving and then...' I trailed off because I had no idea what would happen after that.

Jake reached out to brush back a strand of my hair and then cupped my cheek. 'It's going to be a full-on day for sure. You enjoyed last night, though?' Jake asked me softly, drawing his fingertips down to touch my lips.

'I did,' I replied. 'Did you?'

'You know I did.'

'It will be strange being at the conference today and not being like this,' I said, gesturing to us still entwined.

'Can I keep my hands off you?' Jake pulled me in for a lingering kiss.

'You need to,' I said seriously when we leaned back from each other. Liv's warnings ran through my mind. I watched as Jake looked confused. 'I don't think we want anyone to find out about us here,' I said. 'Hayley is still silent. If we can't make things right, I could lose my job and you could lose an agent. If she found out what we've been doing, we definitely would lose everything.'

'I wouldn't care if she dumps me; you've done more for me these past few days than she would have done.'

'I can't afford to think like that,' I explained. 'I'm just starting out. She could ruin my career before it even starts,' I added worriedly. I was already unsure if she wanted me to keep working for her.

'You really are worried about your career?'

'She was furious.'

'Yeah but we've made progress since then...'

I shook my head. 'Not enough. Her silence speaks volumes.'

'I don't want to ruin anything for you,' Jake said sincerely. 'Hayley won't find out about us, okay?'

'Thank you but how we can salvage things enough to get you a new book deal and for me to keep my job, let alone get a promotion, I have no idea...'

'How about I come up with something? And while I think about it, we make the last moments together in this hotel room count.'

'We can't. I should have a shower and then we need to have breakfast and start the day.' I found myself curling closer around him. I really didn't want to have to leave his warm, strong embrace. Especially now we had agreed we couldn't show any signs of being anything other than colleagues after we left my hotel room.

'Hmm,' Jake said, holding me tightly too. 'Hard to let go of each other, isn't it?'

'I'm so comfy,' I agreed. 'But I know we have to get ready.'

Jake leaned in and kissed me again. I let out a sigh but kissed him back, my fingers threading through his hair as he moved his to my waist. 'I might be addicted to kissing you,' he murmured into my ear.

'Oh yeah?' I purred back. 'I might want you to be addicted to kissing me.' I brushed my lips against his but then I sighed. 'I really should have that shower,' I said reluctantly.

Jake's eyes twinkled then. 'If you really don't want us to let go of each other, we could have a shower together?'

The thought of Jake wet and naked with me was instantly appealing. 'I think that's a very good idea,' I admitted, wanting to prolong us being together for as long as possible. I tried to think if I had ever done that with a previous partner but I definitely hadn't. I probably would have been too worried at being so exposed but last night, Jake had made it very clear that he found me sexy and loved my body, and I hadn't felt nervous or worried.

I extracted myself from his arms finally, my body instantly feeling the loss of his. I wondered if other couples also felt sad when they had to let go of each other and start their days like I did.

Not that we were a couple or anything.

Jake climbed out of bed with me and we stayed naked so that helped the loss of his embrace a lot.

Jake took hold of my hand and led me into the marbled bathroom. The shower was thankfully a large walk-in one so after he turned on the shower, we stepped in it easily together. The water was hot instantly, steaming the room up around us as we got under it.

Jake wrapped his arms around me and looked down at me as water washed over us. 'This was a very good idea,' he said, moving his hands up and down my arms. 'Can I wash you?'

I bit my lip. 'Um... okay.'

'You can't be nervous after everything we've done together?' Jake asked with a smile at my hesitant reply.

'This is all kind of new to me,' I admitted.

'I told you we don't do anything you don't want to do, right?' Jake said, leaning in to kiss me gently.

'I want you to,' I said, more firmly as his kiss gave me a pleasant shiver down my spine.

Jake reached for the body wash in one of those cute hotel bottles and squeezed some out on his palms. Keeping his eyes on me, he started to lather up soap on my body as we stayed pressed together under the hot water. It was incredibly intimate as he washed my skin carefully. When his palms caressed my breasts, I had to lean back against the shower tiles, letting out a sigh. 'What else needs cleaning?' Jake murmured then. He ran one hand down my body towards my thighs. I gave an eager nod and he chuckled, reaching between my legs and stroking me there. 'Do you like that, baby?'

'Yes,' I breathed, arching my back in pleasure at his touch. I looked down and saw he was just as turned on as me. I reached for him and started stroking too.

'Mmm, you know exactly what I like,' Jake said, propping up on hand one the tiles behind me as I clung on to his waist with my free hand. He kept his eyes on me and the eye contact was so erotic that coupled with his touch and our wet naked bodies being so close, I couldn't hold back a loud moan.

'Good girl,' Jake encouraged and I moaned again. 'I want to fuck you against these tiles so badly.'

God, Jake's sex talk was so hot. 'Please,' I said instantly, desperate for him again even though we'd had sex last night. It felt like Jake knew exactly how to turn me on and I was putty in his hands.

'Hang on.' Jake let go of me and I closed my eyes, letting the shower ease the slight ache in my neck from our activities yesterday. Jake stepped out and returned with a condom, slipping it on and returning to me, kissing me with such passion, I felt breathless. He lifted me easily up against the tiles then, our height difference coming in extremely handy, and brushed back my wet hair so he could see my face. 'Do you want me, Freya?'

'So much,' I said.

'I want you so much too,' he said huskily, sliding inside me. We both gasped, smiling at the friction as Jake moved, pressing me into the tiles, and I clung to him, desperate to be as close as possible. He kissed me, then moved his lips to my ears. 'This is better than I could have even hoped.'

'For me too,' I replied, letting out another moan. This felt so good and naughty too. Jake was introducing me to a whole host of things I'd never done with a man. I really had been missing out. Not just in my years of not having any sex but before them when the sex I'd had was nothing like this.

'I don't want this to stop,' Jake said so quietly, I wondered if I had heard him correctly or not but I shuddered against him, lost in pleasure so I couldn't check. But I hoped he had said what I thought he said, and meant it, because I felt exactly the same way.

31

After our shower, Jake had pulled on a hotel robe and slippers, cracked my door and made sure the corridor was empty before giving me a quick kiss and darting into his hotel room next door. When he had gone, I sank down onto the edge of the bed in just my towel and took a few deep breaths. I glanced in the mirror. My skin was damp and flushed, my hair was starting to curl over my shoulders and there was a smile on my face. Talk about a nice way to wake up. I was clean from the shower but also felt slightly dirty in the best way. Jake had spun my world upside down.

How had I gone from not having sex for three years to hot shower sex with my favourite romance author?

My phone beeped with a message so I grabbed it and saw it was from Liv.

> I'm heading to breakfast now, want to join me? I am of course in desperate need of knowing how last night went...

Laughing, I replied saying I'd meet her in the breakfast room in fifteen minutes, then I jumped up and forced myself to stop thinking about Jake. The day outside was grey and not quite the summer weather we'd had so far and the hotel air con was still on in full force so I put on a sweater over one of my dresses, making it look like a skirt, and added boots, leaving my hair to finish drying loose. I didn't bother with too much make-up and headed out of the room in record time. I glanced at Jake's closed door as I walked past. I could have knocked and asked if he wanted to join us but I kind of liked the idea of being able to squeeze in some girl talk before the conference started up again, and I knew I could do with some more time apart from him to compose myself. I was worried that as soon as I saw him again, it would be written all over my face what a giddy state he'd left me in.

I met up with Liv and we sat down with coffee and plates filled with the array of breakfast treats. 'I'll miss this hotel buffet when we go home,' I said, tucking in to my plate happily. I had worked up a big appetite. Jake and I would have to leave before breakfast the next day so this was my last chance to fill up on the delicious selection.

Liv nodded as she ate some of her pancakes. 'Me too. I'm going to put some pastries in my bag for my flight later.' Liv was getting a night flight home so she'd only be at this evening's party for a bit. 'But this is a boring subject when all I want to hear about is your dinner with Jake,' she added, leaning towards me and dropping her voice to make sure no one could overhear us.

I told Liv about Jake's fancy plans that he'd changed when he saw that I was uncomfortable in the limo. 'So, we got pizza and watched a busking trio in Times Square. We even danced to them. It really was a New York moment,' I said, my voice taking on a dreamy quality as I thought back to it.

'That does sound romantic,' Liv conceded. 'And afterwards?'

'Well...' I trailed off, feeling my cheeks heat up. 'It was pretty hot, Liv. He has... moves. I think that maybe I've been missing out all this time on what it could be like in the, uh, bedroom,' I added, stammering a little from embarrassment.

She smiled. 'I felt like that when I got with Aiden,' Liv said. 'And did he say anything about what would happen when you get back to London?'

'No, but we agreed we needed to be careful today to make sure no one finds out. I remembered what you said about me having more to lose than him.'

'Well, good,' Liv replied. 'If Hayley found out, I worry it would make her completely change her mind about promoting you. You know what a stickler she is about keeping things professional with clients. She doesn't like you doing anything for me as we're family; she doesn't want anyone to think I get preferential treatment.'

'I know but I think she has changed her mind already,' I said dully. 'She's been so quiet ever since Jake let slip that article was all true.' I knew Hayley would not look kindly on me having any sort of relationship with Jake. She certainly would feel the same as she did with Liv that it would be a conflict of interest for me to deal with his work, and as her biggest client, that was part of my job. And I worried whether authors, if they knew, would want me to be their agent if I was lucky enough to be allowed to take on my own clients. It was all very complicated. 'I don't know if we can do anything today that will be enough for Jake to get a new book deal.'

'Why can't he just tell everyone why he said those things? Everyone is making up their own story about it. It can't be worse than some of what I've been hearing around the conference!'

I sighed. 'It's really personal, Liv.'

She gasped 'He told you?'

I nodded. 'He did.'

She leaned back in her chair. 'Wow. I didn't realise you had got that... close. I thought it was a holiday fling.'

'I don't know what it is,' I admitted. I wasn't sure whether to tell her that I hoped it could turn into something more because Jake hadn't given any indication that he wanted it to. But he had opened up to me and we had been really intimate. 'I do like him though, Liv.'

She reached across the table and gave my hand a quick squeeze. 'He will be a fool if he doesn't want to see you again at home.'

I raised an eyebrow. 'But you think we're a bad idea.'

'You're very different,' she said carefully. 'Not necessarily a bad thing if you're both on the same page about what you are to each other. Opposites attract for sure.'

Liv took a sip of her coffee while I replayed her words in my mind. I knew we were very different – it was what had made me feel so intimidated by Jake in the first place, and seemed to have been what drew him to me. But what worked here in New York might feel very different once we were back in our usual lives. If we got a chance to find out.

After breakfast, Jake messaged me to meet him before the final conference exhibition so we could strategise. I nervously walked out of the Waldorf into the conference hotel to find him. I wondered if I should ask him what was going to happen once we left New York. Maybe he would reassure me that this wasn't just a holiday thing. Maybe we could try to be together in London if we could work out what to do about Hayley.

When I saw Jake in the lobby, a smile appeared on my face. It was good to see him. Some of my nerves faded into butterflies. I started to go over but then I stopped, stunned. He wasn't alone and the person who was talking to him was unfortunately very familiar. When Jake turned and saw me, there was no smile on his face.

'There you are,' Hayley called over, putting her hands on her hips, her mouth pursed. 'Well, come on,' she added, waving as I still stood on the spot. My boss wore one of her power suits, not a hair out of place, looking calm and cool despite the fact she must not have been long off the plane. I glanced down at my sundress and boots outfit and my stomach dropped.

God. This was a nightmare. Why had she turned up like this? Bracing myself, I walked over slowly, keeping my eyes on Hayley because if I looked at Jake, I was worried I might burst into tears or something equally embarrassing.

32

'I thought you were at your sister's wedding?' I asked once I stood in front of Hayley, my palms already feeling sweaty.

'I was,' she snapped. 'But after Jake told everyone at the panel that he had slagged off romance books, I knew I couldn't trust the two of you to fix things, so I jumped on the earliest flight I could once my sister got married. She's pissed off with me but this needs sorting.'

'I explained to everyone...' Jake started but Hayley held a hand up and he stopped speaking.

'I've caught up on social media,' Hayley said. 'You said there was a personal reason, a secret, that you didn't want that twat Mulberry to find out so you slagged off romance books instead. Everyone thinks it's kind of bullshit. And I agree. Who cares about your personal life?' she asked with a sneer.

'Readers were really hurt by what Jake said so I think they deserve...' I began but this time, she spun around and held up a hand to silence me. The words died on my lips.

'This was all your fault telling Jake that he needed to be honest, wasn't it? You kept harping on about it even at the time.'

'I think it was good advice,' Jake said before I could answer her.

'It was stupid advice,' Hayley responded. 'Because now you've only given half the story so the rumours are crazy as to what you're hiding from everyone. We need to do damage control today. You got a good response when you talked about *When I Met You*, so I think we should focus on that. I'm going to see the conference organisers and see if we can get you a room today where you could read from the new book and then we can show your publishers there is interest out there. No more talk of your personal life or secrets or excuses; that article needs to be forgotten. We need to focus on getting you a new deal.'

'But surely if readers...' I stopped speaking without Hayley needing to say anything this time; the look she gave me was enough.

She leaned in and spoke in a quieter tone as the lobby was filling up with people attending the conference. 'I am taking over, Freya. You have failed at the task I set you and we will need to have a serious talk when we get back to the office about your future with my company. And you, Jake, are my client so follow my lead today and we might still be able to save your career, okay?' She gave a nod then looked at her watch. 'I'm going to find Nora and Christine; you two wait for me here.' And then she faded into the crowd.

My chest sagged and my eyes felt hot as I watched her walk away. I had never felt quite so small in my whole life, and when you're my height, that was really saying something.

'Freya...' Jake began, reaching out to touch my arm with his hand.

'Don't touch me,' I hissed at him. Then I felt bad when I saw hurt flash in his eyes. 'Hayley can't know anything is going on with us; look at how pissed she is already,' I added as quietly as I could. 'She's going to sack me.'

'She's wrong,' Jake said. 'I could see readers did like me telling the truth; I'm sorry I bottled it and didn't come clean properly, then we wouldn't be in this mess. She can't sack you; I won't let her.'

'I don't think anyone can tell Hayley what to do,' I said sadly. 'It's all over.'

Hayley reappeared as quickly as she had disappeared then. 'Christine and Nora have let us have a side room off the main conference hall so although you won't have a stand in the exhibition, you're close and you can read from the new book and sign your backlist for readers. Come on.' She beckoned us and marched off again.

Jake sighed. 'I'm getting tired of her attitude.'

'She's your agent,' I said, following her quickly because if there was a chance to save my job, I had to take it. I would just have to do exactly what she wanted. I didn't wait for Jake; I assumed he was following. If I was honest, I was a bit pissed off with him. I still felt in my heart that my advice had been solid and readers would have welcomed his honesty. I understood it was a very personal reason why he had almost given up on love stories, but I wasn't sure he could get his career back to the heights it had been still keeping his secret, despite Hayley thinking readers didn't need him to be honest. What he had said had hurt; she didn't understand that. I wasn't even sure she liked romance books now despite making her business out of them.

I felt thoroughly discouraged as I walked into the meeting room Hayley had managed to secure. She barked at me to post everywhere on social media to invite readers to hear Jake read the first two chapters from *When I Met You*, and then get her a coffee. Then she fired instructions at Jake, who trailed in the room after me, hands in his pockets, glancing at me as she spoke. I kept my eyes on my phone, though. I couldn't let him distract me any more; I had to focus on what Hayley asked me to do.

It was a tense fifteen minutes where neither Jake nor I spoke but just listened to Hayley, who seemed oblivious to our discomfort. She bossed us and the conference administrators around and then went out into the exhibition hall to bring readers into the room. No one could say no to Hayley so soon the room was filling up. Jake went to the front with Hayley's Kindle, his book loaded up, ready to read from, and I stood to the side with my phone to film it so I could share it online afterwards. I really hoped this would work and get him that book deal. But I wasn't convinced. And it felt like my own career was hanging by a thread.

'Hi everyone,' Jake said, and the chatter in the room died down. He looked at me but I looked down at my phone and started filming. Hayley was leaning against the wall on the other side and I didn't want her to see us have any sort of connection. If she was angry with me now, I knew it would be nothing if she found out we'd been far less than professional while we were here.

'I wanted to thank you all for your support by reading a couple of chapters from...' Jake began, saying what Hayley had told him to. But then he looked at me again and sighed. 'Actually, before I do a reading, I have something to say,' he said.

I glanced at Hayley, who was frowning.

'I know that at the last reader session, you all left with mixed feelings. Because I told you why I acted like I didn't care about romance books or any of you; I wanted to keep a personal secret from getting out but I realise now that by telling half of the story, you can't really understand what was going on. And I might not get another romance book published. I don't want to leave this conference and have any of you thinking that I haven't loved this career, and telling the stories that I have done. If this book...' he waved his Kindle, '...never sees the light of day, I still want to be an author you can enjoy reading. So...' He took a deep breath.

Hayley stepped off the wall and was about to say something but Jake turned to her with such a glare, she paused. I bit my lips to hide a smile. It was good to see her falter just once.

Jake paced for a couple of seconds then stopped and faced the room again. 'I didn't want Davis Mulberry to know what was happening in my personal life but I also wasn't sure I believed in love stories any more because my faith in love had been shattered,' he said. The room was so quiet, you could hear a pin drop. I heard his voice catch. I started to bring my phone down but he saw and shook his head so I kept on filming. 'I began writing romance because I was inspired by my parents. But the happy ever after that inspired me to write books with similar happy endings, and made me want my own one day, turned out to have been far from happy. My parents, who have been married for forty years and who I thought were the ultimate happy ever after... are actually not.' Jake sighed. 'My father had been cheating on my mother for years. On our family, really. He had a second family all along. And I not only found out about them but had to watch my father leave my mother and our family home to go and be with his other family.'

33

A ripple went through the room after Jake's revelation. I could see the pain behind his eyes, and in his voice as he told us about his parents. There were murmurs of conversations as people took in what he had said.

I looked at Hayley, who was completely shocked and seemed unsure what to say or do, and leaned against the wall again, shaking her head. I turned to Jake and gave him a nod of encouragement. He cleared his throat, waited a moment for everyone to settle back down, then he spoke again. 'Yeah, my father had lied to me and my mum my whole life. He had another woman, and children, and he used his job that took him travelling a lot to live this double life. It shook our world as you can imagine. I thought they were the ultimate love story but it was a lie. Does that mean all love is a lie?' Jake shook his head. 'No, but it's taken me a few months to realise that. That conversation with Davis Mulberry happened at my lowest point. I did almost want to give it all up. But after the article that revealed what I said about romance books came out, I realised that I really could lose it all, and that made me see that I didn't want to. That I did still believe in love and I do want to write about it. I have received a lot of messages from readers over the years and I know that I'm not the only one to have experienced a broken heart. So many of you have but you still love reading about love, and I still love writing about it.'

I looked at Hayley. She seemed disappointed. Clearly, she still didn't think this was a good idea. But I was so proud of Jake. I had to help this work out.

I stopped filming, put my phone down and stepped forward. 'I've never been in love,' I said. Jake turned in surprise and I felt all eyes in the room train on me, which made me nervous but I carried on speaking, keeping my gaze on Jake to give me more confidence. 'I have always loved your books because they gave me hope that one day, I will. And if I don't... they are a form of escapism from life, which can be hard, let's face it. They make me happy. I will always want to read a new Jake Richards book.'

Jake smiled at me. It was a slow smile that felt hard won. I smiled back.

A woman at the back of the room stood up then. 'I lost my husband four years ago and one of my friends gave me one of your books. They gave me comfort. They still do.'

Another woman stood up after her. 'I am married and I love reading about couples falling in love because it reminds me of how my husband and I fell in love.'

Hayley waved at me from across the room; she gestured to my phone.

'Oh,' I said. I called out to ask everyone if I could record this and no one objected so I did. Hayley gave me a pleased nod and I let out an exhale. She seemed in a much better mood so she must have sensed things were going well like I did. I could have collapsed with relief but I kept on filming.

A man got up then. 'My boyfriend isn't really romantic so I like the fantasy of reading about men who are.'

'You deserve romance!' a woman sitting in front of him told him over her shoulder. 'I gave my partner one of Jake's books to read and he bought me flowers every week after that.'

Even Hayley raised a smile at that.

More people stood up to talk about why they loved Jake's books and when I looked at him, I could see he was swelling with pride, and it made me happy to see. This was what I had hoped for – he had connected with his readers so they not only believed what he had told them, they understood and wanted to share their stories to show him how much his books had affected them.

Once everyone who wanted to had spoken, Jake thanked them all.

'Honestly, I didn't deserve all that. I'm the one who is grateful to you for reading and enjoying my books. But I'm so happy they mean as much to you as they mean to me. I really am sorry for questioning if what I was doing was worthwhile. For letting my personal life affect something I love. I'm not going to do that any more. Because we need love stories in the world, right?'

There was applause and there were cheers to that, and relief rolled through my body. Jake had won everyone over. I stopped filming and looked at Hayley.

She stepped forward to take back control. She called out to everyone that if they wanted Jake to sign anything or get a selfie with him to form a queue so they could meet him, and pretty much everyone joined it. As Jake met with readers, Hayley came over to me.

'Send me that video and I'll email it to Jake's publishers, and get it posted online so we can make the most of the conference buzz while we're still here,' she instructed me briskly. I waited for her to add something like praise – I mean, it had been my idea for Jake to be honest with readers – but she just stared at me impatiently. I did as she asked then she sat down with her phone so I went over to Jake.

'Well done, it's going so well,' I said after he had a selfie with two readers.

'Yeah?' He turned that sexy smile of his onto me.

'You had the room in the palm of your hand. You won everyone over. I think you saved your career today.'

'Only because I followed your advice.'

I smiled then; it did feel good that he had done that. 'I just hope Hayley thinks we've done well too.'

'If she doesn't, I'll find a new agent.' Jake winked at me then turned back to speak to another reader.

When the queue had finally gone, the three of us were left alone in the room. I could hear the bustle of the conference in the main hall. It was nice to have a minute to breathe and take in what had happened.

Hayley came over before I could speak to Jake alone again.

'Well, I just heard from your editor,' she said to Jake. 'Craig has agreed to a meeting when we're back in London. So, I think we will get that new contract.' Finally, she smiled. 'Good job.'

'We have Freya to thank,' Jake said.

'It was a team effort,' I said, blushing at him saying that in front of Hayley. I really hoped she wouldn't think he was being over the top with me.

Hayley turned to me and nodded. 'It was but when we get home, we can talk about how to progress your career, Freya.'

'Great, thanks, Hayley.'

'Now, Jake, get out into the conference hall; there is an hour left so circulate and make sure this buzz continues. Freya, go with him. I'll go to my room and do some work then I'll see you both at the dinner and party tonight. I've booked a flight home tomorrow a bit later than yours so we'll be back in London soon and we can get that new deal on the table.' She strode off, on her phone before she even left the room.

Jake quickly reached out to squeeze my hand. 'We did it.' We smiled at one another. I liked the word 'we' more than I probably should have done.

* * *

The next hour was crazy. The conference hall was packed and noisy and everyone wanted to speak to Jake about what had happened in the meeting room, both readers and authors. I didn't get a chance to chat to Liv or Tessa; I was walking around with Jake taking photos of him with people, posting online and it was exhausting after Jake and I had stayed up so late the night before. I found myself stifling a yawn.

'You look shattered.' Jake appeared by my side after he'd finished with a group of readers, speaking close into my ear, his hand just grazing the small of my back.

I quickly darted out of his reach in case anyone noticed him touching me. 'Careful,' I warned him. 'Anyone could see, plus Hayley is here.'

'You need a nap before dinner and the party or you'll never make it through; I feel the same,' Jake replied, stepping back from me.

'I'll go straight to my room once we're finished.'

'Why don't we make an escape now, say we have work to do?' Jake lowered his voice further. 'We could nap together.'

'Are you serious?' I hissed.

'It would be far more enjoyable to nap in your arms.'

'But...'

'We won't be able to be alone later now, will we?' he reasoned. Now Hayley was here, I knew he was right. We looked at one another. Even in this crowded room, there was no denying the sparks between us. How could I refuse his suggestion?

'Let's go,' I whispered. We left the hall together and thankfully, no one blocked our path or questioned our slightly early exit. We headed across the road to our hotel and through the lobby towards the lifts.

'It was torture not being able to touch you all day,' Jake said after he'd pressed the call button. He touched the small of my back then and I didn't pull away. 'I can't wait to lie down with you.'

I shook my head. 'You're insatiable.'

'You don't like it?'

'I didn't say that,' I replied.

'That's a relief.' Jake looked behind us quickly as the lift doors opened. He took my hand and pulled me into the lift, leaning down to kiss my lips. Before I closed my eyes, something caught my attention in my peripheral vison. Someone was leaning against a wall in the lobby looking in our direction. I caught the glimpse of a smile but I was too distracted by the thought of being with Jake to take too much notice. The lift doors started to slide shut and Jake pulled me closer, his kiss making me forget all about the person watching us.

34

I fell asleep quickly and easily in Jake's arms and we dozed together until my phone alarm went off to remind us we needed to get ready for the end of conference dinner and party.

Jake snuck out of my room with a quick goodbye kiss without us having any time to talk. So, I had no idea if he would want to see me once we left New York. I got ready and tried not to think about it, but he was on my mind more than I cared to admit. I hadn't really experienced thinking about someone quite this much. It was distracting.

I looked at myself in the mirror and realised I had forgotten to use mascara and then I put my dress on backwards before correcting myself. I kept wondering if I was on Jake's mind too. How did you know if someone was feeling the same things that you were? It was mildly terrifying to suddenly want a man as much as I now wanted him. I had told Liv and Tessa I was being careful but every moment with Jake made that a hard promise to keep.

There was a knock on my door, drawing me out of my head. I went over to answer it and was rewarded with Jake standing there wearing another slick, black suit, and looking exactly like he was doing a James Bond audition later. 'Shall we go to the dinner together? We are sitting at the same table so it won't surprise anyone to walk in with one another, right?' He gave me his charming smile and I was powerless to resist.

'I suppose it would make sense,' I replied, smiling back. 'Let me put my shoes on,' I said, walking back to the bed and sitting down. I knew everyone would be glammed up tonight so I'd brought a fancy outfit with me for the occasion: a silver dress with black shoes and matching bag. I had left my hair loose but added a sparkly hair clip on one side.

Jake edged in slightly. 'You look stunning, Freya,' he said in a low voice.

I glanced up. 'Even though I'm not in your favourite sundress and boots combo?'

'You know I love you in that but honestly, you look good in everything.'

'So do you,' I said as I stood up, my shoes now on. 'It's a shame we can't really go to the party together,' I added a little shyly as I didn't want to come on too strong or anything. I liked the fact he thought I looked good, though. 'But we definitely need to stay apart; no dancing together like we did in Times Square,' I said as I grabbed my bag. 'Hayley will be around us all night, I bet.'

'If that's what you want,' he replied quietly, stepping out into the corridor as I walked out and closed the hotel room door behind me.

I would have killed to slow dance with him again, especially in his sexy suit, but I knew dancing together would make it nearly impossible to hide the fact we were more than colleagues. And the last thing I wanted was for Hayley to notice anything and change her mind about discussing my future once we got back to London. Plus, everything was going so well for Jake at the conference; we didn't want to derail it now. I was sure that the good opinion he'd won would change if people started gossiping about us.

Jake put his hands in his pockets as we walked to the lifts. I was disappointed we weren't touching while we were alone but maybe he was just being ultra careful, and I couldn't fault him for that after I'd asked him to. He glanced at me as I pressed the button for the lobby but didn't say anything. It was maddening not to be able to read his thoughts.

We went down to the lobby and across to the conference hotel side by side but in silence, feeling weirdly distant from one another when just a couple of hours ago, we'd been asleep curled up together. But I told myself that this was for the best, and we'd be in each other's arms again tonight.

That thought would get me through the next few hours.

We walked into the banqueting suite where round tables with white cloths were laid out for dinner, and authors and readers and publishing-industry people mingled together dressed in black tie.

Hayley came straight over. 'I've moved the seating so I'm next to Jake,' she informed us. 'Freya, I've put you over there.' She gestured to the other side of the room. 'See you at the party.' Grabbing Jake's arm, she steered him away and I was left alone. With a resigned sigh, I went to my table. I didn't know anyone on it and I could not only not see Jake or Hayley but Tessa and Liv were nowhere close by either.

The dinner ended up with me sipping wine and checking my phone as everyone at my table knew each other and didn't really include me. I couldn't think of anything to say either so the meal dragged by painfully.

When it was finally over, I wandered into the next room

where the dance was being held. I found the drinks table and grabbed another sparkling wine; I had had a couple already at dinner but I decided I deserved it. After all, tonight was turning out to be less fun than I'd imagined.

I tried to find Liv or Tessa again but ended up circling the room by myself at a loss as to what to do. I saw Jake and Hayley surrounded by people. It looked like they were the favourites of the party. I was glad that things had gone so well but I did feel a bit annoyed that they seemed to have forgotten about me.

I hovered by the dance floor before walking to the side near to a door that led into the bar. I leaned against the wall to sip my wine, wondering how early I could escape to my room. I wondered if Jake would have any time to talk to me tonight or if he might try to come to my room once the party was over. Everyone seemed desperate for his attention, and I wished I wasn't feeling the same way.

'All alone?'

I jumped as a voice spoke in my ear, close enough to be heard over the music. Turning around, my heart sunk in dismay to see Davis Mulberry beside me, drink in hand, with a slimy grin on his face.

'As you can see,' I replied, waving my glass. 'Just having some quiet time.'

'Hmm.' Davis scanned the room. He was wearing a bow tie and it made him look older than Jake even though they were the same age. 'I can't see your client anywhere; aren't you two usually joined at the hip?' he asked, raising an eyebrow.

'He's in demand tonight; Hayley is with him.'

'Hayley is here? How come?'

'Well, she thought she should come as things weren't going great but then Jake told everyone why he said those things about romance books to you,' I said, giving him a glare. 'And everyone now understands.'

Davis rolled his eyes. 'Yeah, I heard his dad ran off and chose another family over Jake and his mum. Looks like the apple doesn't fall far from the tree.'

'What do you mean?' I asked him.

'I can't hear you. Come on.' Davis nodded his head and stepped into the bar room behind us. 'Freya,' he called, beckoning me over his shoulder.

I sighed but pulled myself off the wall and ducked into the room, which was far quieter and empty of people, the bar unused as drinks were being served by wait staff.

Davis leaned one arm in the doorway like he was in a Booktok romance and I kept a couple of feet between us – being alone in a room with him wasn't something I felt 100 per cent comfortable with.

'I mean Jake is just like his father, isn't he? A lady's man. After anyone in a skirt... even if they are inappropriate,' Davis said, the smirk on his face annoying with a capital A.

'What are you talking about?' I said, my cheeks flushing when I thought about me and Jake. But I was sure he was nothing like his father.

'I saw you,' Davis said then.

'Saw what?' I asked, suddenly nervous. He looked way too happy.

'I saw you with Jake earlier in the lift. Kissing. I know you two are sleeping together.'

35

I stared at Davis's triumphant face in horror. I had been aware of someone watching before the lift doors closed when Jake and I went up to my room. Now I knew who had seen us. And it was the worst person possible: Davis Mulberry. The man with a huge vendetta against Jake and who had been unable to bring him down once, and was likely itching to try to do it again. He could tell Hayley about us. And she wouldn't consider promoting me then. She would likely fire me instead.

Panic surged through me.

'Are you joking?' I said, hoping my voice didn't come out squeaky. 'Kissing Jake? What are you talking about?' I added in my haughty voice, hoping that using that tone and by staring into his eyes, he wouldn't sense I was lying. I gripped the wine glass tightly in my hand, wishing I could turn back time and not kiss Jake until those lift doors had fully closed.

Davis sighed as he dropped his arm from the door. 'I hoped you wouldn't lie to me; I saw you two in the lift, so don't kid a kidder. What happened? Jake fooled you into thinking he could do real-life romance as good as he can write about it?'

'Ha,' I said, knowing that I needed to change tack and act like him, not myself. 'Fine, you got me; Jake kissed me,' I said, shaking my head. 'But what you didn't see was after the lift doors closed, I slapped him.'

'You slapped him?' Davis repeated, unable to stop himself from grinning.

'Of course I did! Can you imagine? He's ten years older than me, and we work together; it was highly inappropriate. There is nothing and never will be anything between us,' I said firmly. 'Like you said, Jake can't do an actual relationship and that's what I'm looking for. I don't trust anything he says.'

Davis nodded. 'You're wise not to, Freya; he'd eat a pretty little thing like you for breakfast.'

'You're right. I couldn't trust him, not after what his father has done.'

'Exactly. Jake is just like him.'

I feigned a girly giggle. 'Oh, you're sweet to look out for me, Davis. Maybe we could have coffee sometime when we're back in London, I'd love some career advice from such an experienced person in the industry.' I wondered if I might have overdone it but his chest practically visibly puffed out.

'I would love to give you advice; why don't I get your number and we can—' Davis broke off, looking over my shoulder. 'Oh, hey, Jake, we were just talking about you.'

I spun around to see Jake behind me, wearing a tense expression.

'So I gather,' Jake asked, looking at Davis and avoiding meeting my eyes. I wondered how much of our conversation he had overheard. I really hoped he hadn't heard the bit about his dad or me not trusting him.

'Nice try with Freya here,' Davis said, stepping forwards so quickly, I couldn't back away from him. He slung an arm over my shoulders. I saw Jake tense as much as my body instantly did. He still wouldn't look at me, though. 'But mate, she needs a real man.'

'You wouldn't know what a real man is like,' Jake said through gritted teeth.

I felt I needed to diffuse the situation and fast. Hayley was only feet away. Everyone at the conference was on Jake's side again. If he started a fight with Davis, it would all be over. I threw on a smile. 'It's sweet, you both wanting to look out for me; I am a big girl, though.' I stepped out from Davis's arm. 'Why don't we go back to the party? I need a refill.' I waved my now-empty glass. I hadn't even noticed I'd drained another one. I was now feeling decidedly light-headed. 'Davis, can you get me one then maybe we can dance?' I asked him, fluttering my eyelashes in his direction. I was disgusted with myself but I knew I needed to get rid of Davis before Jake exploded.

Davis smiled at me. 'Sure thing, gorgeous.'

'I'll follow you in a minute,' I said, handing him my empty glass.

'Don't be long.' Davis brushed past Jake. 'Looks like you've lost your touch,' was his parting shot as he went back into the party.

I exhaled. 'Thank God I got rid of him.' I looked at Jake, who finally met my gaze. 'You almost ruined the whole thing.'

'Ruined what, Freya? You coming on to that twat?' Jake demanded, the anger in his tone taking me back.

'Huh?' I started at him, confused. 'He saw us kiss in the lift earlier; I was acting like I didn't want it...'

'And why would you?'

'What do you mean?' I asked, the sharpness in his tone taking me back.

'Why would you want me to kiss you when I'm just like my father?'

'Oh.' My stomach dropped that he had heard me. 'I only said that because Davis—'

'Because you don't trust me.'

'I didn't want him to go out there and tell Hayley about us!' I said, moving closer and trying to reach for Jake.

He stepped back, though. 'You said we have to pretend nothing is going on,' he reminded me. I dropped my arms to my side. 'Maybe it was never pretend, though. Yeah, you might have wanted to make sure Davis doesn't run his mouth to Hayley about us but you haven't given me any indication you want anything to happen after we leave here. In fact, you just want to make sure no one finds out about us. And I thought that was to protect your career, which I 100 per cent want to do too, but maybe you don't think I can do relationships because of my father. Maybe you just wanted a holiday fling.' Jake shrugged as though he couldn't care less either way.

His words felt unfair. 'What do you want? You haven't said anything about us after this trip either,' I pointed out.

'I just walked in to find you flirting with Davis!' Jake snapped. 'Talking about meeting up with him in London, asking him for his advice... Were you just using me, too, to help your career? Using this trip and me to get into Hayley's good books? Maybe you thought I'd be honest with everyone like you wanted if you slept with me!'

I stared at him, stunned at what he had just said. 'You think I could do that? I'm that kind of person?'

'You just seem desperate to make sure no one finds out about us.'

'I have things to lose; you don't,' I snapped back then,

annoyed that he didn't understand why I had to do that. Hayley wouldn't drop him as a client but she could sack me.

'Don't worry, you won't lose anything.' Jake turned to go, then looked back at me, his expression and voice cold. 'Whatever this was, we should just leave it here in New York; you're right. We're too different.'

'What do you mean?' I asked, trying to follow him, hurt that he thought I wasn't good enough for him after all. Talking about our differences... Of course I was aware of them but in his arms, I thought they didn't matter. Now Jake was shoving them in my face.

'This wouldn't work in the real world, let's face it,' Jake said. 'We had fun, sure, but we should go back to just being professional.'

I stopped trying to follow him. I narrowed my eyes. I was furious. And more than a little bit tipsy. 'That's fine with me,' I replied coldly. 'You're right. We would never work in the real world. Let's keep things strictly business between us from now on.'

'Goodnight, Freya,' Jake said and with a tight nod, he left the room and went back out into the party as if we'd just ended a work meeting and not basically broken up.

I stared after him in shock at how the last few minutes had changed everything. I could blame Davis Mulberry but maybe he had just expedited what would have happened anyway. Jake thought I'd slept with him to get ahead at work. And I had no idea if he'd ever wanted more than a holiday thing with me. I had wondered if we had a chance after New York but clearly, that was never going to happen.

Walking back out into the party, I knew I couldn't pretend all was okay and I certainly didn't want to have to entertain Mulberry or face Hayley in this state. I looked around. Jake was with Hayley again, their backs to me. They clearly weren't looking for me. I wasn't needed any more.

I hurried along the edge of the wall for the door, keeping my head down and avoiding eye contact with anyone. Once out of the banqueting suite, I pulled my heels off and clutched them in one hand, scooped up my dress in the other, and like Cinderella, I made a mad dash across to the Waldorf so I could get to my hotel room and cry in peace.

But unlike Cinderella, I didn't drop a shoe on the floor, I narrowly avoided stepping on a discarded, half-eaten pizza on the pavement, and there was no Prince Charming trying to catch me.

36

> Where did you get to last night? I missed saying goodbye. I'm at the airport ready for my flight home boo!

I was wide awake when Liv messaged me later that night. I saw my phone light up and for a crazy moment thought it might be Jake asking to talk. I couldn't face telling Liv what happened between us so I just replied to say I'd call her when I got back to London. I really didn't want to, though. I definitely wasn't up to hearing a 'told you so'.

The night had passed with me staring at the ceiling or the clock, and then it was time to get ready for my early flight, and panic set in because Jake and I were meant to be travelling to the airport together. Plus we'd be sitting in neighbouring pods for the flight home.

How the hell was I meant to face him after our argument at the party?

Slowly, feeling like a zombie, I threw my things into my suitcase, annoyed with myself for napping with Jake yesterday when

I should have been packing, and then I had a lightning-fast shower. I tried really hard not to think about him while I stood under the hot water but how could I forget our steamy shower together? I cursed the man for being so hot. I knew it would be a long time before I forgot how his touch had driven me crazy. Or how much of a wrench it had been to leave his embrace. How good his arms felt around me. How much his kisses had thrilled me. And how when he'd looked at me, the rest of the world had disappeared. He'd made me feel things I wasn't sure I'd ever feel in real life. The stuff of a romance novel.

Or so I had believed at the time.

It had all been fleeting, though. It was gone in a flash. Pulled away from me like ripping the duvet off a bed when it's time to change the sheets.

And now I was back to believing romance was officially dead. And I'd never find the kind of love I read about in books.

Maybe I had been right after all – it just didn't exist.

My hair was still damp as I pulled on a dress and boots and packed my hand luggage but I didn't care. I went down to the lobby in a daze, checking out at reception then walking towards the doors to wait for Jake and the car I'd booked to take us to the airport. I sighed under my breath though when I saw Hayley sitting in one of the chairs with her laptop. She waved me over as soon as she saw me. How did she look so perky at this time and after the party as well?

'I was waiting to see you and Jake before you leave... Ah, there he is.' She waved over my shoulder. I tried not to but I looked back and my eyes met Jake's briefly. His face was expressionless so I kept mine the same. He reached my side and I forced myself to keep my gaze on Hayley although I desperately wanted to know if he was looking at me. 'I've arranged the meeting with your publishers, Jake, and added it both to your calendars. I'll need you

there, Freya, in case they want any information about the conference before I got here. Get as much rest as you can once you get
back so you both can be on your A games in that meeting. I will
get you a great deal, Jake, after the success here.' Hayley smiled
with satisfaction. 'Hadn't you both better be getting to the airport?'

I shook myself out of my trance and glanced at my phone.
'Yes, the car has arrived – it's waiting for us outside. I'll see you
back in the office then, Hayley,' I said, my heart sinking at the
thought of having to go to this meeting with them both. I kind of
hoped I wouldn't have to see Jake for a long time once we were
back in London. No such luck.

Hayley just nodded then went back to working on her laptop.

I glanced awkwardly at Jake. 'Okay then.'

'We should go,' he replied.

'Yep,' I said and I set off for the hotel doors, feeling Jake close
behind me. My body felt so attuned to him after all the intimate
time we'd spent together. It seemed so strange to feel so distant
from him now.

Outside, the driver of our car took our bags and then held the
door open. I slid across the leather seat and Jake sat beside me,
instantly pulling out his phone. So, I turned to look out of the
window, wishing his scent wasn't as appealing as it was. We set
off for the airport and the journey reminded me of the one here.
I had planned to be super professional with Jake. That had failed
completely but I was determined to not fail this time. I didn't
want him to think I was at all bothered by what had happened.
Was this a little bit childish? Perhaps. But we needed to go back
to how we used to be otherwise Hayley was going to smell a rat,
and I sure as hell wasn't going to let him derail my career now.

As we drove out of the city, my heart felt heavy with having to
leave New York. I had loved being here. I wished it wasn't now

tainted with memories of me and Jake but I vowed I'd return one day and replace them with better ones. I watched as the skyscrapers rolled past the window; the morning sun was just becoming visible in gaps between the imposing buildings, casting a pale glow over the city. Jake had dulled my shine at seeing New York on the way here with his grumpy attitude, and now beside me again, he was doing exactly the same thing. And it pissed me off.

Jake cleared his throat then. 'How do you feel about Hayley wanting you at this meeting?'

Involuntarily, my head turned around. He was looking at me and the sudden eye contact made my breath hitch.

'I know things are...' For a second, his confidence seemed to fail him and he trailed off before clearing his throat again. 'But it would be good for your career, wouldn't it?'

'I didn't think you'd care about my career now,' I replied. I shrugged. 'But yes, I have no choice. And we have to get back to being professional with each other so we might as well start as soon as possible,' I said, turning back to the window.

There was a short silence. 'Okay.'

We didn't speak for the rest of the journey to the airport. I ached with wanting to erase our argument but even if we could get past what happened last night, I wasn't sure there was any point. My career needed to be my focus now. We were miles apart even next to each other in this car, and that made me hold back from reaching out to him either literally or figuratively. Maybe Jake felt the same way as he didn't make any attempts to speak to me either.

Once at the airport, we got out, grabbed our bags and made our way through all the checks to the first-class lounge. It was still early and the airport was quiet, which suited me as my head ached. I grabbed coffee and a pastry and sat down, hoping I could sleep on the flight.

Jake went to the buffet and when he came over, hovered near my table, unsure whether to join me or not. I stayed silent as I watched, wondering what he was going to do. Jake started towards me then but he didn't see there was a slight bump where the lino floor turned into carpet tiles and his shoes caught the line. He tripped forward, the tray shook and as if it was happening in slow motion, it slipped out of his hands, sending the coffee, plate of scrambled eggs, sausage, bacon and beans, and the pot of fruit and yoghurt all over the floor, shattering the plates and the cup, and even though Jake managed to right himself and stop falling to the floor along with it all, he did get splashed by the baked beans.

Everyone in the lounge looked over at the noise.

Jake cried out 'fuck' as his trousers got covered in food. And I bit my lip hard to stop myself from laughing. The sight of Jake like this was priceless, though. I had embarrassed myself spectacularly in front of him on the way here and miraculously, the universe was throwing me a bone for once and this time, it was him.

Jake looked at me biting my lip. 'Don't say anything,' he growled before turning and half-running for the toilets. A member of staff came over to clear up the mess with an annoyed titter. I turned away and let out a snort. We had talked about my falling over in front of him as a meet-cute situation. Things could have been very different if we'd just met this morning. I would have likely swooned at meeting someone so good-looking and equally as clumsy and chaotic as me.

But I knew this was an anomaly. Jake wasn't like me.

Still, I would remember this moment and if I felt sad about us ending whatever had started in New York, this would help.

If only just a little bit.

*   *   *

The flight from New York to London was a parallel of the flight from London to New York. Jake and I sat in our separate pods and did our own thing for the hours spent in the sky. Before our trip, I didn't know that Jake could be different to the man I thought he was when we first met. Back then, he said he was bitter from his dad's betrayal, and I completely understood why. Like me wondering if love was all a lie, Jake had thought love was real and then that belief had been shattered. By the person closest to him. It had made him cold, reserved, stand-offish even.

But in New York, he had finally been honest with me and himself, then his readers. All of that felt completely pointless now because when I looked over at him on the plane, he had shut down again. Maybe I had just imagined him changing. Or it had happened but after our agreement, he had gone back into his hard shell?

Jake closed up his pod soon after take-off so I couldn't even glance over to see what he was doing. I tried to sleep or watch a film on my screen but I was too restless for either. I couldn't even enjoy first class the second time around.

When the plane started its descent to Heathrow, Jake opened his pod and put his seatbelt on without looking over at me. That told me he hadn't been thinking about me on the flight like I had been thinking about him. I put my seatbelt on, looked out at the fluffy clouds over London and resolved to put him out of my mind. I would think of him as someone I had had a fun holiday fling with, and that was it.

'You are a good girl, aren't you, Freya?'

I shook my head to try to clear it of dirty thoughts about our time in my hotel bed. Great sex didn't equal a great relationship, did it?

The plane dipped again and the approach to Heathrow began. I breathed a sigh of relief that soon, I would be off this plane and back in my room in my flat, far away from Jake. And when I next saw him, it would be for work, and I needed to go back to being just professional with him.

And not think about being in Jake's arms ever again.

37

'You won't believe the gossip I have for you!'

I jumped as Liv made her announcement the following day, suddenly appearing by my table in Starbucks, sounding far brighter than I felt. 'What?' I asked sleepily as I took another long drink of my vanilla iced latte. She sat down opposite me with her iced coffee and handed me one of the muffins she had bought. I felt sluggish with jet lag. Once I'd got through Heathrow and found my case, Jake had disappeared so I got the Tube by myself to my flat, where I slunk into my bedroom, closed the door and flopped on my bed.

I had felt a weird twinge then. There was no one in my shared flat waiting for me to come home, no one to debrief the trip with, and I had let self-pity wash over me. I'd slept most of the day so I'd struggled to sleep at night. Liv had suggested a coffee so I'd crawled out of my flat to meet her at lunchtime, keen to see a friendly face again. And to talk about work tomorrow because I was really nervous at having to see Jake again and act like we'd been nothing to one another in New York. Hayley could never find out about us but it was going to be so hard to move past the feelings I'd been starting to have for him.

Liv had a sip of her coffee then propped her elbows up on the table to look at me. 'It's about our least favourite person – Davis Mulberry.'

'What about him?' I asked, pushing through my sluggish mind in a panic. I didn't want to ever see or hear about Davis Mulberry again but if he had been gossiping about me and Jake... 'What happened?' I demanded of Liv.

'After we left the end-of-conference party, all hell broke loose, apparently. Tessa phoned me before I came to meet you to tell me about it. We missed a scandal. Typical that I had to leave for my flight and you... Actually, why did you leave the party early? Were you with Jake?' She wriggled her eyebrows suggestively.

'No!' I snapped.

Her face fell.

I couldn't bear to tell her about me and Jake ending just yet so I waved my hand. 'Sorry. Jet lag is killing me. What did Davis do and say?' I asked, really hoping he hadn't mentioned us. Hayley hadn't said anything, though and surely, she would have if she had found out?

'Well, according to Tessa, Davis got more and more pissed as the night went on. And he started telling the conference organisers the whole event had been rubbish and crime events are so much better, and maybe they should come to one so they can improve their conference. Then a few attendees got involved to tell him he was wrong and he got really angry and pushed over one of the tables with drink on. It was chaos, apparently.'

'Blimey. I knew he was a bit of a twat, but that takes the biscuit! He didn't say anything about me and Jake, did he?'

'No.' Her eyes widened. 'Why, did he know about you two?'

'What happened then?' I asked, wanting to put off telling Liv about what had happened with me, Jake and Davis.

'The hotel called security and he was escorted out!'

'God,' I said, shaking my head. 'How embarrassing for him.'

'I know, right? He won't have anything to lord over Jake now after this. It's *his* reputation in tatters now!' Liv grinned. 'Couldn't have happened to a nicer man, right?' She frowned. 'Are you okay, Freya? You aren't yourself today.'

I sighed, unable to put it off any longer. 'Me and Jake... Whatever it was between us, it's all over now. And it could be why Davis Mulberry had such a meltdown. The three of us had a row at the party. It was horrible, Liv. And now I have to have a meeting with Hayley and Jake at his publisher's tomorrow and pretend I haven't seen the man naked!' I cried out, causing a couple of people at neighbouring tables to look over at me in shock. 'Oops,' I said, ducking my head.

'Don't worry about them,' Liv said. 'Are you okay? How can it be over? I saw the way Jake looked at you. Hang on, what happened with Davis then? Did he do something to break you guys up?'

I gave Liv the blow-by-blow account of what happened at the party. 'I wish I could just blame Davis but Jake clearly never trusted me. He thought I was using him to help my career. And that I think he's just like his father. Maybe I didn't trust that he wanted anything serious with me. So, I guess maybe I didn't trust him either.' I shook my head. 'I need to focus on my career now. I need to get through this meeting at the publishing company, and hopefully, then Hayley will promote me. And I can forget all about Jake Richards!'

'Oh, Freya,' Liv said with sympathy. 'I'm sorry it didn't work out.'

'You told me to be careful, and you were right,' I said dully.

'Are you sure you and Jake can't talk and—'

'No,' I cut in firmly. 'I'm done humiliating myself with that man. He doesn't want a relationship with me. It was just a fling. I need to move on, Liv. But how can I get through this meeting?'

'You can get through it,' Liv reassured me even though she looked concerned. 'You need to treat Jake like he is still what he was to you before New York. Just Hayley's biggest client. And you need to show her how much you deserve that promotion.'

I nodded along with her pep talk and hoped I could pull it off.

'You were amazing in New York. I mean, you've saved Jake's career! That was down to you. You got him to be honest, and everyone reacted really well to it. He did that because of you. Just channel the same energy.'

I gave her a weak smile. New York had been a success on the professional front. I needed to remember that, and try to forget the failure on the personal front. I drained the rest of my coffee and felt a little bit more awake. 'You're right. Thanks, Liv. If what happened with Jake taught me anything, it's that I should have been more professional, and less like myself. Being myself might have saved his reputation but it had made me risk my heart on someone who hadn't been worth that risk.'

'What do you mean?' Liv asked with a frown.

'I'll do everything Hayley wants, be who she wants me to be, and leave the old "wears her heart on her sleeve" Freya behind. I'm going to turn over a completely new leaf. I will be a complete boss bitch like Hayley. The old Freya is dead.'

'Hang on...'

'I follow my heart too much; I always have. It's time to follow my head instead.'

Liv didn't look convinced but I ignored her negativity. I knew what I had to do. I jumped up. 'I need to go shopping and buy a new outfit for tomorrow's meeting. Wish me luck!'

'But, Freya...'

I was already walking away from her. 'I'll call you and tell you how it went,' I told her over my shoulder.

She sighed but called out to wish me luck and with a parting wave, I walked out of Starbucks and left her there, determined to make tomorrow's meeting go the best it possibly could.

38

'Now, Jake's publishers will definitely want to play hard ball with us so we need to make sure they know how successful the romance conference was for him,' Hayley said to me the next day as we talked through the meeting we were about to have at Jake's publisher's office.

I sat in the chair on the other side of her desk as I had done so many times in the months I'd worked here but this time, I was trying to act like an agent like her, and not like her assistant. When I had walked in wearing my new outfit, she had done a double take and given me a smile, which I took to be a big compliment. I had chosen a black suit – straight-leg trousers and a blazer with a white blouse underneath – and I wore black court shoes with a heel. I was trying to channel Hayley's power suits and the outfit definitely made me look older and more professional. I felt smart, if a little uncomfortable and unsure if the outfit was flattering on me.

But I told myself that didn't matter. I didn't need to look good, just capable. Like I could be a powerhouse agent just like Hayley was.

'We need to big up how much readers loved him being honest about his personal life, and how they are now clamouring for his next book,' Hayley continued. 'Sharing what happened with his father was gold dust. I've had so many requests for interviews so lots of publicity opportunities are there for the taking with a new book. His publishers will love that. And I might even pitch a non-fiction book idea to them. Maybe something about not making the same mistakes as your parents in marriage and relationships.'

I looked up in surprise. 'Would Jake want to write a book like that?' I asked, thinking that with how reticent he'd been to even talk about his father, I couldn't imagine he'd want to write a book about it. And what would his poor mum think?

Hayley frowned. 'I haven't talked to him about it. But he wants his career back on track, and we want to make money... This is a real opportunity; we have to seize it.'

'Surely it's up to Jake what he writes—'

'Freya,' Hayley cut in impatiently. 'Who is Jake's agent?' she demanded, eyebrow raised.

I flinched at her tone and the look on her face. 'You are, of course.'

She nodded. 'Exactly. Now, you went rogue in New York, which we very much need to talk about, but I was pleased you finally showed initiative and did exactly what I asked you to do. Now his publishers are keen to discuss a new contract, it's my turn to do my job.'

'I'm just glad to be in the meeting,' I said meekly.

'It will be good for you to see how to pitch and negotiate for your own clients one day,' Hayley said, beaming at me like I had pleased her. I relaxed a little bit in my chair. 'So, I want you to listen and take notes, and not say anything unless I tell you to.

And for goodness' sake, don't mention the disaster that was the first panel session. We are focusing on what went well.'

'Definitely,' I said firmly.

Hayley eyed me across her desk. 'Remember that whatever I say in there is to get Jake the best deal possible, okay? Sometimes as an agent, you need to sprinkle a little bullshit over things like icing on top of the cake. Just to make sure you get what you want.'

I was unsure what she meant. Was she going to lie about something to get Jake a better deal? 'But Jake's book is brilliant and—'

Hayley waved her hand. 'No need to fangirl without him here to hear you, Freya. The book is fine, a little mushy for my taste but that's what he does so well, and why he is so popular. His publishers will eat it up, I'm sure. I expect the full red-carpet treatment for him today.'

'But you said you thought it was one of his best books...' I said, remembering what Hayley had said in her office with Jake before we went to New York.

'Of course I had to tell him that,' she said with a chuckle. 'You need to get stronger or this business will chew you up and spit you out. Learn from me and you'll do fine. If all goes well today, we can talk about the next steps for you and your career.'

I smiled. 'That would be great, Hayley, thank you.'

She stood up. 'We should make our way over to meet Jake. I think we can get him one of his best deals so far.'

I stood up too. 'Wow, just because of what we did at the conference?'

Hayley picked up her Louis Vuitton bag and swung it over her shoulder. I tried to hide my H&M bag behind my back. 'Taking credit for what your author did? You are learning from me. Let's go.'

I followed her out, confused as to whether she was praising or criticising me. Hayley was such a formidable character that if I was learning from her, I assumed that was good for my career. She strode through the office, full of confidence, and I hoped one day, I'd feel just as confident.

* * *

We met Jake around the corner from his publisher's office outside a Starbucks. It was a warm summer's day and my suit was making me hot and bothered. When I saw him standing there, hands in his pockets, the sun beaming down on his dark hair, I felt decidedly sweaty. Jake was in a linen suit and his facial hair was slightly scruffy. Annoyingly, it suited him as much as when he had it styled to perfection.

'Jake,' Hayley said, giving his hand a firm shake. 'Ready to give them hell?' she asked, her eyes twinkling.

'Lead the way,' Jake replied, but didn't return her smile. He glanced at me and did the same double take Hayley had done. 'Freya?' he said, but it sounded like a question.

I nodded. 'Hi, Jake,' I said, keeping my eyes on a spot just over his shoulder so we didn't make full eye contact. That might have made my new cool, calm demeanour crumble.

'Enough chit-chat,' Hayley said. 'We need to be on time.' She set off but Jake kept looking at me.

'What?' I said, uncomfortable at his scrutiny, snapping my eyes onto his for a second. I felt a jolt of electricity that I tried desperately to ignore.

'Nothing.' Jake shook his head and set off after Hayley, shoving his hands into his pockets.

I sighed but hurried after them, wondering how things had got so awkward between us so fast. This man had been naked in my bed but now we were barely speaking. I hated it but I tried to push the memories of New York out of my mind. I had to focus right now. I just needed to be the consummate professional in this meeting, and then get out and hopefully never be in such close contact with Jake Richards ever again.

His publishing company was in a Victorian building in the city. They had published some of my favourite books and this was my first time inside. There was a delicious old-book smell and the walls were lined with them as we were walked across the open-plan office floor by the receptionist and shown into the boardroom to wait for the team that looked after Jake's books. There were old sash windows and the floor was polished wood: a nice change from the usual carpet tiles in offices. The long, shiny, wooden table had been laid out with water for us, plates of cakes and biscuits and Jake's books scattered around. On the TV screen at one end was a presentation ready to be played.

'Jake! Hayley!' A man in a grey suit with strawberry-blond hair walked in, followed by four other people. 'It's a pleasure to see you both again.'

I knew the man was Jake's editor, and the head of the publishing company, Craig Blanc. He greeted Hayley and Jake like old best friends though I knew that, just last month, he had been avoiding her calls. Hayley's 'bullshit' phrase swirled around in my head. There seemed to be a lot of it about to happen in this room.

The door closed and we were trapped together for an hour.

'Well, well, well, what a week you've had,' Craig said once we were all seated at the table. I was next to Hayley with Jake on her other side, and it was a relief to have her in between us. Craig sat opposite us with his colleagues, who he had introduced but I'd missed most of their names because I'd been trying to not think about being so close to Jake again. 'We've heard amazing things from the conference. Hayley, you told me that Jake could turn around his reputation and boy, did you pull it off this week. You kept your strategy quiet, though. We had no idea what Jake was going to reveal.'

'I didn't—' Jake started to say but Hayley leaned forward in her chair and interrupted him.

'Thank you, Craig. I decided before the three of us went to New York that we couldn't stick to the same statement we had been using about that article. I realised Jake's readers are a sentimental bunch and would love to hear the true story from him. I knew the conference would be the perfect opportunity to come clean, and get everyone back on his side,' Hayley said, a sweet smile on her face.

39

My head swivelled around to look at Hayley in shock. Not only was she claiming that we'd all gone to the conference together with a strategy in place to save Jake's reputation; she was taking the credit for it. She was telling Craig that it had all been her idea! I thought about her saying that I should just sit and take notes so I could learn from her. Had that been because she knew she was going to pretend the romance conference going so well was all down to her?

'Hang on—' Jake started to speak again.

'Jake,' Hayley cut in again, turning her smile on to him. 'Why don't you tell everyone how your readers reacted to you at your event? When you told them all what had been going on these past few months... I know we all saw the buzz on social media but there is nothing like a first-hand account.' She waved her hand. 'Go ahead, don't be modest.' She laughed a little bit. I hadn't realised quite how phony her laugh sounded before now.

Jake hesitated and leaned back slightly to look at me behind Hayley. I couldn't fathom his expression but he seemed to be looking at me for some kind of cue. I was still stunned at what

Hayley had said but she had pointed out she was Jake's agent, not me, and that we would discuss my career after this meeting. Did I actually have any other choice here but to sit and listen to Hayley bigging herself up? Wasn't that what she had basically told me she would do, and it would be for the purpose of Jake getting the best deal? I knew that was in all of our best interests so I gave Jake a firm nod, hoping he would take that as encouragement to tell the story Hayley wanted him to.

Jake seem to hesitate but finally, he cleared his throat and looked across the table. He began the story of what happened in New York and as he told it, he made it sound like we had planned it all along and we hadn't had a disastrous first couple of days at the conference. Jake was, of course, a brilliant storyteller so everyone was in the palm of his hand.

'And Jake was the talk of the conference after that,' Hayley said triumphantly after he had finished. 'Wasn't he, Freya?' She looked across at me.

I nodded along quickly. 'Everyone was talking about it and so many readers came up to him asking about when there might be another book out,' I said, relieved I didn't need to lie about that. It was just frustrating that Hayley wasn't telling anyone that I had been the one to encourage Jake to be honest. I wouldn't have minded her taking the credit exactly if she had at all been supportive at the time but she had wanted Jake to keep lying, and had been really unhelpful when things had gone wrong at first, basically telling me I'd failed. Then she'd turned up and almost fired me, tried to take over but when Jake had done what I suggested and it had worked, she had changed tack completely. Now we had been successful, it was like she couldn't remember not being on board.

Or was hoping that we wouldn't remember.

But I did.

'And they would be thrilled to know that he has a book all ready to go,' Hayley said after beaming at me like she was really proud.

I had looked up to her but now I wasn't sure I could trust her. First Jake, now Hayley. My head and heart hurt.

'*When I Met You*, as you all know, is Jake's best book so far. It's bound to be a bestseller,' Hayley added.

Again, her words galled me. Just an hour ago in her office, she had dismissed my praise of his book.

Craig nodded eagerly. 'As soon as you sent it to me, I knew it would be a hit. It's a brilliant book. Didn't it make you cry, Rachel?' he asked his colleague.

I tried not to react but, again, I knew this was a lie. When Hayley had sent Jake's new book over, the article furore had been in full swing, and Craig had ignored it, left it sat on his desk for two months because he wasn't bothered about publishing it. And when he'd finally read it, he had side-stepped talk of a new deal until now. Now opinion was back on Jake's side, Craig's attitude had taken a 360-degree turn.

This meeting seemed so fake.

Then I looked down at my outfit in dismay. Was I now just as fake?

I tried to shake off my thoughts and focus on what Craig was saying about their plans for Jake's books, but my mind was racing. I really wanted this to be my career but now I was questioning at what cost I was willing to make it happen.

'We are so happy you're still on board with us,' Craig said then.

Jake let out a loud exhale that turned all heads in his direction. I looked at him too, wondering what was on his mind, and if his thoughts were at all similar to mine. 'I haven't said that I am.'

Hayley threw a sharp glare at Jake but he kept his eyes on

Craig and ploughed on regardless. I couldn't help but admire his bravery because if she ever looked at me like that, I'd want to shrink like a tortoise retreating into its shell.

'Um... what do you mean?' Craig asked uneasily, his confidence suddenly shaken. I was kind of pleased about that.

'Well, you weren't exactly supportive over these past six months,' Jake replied. 'I thought you didn't want to publish this book. I know we are skirting around that fact but I think it's important to put it out there. I made a mistake, yes, but I didn't appreciate the way you all tried to wash your hands of me.'

There were sharp intakes of breath, murmurings and tense expressions all around the table at Jake's words. They were completely true but everyone was shocked he had uttered them.

'Jake, I think—' Hayley began, but Jake cut her off.

'I'm sorry, Hayley, but if I am going to re-sign here, I need to make sure that something like this won't happen again. That we can work though any issues together. And as we've discussed, what happened at the conference has increased interest in my new book, and the backlist has gone up the charts on Amazon too, so I would need my new deal to not only reflect this but the fact that these past few months, you haven't been at all bothered about me or my career.'

Craig went pale. 'Jake, come on, it wasn't like that; you have to understand that—'

'I do,' Jake cut in again, taking no prisoners. I bit my lip in case I started cheering or something. I had always admired Hayley's style but now I could see just how much of it was based on manipulating people and situations, whereas Jake was telling the cold, hard truth. I had found him intimidating but now I just admired the hell out of him. It was making him even more attractive to me but I tried hard not to think in that direction and keep my thoughts on professional ground. He was making that bloody hard, though.

'I understand completely what has happened,' Jake continued. 'And as I say, that has made me need to think very carefully about bringing this book, and my next ones, to this company again. I need to be sure the new deal you offer me is right for me now and for the future. So, I look forward to receiving it from you and I'll then think it over very carefully.'

Hayley eyed Jake for a moment and then turned to Craig. I could almost see her brain ticking over. Jake had gone rogue but she wasn't going to let that stop her from taking back control of this situation. She gave a firm nod. 'Exactly. I couldn't have said it better myself, Jake. We have discussed the fact that several other publishers have been in touch in the past couple of days to ask whether Jake is still under contract with you, and I have told them that currently, that is not the case.'

Craig was now ghostly white. He leaned forward and cleared his throat. 'Now, Hayley, Jake, you know that we definitely do not want to lose you. As you say, your backlist is doing so well, and a new book will only help that further; we could re-brand all your titles and tie them into your new release. And we can set up TV appearances and arrange a book tour, capitalise in every way we can on the publicity you got at the romance conference. And I can assure you both, we are fully committed to Jake's career and the new deal we offer will most definitely reflect that commitment. I only ask one thing: will you wait for our offer before you talk to any other publisher?'

I saw Hayley put her hand up under the table to make sure Jake didn't answer. He leaned back in his chair and crossed his arms.

Hayley took her time to respond. I found myself holding my breath. Finally, she sighed. 'You're asking a lot, Craig, but we are very loyal to you as you know so as long as you get us the deal by end of play tomorrow, we can do that.'

'Tomorrow? I need to...' Craig began, eyeing his team in what seemed like something close to panic.

'Get it sorted. Excellent.' Hayley clapped her hands together, making everyone jump a little bit. Then she stood up. 'I have calls to make so thank you for the meeting, Craig. Looking forward to hearing from you tomorrow. Jake, Freya, shall we?'

I scrambled to get up and grab my things as Hayley swept towards the door. Jake followed at a brisk pace and I hurried after them, hearing the team calling out goodbyes and thank yous behind me. We walked to the lifts and jumped in one heading back down to the ground floor.

In the lift, I took in a couple of breaths, unsure how to even feel after that meeting.

'Hayley...' Jake began.

She held up a hand. 'You know by now to trust that whatever I do is the best thing for your career, Jake. So, trust me.'

Jake looked at me but I kept my eyes on the lift doors.

After we had reached the ground floor and walked out of the building, Hayley turned to us. 'I'm off for a lunch meeting. See you back at the office, Freya. Jake, I'll call you as soon as Craig gets in touch.' She air-kissed us both then strode off, disappearing into the city and leaving me and Jake together on the pavement.

'We need to talk,' Jake said after a moment of us watching her go.

40

I hesitated as Jake looked at me. 'What do we have to say to each other?'

'For starters, what's going on with you?' he asked.

My eyebrows shot up. 'What are you talking about?'

'Freya, in that meeting, you were completely unlike yourself!'

'And you know me so well?' I asked him, feeling instantly defensive at his tone.

'I know you well enough to be confused about what happened in that meeting. You let Hayley act like everything that happened in New York was down to her! You let her take all the credit for your hard work. She made it seem like not only was she there all along but it was all her strategy to begin with. When we both know she had basically washed her hands of us!' He looked as exasperated as I felt, but it made me annoyed.

'Well, you didn't say anything either,' I pointed out. 'You went along with her too.'

'I wanted to set them straight but you didn't seem to want me to do that. I was confused what was going on. You were so different in there. I mean...' Jake gestured to me. 'You even look like Hayley suddenly. What's going on?'

My blood started to boil at his attitude when he'd made it clear we were nothing to each other. I snapped, 'Why do you care? I'm just Hayley's assistant to you!'

Jake looked taken aback. 'If you really think that...'

'What else am I meant to think?' I demanded. 'Ever since the party in New York, we've avoided each other. We said we'd go back to how we were before. And that meeting was exactly like we were before. Hayley is your agent so she took control to nego-tiate the best deal for you. She's promised to help me become an agent, and told me to follow her lead. So, I did my job, Jake!' I could see some passers-by looking at us and I realised I'd raised my voice more than was acceptable, but Jake really was winding me up. 'And you did what she wanted too!'

'I made sure they knew how pissed off I was with how they've been treating me these past few months. I'm not keen on re-signing but Hayley thinks I'll get the best deal with them so—'

'Exactly,' I interrupted him triumphantly. 'You did what she told you to, like I did, so why am I in the wrong?'

Jake stared at me for a moment, then pushed a hand through his hair with a sigh. 'Why are we doing what she says though, Freya?' he asked in a softer, calmer tone. 'We were the ones who turned things around in New York, not her. We did it together. We made a good team, didn't we?'

I sighed too. 'Yeah, we did. But that's in the past.'

'Is it? I don't know about us personally but work stuff, Freya, we should really think about it. I meant what I said that you'd make a good agent. You're honest and loyal and you know what readers want. You gave me some bloody good advice. And I liked how you were always yourself. This...' He gestured to me again. 'Today, this wasn't you. I know you don't care what I think, that

I'm nothing more than someone you work with now, but as an author, you could take my advice. I don't think working with Hayley is the best thing for you.'

I hesitated. Jake spoke sincerely like he cared about me but I knew that he didn't so it just made it harder to accept what he was saying. It made my heart ache for those moments back in New York when I was in his arms feeling like there was just us two in the world together. Now, I had woken up from that dream. Now, the world was very much in between us.

'Hayley is successful,' I said, shaking my head. 'She wants to help me be successful too.'

'Does she, though?' Jake countered. 'She certainly was comfortable with taking credit for your work back in there. Does that seem like someone who wants to support and guide you? Just be careful, Freya. Whatever you think of me, I don't want Hayley to treat you badly.'

'Why are you making me feel like I've done something wrong?' I asked, hoping I wouldn't start crying.

'Freya...' Jake lifted his arm like he was going to touch me but then he hastily put his hand back down. 'I'm trying to get you to see that you should be yourself. Remember how you pushed me in New York? You wanted me to be honest. And you were right. I'm trying to do the same for you here. Be honest with yourself about what you really want. Do you want to be like Hayley, or do you want to be yourself? Who was the one who fixed my career, by the way. Remember that, okay? You did it, not Hayley.'

My body suddenly craved his touch all over again. I wanted to crawl back into his embrace and let him hold me and make it all okay. But I knew that was impossible. Jake was making it really hard for me not to miss what we had together the past few days. Suddenly, all the confidence I had summoned before our meeting felt like it had been sucked out of me.

'I don't know what I can do,' I admitted, my anger fading fast. I had given him some home truths and that was what he was doing for me. I couldn't be annoyed about that. And what if he was right?

'We both have a lot to think about,' Jake said. He gave me a sad smile. 'I wish things were different.'

I didn't know if he meant between us, or all this complicated work stuff, or both. And I didn't want to hear the answer in case he didn't think about us at all any more. I might have accepted things were over but if he regretted everything, that would hurt a lot.

'You can always call me, Freya. I mean that,' Jake added quietly. 'I'll see you soon.' He headed off then, walking away slowly. I watched him go, thoroughly confused. He had been so harsh with me at the party and we'd both said things we couldn't take back but now he seemed worried about me.

My phone rung then and I started walking in the opposite direction to Jake. I answered it without looking at the screen, assuming it would be Liv asking what happened at the meeting. I really didn't want to tell her.

'Freya, is that you?' a man's voice spoke.

'Who's this?'

'Um... it's Davis Mulberry. Please don't hang up,' he replied, adding the last bit hastily as I did almost do just that. 'I persuaded the receptionist where you work to give me your number.'

'What do you want?' I asked dully, wondering if this day could get any worse.

He cleared his throat. 'Freya, will you meet me for coffee? I have a proposition for you,' he said, sounding a little bit less confident than he had in New York.

I snorted. 'Are you serious? Listen, there is nothing to tell about me and Jake now...' I began but he cut me off.

'So, you admit that there was something to tell?'

I cringed at my slip-up, forgetting that I'd told Davis I had slapped Jake after the kiss in the lift he had seen.

'It's okay,' he added, quickly before I could think of what to say. 'This isn't about you and Jake although I am curious...'

'Whatever happened between us, it's over now,' I replied, firmly. 'So, if you try to tell Hayley anything...' I began, really hoping he wouldn't do that.

'I won't,' he said quickly. 'I never actually would have; I was just trying to wind you both up.'

'Nice,' I replied. 'Well, it worked; we are broken up for good. So, if you're not going to threaten me again, why are you calling me?' I carried on walking towards the office. The thought of going back to work and seeing Hayley again later wasn't very appealing but I didn't have any choice. Suddenly, the outfit that I'd previously felt super professional in felt restrictive and strange. I wondered if Jake was right that trying to be someone different wouldn't work in the end or if I should just ignore his advice.

'I need your help.'

My eyebrows shot up into my forehead. 'You need my help,' I repeated incredulously.

Davis sighed down the phone. 'I suppose you've heard what happened in New York...'

'I did,' I replied, trying to focus on what Liv had told me, pushing Jake away from my mind. 'You upset the conference organisers and then pushed over a table and had to be escorted out, something like that?'

'Something like that,' he said. 'I have a bit of a problem knowing when I've had enough to drink and once I've had too much, I can't filter myself very well,' he added uncomfortably.

'I'm not sure you filter yourself very well when you're sober,' I replied.

'Freya, this is why I need to speak to you. You're honest, and that in our business is pretty rare. Please. I promise I'll make it worth your while.' He coughed. 'I didn't mean that to come out like an innuendo, I swear. This is a mutually beneficial career situation. I know that I was a bit... flirtatious in New York.'

'I'd say creepy,' I said flatly.

'God, Freya, I'm sorry. Will you please meet me? Hear me out? Nothing creepy will happen.' He chuckled then. 'I don't think I've ever promised a woman that before.'

'Maybe that would help your chat-up skills,' I mused as I crossed the road, the office in my sight then. For the first time since I got the job there, I was kind of dreading going into work. Thankfully, Hayley was out for at least a couple of hours. I had no idea what to say to her about what had happened in Jake's meeting. I felt myself slow down a little bit.

'See? You're brutal and I need that right now.' He sighed. 'I'm sorry I was like that with you in New York. I actually have a girl-friend. I was just trying to push Jake's buttons by talking to you,' Davis said. 'Please meet me, Freya,' he added in a pleading tone.

I had no idea what to say. I didn't trust the man but he sounded sincere about needing my help, and I was a little bit intrigued. It helped too knowing he had a girlfriend and wasn't hitting on me, I supposed. 'I don't know...'

'You mentioned needing career advice; this will be even better than that.' Some of his usual arrogance crept into his tone. But then he added, 'I would be incredibly grateful.'

'Fine,' I said finally. 'I'll meet you but if you are anything less than polite, I'm leaving.'

'Thank you!' He told me where and when to meet him, then we hung up. I really wasn't sure about this but with everything feeling like it was up in the air, I reasoned I didn't have much to lose.

I carried on walking to work and when I got into the office and sat down at my desk, an email came through from Hayley.

> I won't be back into the office today. Hold the fort. Let's meet first thing tomorrow to catch up.

I let out a slow exhale. At least I wouldn't have to see her again today. Now all I had to worry about was meeting Davis Mulberry later. My eyes fell on my Kindle and I thought about Jake's book. I told myself I shouldn't be worried about him. He was just another one of our authors now.

But his words echoed through my mind for the rest of the day regardless.

You can always call me, Freya. I mean that.

41

Davis Mulberry and I met after work at an outside café close to the Tube. The summery afternoon had encouraged a lot of other people to do the same and the tables were all full. Davis was there waiting for me at one, wearing a short-sleeved shirt and light-coloured trousers, a cup of coffee in front of him. I grabbed an iced lemonade, not wanting caffeine so late in the day – I was already thinking I wouldn't sleep well after the day I'd had – and then joined him at his table.

'Freya, thank you,' Davis said, breaking into a relieved smile as I sat down opposite him. 'I wasn't sure if you would actually turn up or not.'

'I wasn't sure myself until I actually got here,' I admitted. I'd kept changing my mind the past hour as to whether this was a really bad idea or not. At least he appeared to be sober. 'What's going on?'

'My publishers aren't happy with me after what happened at the conference. My agent has tried to do damage control but they're talking about pulling my next book, which is meant to be out next month. It's ridiculous,' Davis said, shaking his head. 'I didn't even do anything *that* bad.'

I gave him a sceptical look. 'You had to be escorted out by security.'

'Okay, I know I fucked up. But what do I do now?'

After a beat, I responded, 'I'm sorry but why are you asking me?'

Davis leaned forward. 'Because you helped turn things around for Jake bloody Richards! He came to the conference in the doghouse with every romance reader in the world, and now everyone is saying he'll have the biggest book of his career once it comes out. He's the darling of the literary world again.' Davis groaned. 'Totally undeserved in my opinion but there we are. Life isn't fair, is it?'

I shook my head 'Slagging off Jake to one side, I'm still confused why you wanted to see me.'

'Because I want you to help me like you helped Jake! Restore my reputation, save my career, persuade my publishers to still bring out my book, get me to the top of the bestseller list. What do you think?'

'Even I could do that, why would I?' I challenged. I took a sip of my drink. 'I don't know if your career should be saved!'

'Have you read any of my books?'

'No,' I confessed. 'I only read romance, sorry.' I shrugged. I wasn't really sorry at all.

'And you say I'm prejudiced.' Davis reached down to his briefcase and pulled out a book. 'I brought along a proof copy for you. Why don't you read it so you can make an informed judgement?' he challenged me then, sliding it across the table towards me.

I stared at it. 'But why?' I asked again, still confused as to what he actually wanted from me.

'I told you – we can help each other,' Davis said. 'I told my agent about you and what you did for Jake, and he agreed to let me talk to you. He is only a couple of years away from retirement and is looking for new blood to join his agency, to take over his clients when he leaves, and he said you're exactly the kind of person he's looking for. If you can help us get my career back on track, he will hire you and show you all the ropes and who knows? You could be running his agency one day, if that's what you want.'

To say I was stunned was the understatement of the century. I stared back at him.

'You do want to be an agent yourself, don't you?' Davis prodded me when I didn't respond. I felt like I couldn't speak just yet. 'Freya?'

'Um... yes. I want to be an agent,' I said finally. 'But I work for Hayley Harper. She's my boss, and mentor. And she's going to help me become an agent one day. After everything in New York went so well.' I tried to ignore the voice in my head reminding me that she just took credit for everything I had done there. And Jake telling me not to trust Hayley so blindly.

'Oh well, that's good,' Davis said, stuttering a bit. 'But as I said, my agent, Simon really wants to groom someone to take over. And you'd be perfect. Are you not tempted even a little bit? I really could use your help. Has Hayley said when you'll be able to take on your own clients?'

'No, we're going to speak tomorrow morning.'

'Okay, well, will you think about what I've asked and see how you feel after your meeting?' Davis tapped his proof which was still on the table. 'And maybe you could just read a couple of chapters tonight? See if this is a book that you think should be published or not.'

'I'm really not sure I can help you,' I reiterated. I wasn't sure I

wanted to either and I was certain he realised that after our interactions in New York.

'Don't decide yet,' Davis begged me. 'Tell me tomorrow,
please?'

He seemed so desperate, I felt bad just shutting him
completely down. Despite the fact he likely deserved it. His
proposal was unexpected and I didn't want to hurry and say no
and then regret it. I knew I needed to pin Hayley down tomorrow
as to what was going to happen with my career and then I could
feel confident in turning down Davis's offer. So, I nodded. 'Okay.
I will think about it.' I picked up the proof and read the title: *He's
Behind You*. I never really fancied reading a thriller but I was
curious as to what his books were like. I eyed him as I put it in
my bag. 'Are you really worried?' I asked.

Davis shifted in his seat, avoiding my eyes, but he nodded.
'Simon is worried too. My publishers think I'm now a bad bet.
And I'm not sure how to convince them otherwise. I know that I
can be arrogant but I do care about my career and I know that
I'm in trouble.'

I was surprised by his honesty. 'Okay, let me think about it.'

'That's all I ask. Thank you.' Davis took a sip of his coffee and
then he grinned at me. 'So, you and Jake are really over?'

I rolled my eyes. 'Don't ruin it all now by coming on to me!'

'I wouldn't. I told you, I have a girlfriend, and I'm head over
heels for her. I was never really interested in you, Freya, no
offence. I just knew it would wind Jake up as I could tell he liked
you.'

'He doesn't any more,' I said, unable to hold back the tinge of
bitterness to my tone.

'What's changed so quickly?'

'We had an argument after we spoke at the party,' I said,

nodding at him. 'I think we're too different to make it work. It's better we keep things professional.'

'I spent years not telling the woman I just mentioned that I liked her, and we lost all that time we could have spent together, if I hadn't been worried about her rejecting me. Just don't make that mistake too.'

I raised an eyebrow. 'You're advocating for Jake Richards now?'

'No,' he replied. 'Definitely not. I don't see the appeal. But the things I said about him and relationships, I was just trying to push his buttons, and put you off him. I don't know anything about how he treats women or whether he wants a relationship or not.'

I was annoyed at myself for listening to Davis but I knew I couldn't really blame him for things ending so abruptly between me and Jake. He said I didn't trust him and he couldn't trust me. That was on us, not Davis. 'Well, you shouldn't tell lies about people. If we ever were to work together, I would expect you to be honest with me, Davis. But I think me and Jake just don't work in the real world.'

I wished we did. I wasn't going to share that with Davis Mulberry, though.

I stood up, not wanting to talk about Jake any more. 'I'll call you tomorrow,' I promised.

Davis stood up politely. 'Thank you, Freya. And I know I have thought about myself too much in life but I get the feeling you are the opposite. So, if you take one piece of advice from me, it's to think about what would work best for you right now, okay? And do that. You're honest with other people, right? Sometimes, you have to be honest with yourself.'

It was similar to the advice Jake had given me. I wasn't sure if either of them was right but as I left the café to head towards the

Tube, I knew that today had left me feeling uneasy. I had tried to do what I thought would get me ahead in my career and I had no idea if it had worked, but it had felt inauthentic. I'd been so pissed with Jake at lying to his readers, but was I lying to myself?

* * *

When my alarm went off the following morning, I groaned out loud as I rolled over to stop it on my phone. It was 6.30 a.m. I had been up until past 2 a.m. reading Davis's book and then it took me a while to actually fall asleep as my mind kept repeating what had happened yesterday over and over.

I looked at the book, which was beside me, after I had finally put it down and tried to go to bed. I was actually hooked on it. It was about a woman who had a stalker. She was determined to find out who it was before they made good on their threat to hurt her. It was unsettling and compelling. A lot darker, of course, than my usual reading material, but I really wanted to know what was going to happen next. Davis was arrogant but I already thought he was right and that this could easily be a bestseller. If his publishers were still interested in putting it out into the world, that was.

But I had to focus on my own career dilemma, not Davis's. I was due to meet with Hayley and after yesterday, I needed to make sure she was actually still on my side. I didn't want to be influenced by either Jake or Davis. I needed to make up my own mind about what to do next. All I knew was that I wanted to be a literary agent one day, and I had to work out how best to make that happen.

After climbing out of bed, I hurried into the bathroom for a quick shower and then got dressed for the day. I hesitated about what to wear. I had bought two new outfits to fit my new boss-bitch attitude but yesterday, I hadn't felt like a boss bitch at all. I had been confused and kind of pissed off for most of it instead.

I stared at my wardrobe and thought about when I had felt most confident. And the night in New York when I told Jake I wanted to meet the man he really was, the moment that had pushed him to be honest about his personal life, and to open up to both me and the world, came to mind. I hadn't hesitated that night to tell the truth. That surely was more of a boss-bitch moment than wearing a suit I didn't feel good in to try to look more like my boss. Or allowing her to take the credit for my work.

So, I put on the dress and boots I had worn in New York, I left my hair loose and did my favourite make-up, finishing it all off with a spritz of my sweet, summery perfume. Then I looked in the mirror and told myself that even though I looked different to Hayley, that didn't mean I couldn't do what she did. And both Jake and Davis Mulberry had told me I had the potential to be a good agent. They liked it when I was honest. I hadn't been honest with Hayley at all yet. I had always known I was intimidated by Jake but I realised now just how intimidated I had been by Hayley. She was formidable and made me feel like an incapable adult because I didn't have my shit together like she seemed to. But watching her yesterday had made me wonder if I did really want to be like her.

This morning, I needed to listen to my gut and do what I wanted to do, not what anyone told me I should do.

42

When I arrived at work, Ellen on reception waved me over eagerly. 'Hayley is in a great mood; I think it's something to do with Jake Richards,' she said with a big smile. 'I still can't believe you survived five days in New York with him. How was the meeting yesterday? Was Hayley a superstar? I bet she gave them all hell.'

'Um...' I said, wondering how honest to be with her. 'She was a tough cookie for sure,' I added cagily. 'I wonder if his publishers have sent in their offer for a new deal then.' Glancing towards the office, I could see Hayley's door open as though she was waiting for me to come in. I knew she would want to gloat if an offer had been made especially if it was as good as she'd been hoping for.

'Go and find out then tell me,' Ellen encouraged. The phone started ringing. She sighed. 'No rest for the wicked. What are you waiting for?' she added as she picked up the phone, frowning.

'Oh, yeah, okay,' I mumbled, finally setting off towards the office, nervous for what was about to happen. I dropped off my things at my desk, switching my laptop on, before Hayley called out, beckoning me into her office as I was expecting she would.

Taking a deep breath, I walked over, closing the door behind me when I went inside.

'Well, we did it,' Hayley said as she leaned back in her chair. I sat down on the other side of her desk. She smiled. 'Craig emailed me at 8 a.m. with their offer. A new six-book deal for Jake worth seven figures. The best we could have hoped for, Freya. We killed it in that meeting. I knew we would.'

This time, it was 'we'. Yesterday, she had acted like it was all 'I'. So, which was it really? I forced out a smile as Hayley watched me expectantly for a reaction.

'That's great news,' I said.

'Isn't it? You played it perfectly in that meeting,' she continued. 'We make a good team, don't we? I need to call Jake and tell him the good news...'

Now was my chance. While she was in such a good mood. I needed to know if she would make good on her promise to advance my career. She thought I had done well in the meeting, and even if she had taken credit, she knew that my trip to New York with Jake had resulted in this great new offer for him. I leaned forward in my chair and summoned all the courage I could muster. 'Before you call Jake...' I cleared my throat. 'You said we could talk about my career. You know I really want to take on my own clients and become an agent myself. What are the next steps towards that? I am really keen to make progress here.'

Hayley nodded. 'I know. I admire your ambition. You remind me of how I was at your age. Eager. I like it. And as I said, I was impressed yesterday. You did what I asked you to. In another six months, we can start looking at you taking on your own clients, I have no doubt about that.'

I absorbed what she said with a sinking feeling in my stomach. 'Six months?' I repeated. That wasn't what she had indicated when I got back. I knew I had only worked with her for that amount of time but I had proved myself, surely? I thought she might let me take over one of her clients or at least take the lead with one or two. 'There's nothing we could do before then to start that process?'

Hayley sighed like I was starting to irritate her. 'Freya, you have to understand that my clients are extremely important to me, I have to always think about their best interests, don't I? So, you have to trust me that I know what I'm doing. We will get you there. It will just take time. For now, I need you to be my assistant. Now, I really have to call Jake and tell him about the offer so we'll talk later, okay?' She reached for the phone on her desk before I could respond, effectively dismissing me. Conversation over.

Slowly, I stood up, utterly deflated. It felt like she had gone back on her word. Like she had let me think things would move quicker to get me on side in that meeting. To make sure I played ball and let her take the credit for Jake's return to popularity. No one in that room yesterday, apart from me and Jake, had any clue that Hayley had had no say in what he told readers at the conference. Now his publisher had made Jake a new offer, Hayley no longer needed me on side so she had come clean about her plan. And that was for me to keep being her assistant, and to hold me back from taking on any other responsibilities for another six months. At least. Could I trust that she would let me even then?

I watched as she started to dial Jake's number, not interested in talking to me any more. Any plans of me being a boss bitch had disintegrated. I slunk out of her office, closing the door, feeling small and like I had been used.

I saw Davis Mulberry's book poking out of my handbag when

I went back to my desk, tempting me in a way I never thought possible from that man. But there was something stirring in my gut. I hadn't respected Hayley's decision to encourage Jake to lie about the article, to pretend he hadn't dissed romance readers, and my instinct to have been honest with those very readers had been the right one. I knew Hayley had tons more experience than me but I had learnt that didn't always mean her instincts were better. I sat down at my desk and looked around the office. I would be in this place for another six months, she had just assured me of such, but I had an opportunity to do something else. Did I want to take it? I grabbed my phone and asked Davis to set up a meeting with his agent, Simon.

My fingers hovered on my phone after that and I found myself scrolling to Jake's number. I wondered what he thought of the offer Hayley had put to him, if he was going to accept, what he would say about Davis Mulberry approaching me for help. It was annoying that I wanted to hear his opinion after everything that had happened between us.

With a sigh, I put my phone back on my desk and opened up my emails to start work, knowing that it was better not to contact him and confuse things any further between us.

* * *

That evening, I curled up on my bed to finish Davis Mulberry's book. As the female main character started to realise who her stalker was, she drew closer to her neighbour who she'd been worried might be the one threatening her. It turned out, he had started to notice what was going on and wanted to help her. As the book got closer to the end, I was shocked to find out the identity of her stalker and the final showdown was epic. The woman she thought was her best friend was the one who had been terrifying her. It was a great twist. And when she told her neighbour she had feelings for him, they had a great love scene that surprised the hell out of me. Davis Mulberry had not only included a touch of romance mixed in with his gripping thrills and twists, but had actually done it well.

I closed the book as the night faded into the early hours of the morning and I felt that not only should this book be published despite Davis's bad attitude, but it could be his biggest hit. And maybe if everyone knew that Davis not only didn't actually hate romance but had included it in the book, he would be forgiven for what happened at the conference. I thought about his long-standing feud with Jake. All the times he had belittled the fact Jake wrote romance and questioned how easy it was to write. This was a big turnaround to write it himself. Was it down to the woman Davis had opened his heart to? I had to find out. If Davis Mulberry could believe in love then why was I finding it so hard? Why was Jake finding it so hard?

Rolling over, I turned off my bedside lamp and crawled under the covers, yawning after reading for so long.

I wondered if Jake was awake or asleep. If he ever thought about me at night. I couldn't help but hope he did even though it seemed impossible. He didn't trust love any more. Why did I think he'd ever trust me? He thought we were too different to ever work. I had agreed with him. I hadn't been sure he really liked me. I had walked away from him at the conference. But our time together kept coming back to me regardless. The way he had looked so disappointed after the meeting with his publishers haunted me. It had made me realise I was disappointed in myself.

But that was about to change.

43

The Simon Langley Literary Agency was in a very different building to my current place of work. Sleek and next to the River Thames, it felt more modern and had a good buzz to it. Simon's office was up high, offering an impressive view of the city. I looked out of the huge window in reception while I waited and ticked off all the landmarks I could see from there. And it was most of them.

'Freya, thank God you're here!' Davis came into reception. He was wearing a smart suit and looked nervous but smiled when he saw me. And held out his hand for a firm shake. I followed him through into Simon's office. He stood up and came to the door to greet me. He couldn't have appeared more different to Hayley – a man in his sixties with salt and pepper hair, a warm smile, wearing jeans and a t-shirt.

'Freya, Davis has told me so much about you. It's lovely to meet you.'

I returned his smile and shook his hand. 'I dread to think,' I replied.

Davis chuckled. 'I told you – she tells it exactly how it is.'

It was still jarring to hear people complimenting my honesty. I had thought I needed to change that. We all sat down in the sofa area of the large office. It still managed to be cosy, with a huge bookshelf, a floor lamp and lots of plants. The view behind Simon's desk was hard to stop looking at too.

'I finished *He's Behind You*,' I told Davis after I had turned down any refreshments. 'And it's great. But I was surprised by the romantic part after everything you said at the romance conference.'

Simon shook his head. 'We said yes to the invite for Davis to join the panel there because we were planning to post a snippet of the romance scenes to surprise everyone afterwards. But at the party, as you know, things went awry so we held off doing that. And now his publishers are on the fence about even publishing the book.' Simon was quiet and calm in how he spoke but his body language screamed of being disappointed in his client. I glanced at Davis and he looked abashed, a far cry from the arrogant author I had encountered at the conference.

'I can see why you wanted to be at the romance conference now,' I said, things clicking into place. I knew they had been trying something new by inviting authors of other genres to do that panel with Jake but as Davis had been so critical about romance, I had been confused why he had accepted. Now, it all made sense.

'That would have been great publicity for the book.' I raised an eyebrow. 'But why were you so condescending about romance books while you were there? You told Jake on the panel that romance was really easy to write compared to crime and thrillers.'

Davis sighed. 'I know. It's Jake. He gets my back up and

pushes me to be a dick. It all started at uni, this rivalry... I can't help but wind him up.'

'Your rivalry is ridiculous,' I replied, annoyed with them both, frankly. 'You have damaged your careers because of it. Is that what you want? To give it all up?'

'Christ, no!'

'Did you find the romance easy to write?'

He avoided my eyes and shifted in his chair. 'No. It was really hard. It was the part of the book I spent the most time on to make it just right.'

'You know who could have given you advice for it? Jake Richards.'

Simon nodded. 'I told him that.' He leaned forward. 'We know you really helped Jake get back into favour with his readers. We are now in a similar situation. Is there anything Davis could do, do you think?'

'Personally, I am on the fence at wanting to help you, Davis. Professionally, I do think this is a great book and I would love to see it out in the world.'

I sighed then. It was difficult. Was I being like Hayley if I helped him? Or if I helped him on my terms, was it both a good move for my career but also something that went along with who I was, and not who I thought I should be?

'What I think you should do is tell your readers that not only do you not think romance is easy, but you've included it in your new book because you were inspired by Jake Richards.'

Davis choked a little bit. 'What?'

I nodded. 'This feud needs to end. Jake is really popular right now. If you make up with him and talk about how he's inspired you, I think both you and his readers will love it. Say you've become a romance fan and have included it in your book. I noticed there is no dedication in the book. But you mentioned you're a believer in romance now in your personal life. Hasn't your girlfriend helped to inspire a romantic side to you?'

'Let's not get crazy now,' Davis said but he did smile at the mention of her.

'You could dedicate it to her. Talk about that too. Humanise yourself after the mess-up at the conference. Tell your publisher your plan and hopefully, they will stop threatening to pull the book.' I looked at Simon. 'What about asking Jake to read and do an endorsement quote too?'

'He wouldn't,' Simon replied quickly.

I shrugged. 'He might do if you end the feud,' I said to Davis. 'It's up to you. But I think it's the only way to turn around opinions right now. I'll be honest: at the conference, I found you arrogant and annoying. I think a lot of people do.'

'God, Freya, you don't need to be *that* honest,' Davis said, folding his arms across his chest.

'Actually, I think she does,' Simon said, giving me an approving look. 'I haven't always been as honest with you as I should have been. We're old friends and go back years, but as you got more successful, you did become different to the man I first met as an aspiring author. And sometimes, I have been worried you're changing into someone that might become too difficult to work with.'

Davis looked shocked. 'Mate, you should have said... I hold my hands up, I know I haven't been easy to work with sometimes. Honestly, this job is so stressful and I tend to act out when I'm stressed. And drink too much. In fact, I'm wondering if I need to quit the booze altogether.' He turned to me. 'Freya, I hate to admit it but you've given me some great advice. Whether I can actually follow it all through and get people back on my side, I don't know. But I want to try. I have to try. I believe in this book and I want to see it on the shelves. Even if that means resolving things with Jake bloody Richards.' But he winked at me and I knew he realised it was what had to happen.

Simon smiled. 'Well, Freya, you've won Davis over so how could you not win me over? I know you might be happy with Hayley Harper but you are just what I've been looking for here. I'm about to start the journey towards retirement and I want to bring in some new blood that can make that happen. I think we'd make a good team until then. And you certainly seem able to handle Davis.'

'If you can handle Davis, you can handle anyone,' I said with a laugh. Luckily, they both chuckled along with me and Davis didn't seem to take it personally.

'If I could persuade you to leave Hayley, you could come and work here. We could co-agent Davis and a couple of my other authors for a while, then you could start to take on your own clients and, with time, take on some of mine too. I have no doubt you have the skills to be a great agent, and I want to help make that happen. I would give you a pay rise, of course. And you could start here as soon as you wanted,' Simon said. 'What do you think?'

I started at him in shock. 'Huh?'

'Davis told me you were honest and capable and ambitious, and I have seen that today for myself. I think I could be a good mentor to you. But you'd also help us here. We may have become a bit stuck in our ways. You could be the breath of fresh air we need. And Davis certainly has warmed to you. I think all of our clients would do so as well.'

'Wow.' His offer started to sink in. I glanced at Davis, who was beaming with what looked remarkably like pride. 'You would let me actually look after clients?' Hayley was set against that, and I knew she wasn't a woman to change her mind. Simon was offering me what I wanted so much sooner, and I liked him instantly.

Simon nodded. 'I would. How about I take you on a tour and give you some of our clients' books and you can have a think about it? But if you're completely happy where you are, I understand if you don't want to even do that...'

I shook my head. 'I want to do that. I definitely want to consider your offer.' The thought of leaving Hayley was terrifying. Even telling her about this threatened to bring me out in a cold sweat. But I was getting a good feeling in Simon Langley's office, and I had told myself to listen to my gut from now on. My gut was telling me this could well be my future.

Davis pulled his phone out. 'I'm going to phone Jake right now, see if he'll meet me for a coffee. I'll tell him this is all your fault.'

Davis left Simon's office so quickly, I couldn't stop him. I wasn't sure how Jake would react to hearing from Davis or my involvement in encouraging it, but I hoped he would be happy that I was being myself again. Part of me wanted him to also be proud of me but I knew I needed to stop thinking like that. If I did leave Hayley's agency, we wouldn't even have a professional relationship any more. I would be moving on from Jake Richards and even though that was sad, I had to make the best of this opportunity.

'Ready when you are,' I told Simon.

After he had shown me round and given me a tote bag full of books, I promised to think about his offer and get back to him ASAP. I left his office, stepped back onto the London streets, hot from the midday sun, and walked around in a daze, thinking over everything he had said. I knew this was the right move. But it was terrifying too.

I pulled out my phone to message Liv.

> SOS. Can we meet for a glass of wine tonight?
> So much to tell you!

She replied instantly.

> Tell me where and when...

44

Liv and I met that evening in our favourite bar. It was warm so we sat outside at a small, round table with a glass of wine each as London livened up for the night. I told her what had happened with Davis and Simon and asked for her advice.

'Wow, Freya, that's amazing,' Liv said, her eyes lighting up. 'That's exactly what you've been wanting.' Then she frowned. 'But, hang on, Hayley is going to give you the same opportunity, isn't she?'

'I thought she was but...' I told her about the meeting we'd had with Jake and his publishers, how Hayley had taken all the credit for what had happened in New York, and that I needed to wait another six months to do anything more than be her assistant. 'It's not that I think I don't have to pay my dues... it's that she promised me that if I was successful at the romance conference, she would further my career. Now she's just gone back on it all.'

'That's not on. She's gone down in my estimation now.' Liv sighed. 'I did worry the other day when you said you wanted to be like Hayley. I think you're great just as you are. And I always knew you'd be a successful agent one day. I just thought Hayley would help you get there.'

I nodded. 'Me too. But I don't think she wants to. Not yet anyway. And I did think I needed to be like her. But then I think about the whole thing with Jake – she didn't help his career after that article came out. I followed my gut and it worked. Hayley wasn't any help at all there. I thought I admired her, you know? Now, I'm not so sure. She seemed fake in that publishing meeting. I never want to be fake. I would want to support my authors but I'd have to be honest with them and myself, and whoever we're working with.'

'Authors appreciate honesty,' Liv said. 'Sometimes, you're promised the earth but then it never happens. I'd rather be told the truth and then I can manage my expectations.'

'I'm glad you think so too,' I said, smiling at her. 'But could I really do this? Leave Hayley and work with Simon? It would be such a leap, such a challenge, and Hayley is going to be furious when she hears about it...' I bit my lip. The thought of telling Hayley I was leaving for another job scared the shit out of me. But the thought of the new job was so exciting, even if it would be a challenge. I really didn't want to run away from something I had wanted to do ever since I fell in love with romance books just because I was scared about it.

'Of course you can do it!' Liv said firmly. 'You'll be amazing. And Hayley will have to suck it up. Don't worry about her, only about yourself. You will be great at this. In fact, I'd love you to be my agent!'

I laughed. 'Yeah, and leave Hayley when I move to Simon's agency, can you imagine?' She giggled along with me. 'God, what would she say?'

'I dread to think,' Liv said. Then she eyed me across the table. 'Have you spoken to Jake about it all? I bet he'd be chuffed to hear Simon has offered you this job.'

'No, we haven't spoken since the meeting. He was frustrated that I went along with what Hayley wanted. And he was right. I told him to be honest then did the opposite myself. I think he'd tell me to go for this new job like you have.'

'I think so too,' she agreed. 'Does his opinion still matter to you?'

I had a sip of my wine as I considered that. 'I don't know. I want him to think well of me, I guess. We seemed so close for a while. I don't like the idea of not seeing him ever again but if I leave Hayley, when will I?'

'You could reach out and tell him about what's happened...'

'I have enough to worry about with telling Hayley. No, Jake and I are in the past. I need to look to the future now.'

Liv looked a little bit sad but she raised her wine glass. 'And it will be a great future, I have no doubt. Here's to your new opportunity.' We clinked our glasses and both had a sip. I did feel a lot better now I'd spoken to Liv and she didn't seem to think this was a crazy idea. She was encouraging. And my gut was telling me to go for it. Now I would have to talk to Hayley.

I hoped I'd make it through doing that in one piece.

* * *

After not sleeping and putting my dress on back to front, I eventually stumbled out of my flat and got the Tube to work. I had a large coffee on the way to wake up but that made my nerves about seeing Hayley double. I was a jittery wreck by the time I turned into the road where our building was. I was half-inclined to call in sick and try this another day but I had emailed

Simon last night and told him I wanted to take him up on the job offer, and he'd been delighted and told me to let him know as soon as I had spoken to Hayley. I couldn't chicken out now, as much as I really wanted to.

Walking towards the building, I saw a man heading towards the doors and when I got closer, I recognised who it was. I paused on the pavement, hoping he hadn't seen me. But as he went to open the door, he looked my way and froze also.

'Freya,' Jake said, letting go of the door. He turned and waited so I reluctantly walked towards him.

Jake looked nothing like his usual cool, composed self I realised as soon as we faced each other, just a couple of feet between us. His facial hair was unkempt today like he needed to shave, there were circles under his eyes and his skin looked pale despite the warm week we were having. His shirt had a button undone and the laces on his shoes were untied. I felt a weird urge to hug him. It looked like he needed one in the same way I did. My body seemed to want to lean into his, although I made sure it didn't.

'Hi, Jake,' I said softly, wishing he would smile at me and look at me like I was the only woman for him like he had done before. But there was no smile or softness to him this morning. He looked on edge and almost angry. Back to the intimidating man he had been before that electric kiss we'd had against my hotel-room door.

'I had an interesting chat last night with Davis Mulberry,' he said coldly. 'You didn't think I deserved to know that not only are you working with that twat now, but clearly, it's been him you were after all along? And now you've got your happy ever after finally!'

I stared at him dumbfounded. 'What are you talking about?'

'Davis was Freya this, and Freya that, singing your praises, saying he wants to end our feud, that I inspired his latest book and he was wrong all along about romance. He's now in love and going to dedicate his book to the woman of his dreams...' Jake ran a shaky hand through his hair. 'So, we didn't mean anything to you? Now you're with Davis, and I'm supposed to be pleased for you both?'

I was thoroughly confused. 'Davis told you we're together and he's going to dedicate the book to me?' I had to check in case Davis had actually turned out to be a worse man than I'd ever thought he could be.

Jake stared at me then shook his head. 'He was after you the whole time in New York! Of course it's you that he was talking about.'

'It's not,' I said quietly. 'Davis was just trying to wind you up in New York. He was never really interested in me. I've told him he's arrogant and annoying, and he needs to sort himself out. I've been offered a job by his agent and I'll be working with him, but there has never been, or ever will be, anything between us outside of work. Davis has a girlfriend who he loves and will be dedicating the book to. I told him that the two of you need to sort things out as you've both almost ruined your careers over your feud.'

I moved around him and went to the door, grabbing it then glancing back at his surprised and confused expression.

'Jake, whatever you think, you need to know that I had a great time in New York with you. I really liked you and I hoped that maybe we were starting... something. I know now you didn't feel the same but don't make me out to be someone I'm not. I only had eyes for you.' I hoped my voice hadn't wobbled but I thought it probably had.

Jake stared at me. He was silent and his expression unreadable. I longed to know what he was thinking. Had he wanted me as much as I had wanted him?

When he still didn't respond, I decided that was my answer.

I looked away from those piercing eyes of his and tried not to show how disappointed I was. 'I hope you will make peace with Davis. Now, I need to talk to Hayley about the job offer I've had, and I'm frankly terrified.'

45

I yanked open the door and hurried through it, towards the lift, my heart pounding from being honest with Jake. It was one thing telling him what I thought on a work front, but opening my heart was a whole other level of honesty and vulnerability. It wasn't easy but I felt better for having done it. Now Jake knew I had really liked him.

Maybe what happened between us was a good thing. I had been so worried I'd never have anything close to feelings like the characters had in my favourite books, but Jake had shown me that it was possible to have a strong attraction and pull towards someone, to have amazing sex and to feel like the two of you were the only people in the world when you were together.

Luckily, Jake didn't follow me so I got into the lift and the doors closed. I leaned against the wall with a sigh. I didn't need that stressful interaction on top of having to deal with Hayley. I straightened up as the lift reached the fifth floor and told myself if I could tell Jake how I felt, I could definitely tell Hayley. Taking a deep breath as the doors opened, I walked through, shoulders straight and head high.

'You look like you're on a mission!' Ellen called out from behind her desk.

'I am,' I said, not slowing down to chat in case my resolve cracked. She stared after me curiously as I went to my desk to dump my things then went straight to Hayley's office, knocking on the open door to make my presence known.

Hayley was at her desk, typing on her phone. She waved me in without looking up as she carried on typing, her long fake nails making a tippy-tappy sound on it. I didn't sit down opposite the desk though in my usual chair. It felt like I might have the slightest chance at not chickening out if I remained standing. Plus, this way, I actually appeared taller than her too. I kept my hands behind my back so she couldn't see me wringing them with nerves.

Finally, she put her phone down on the desk and rolled her eyes. 'All my sister wants to talk about is her wedding,' she said. 'She keeps on about me leaving early to go to New York but I was there to see her get married. And she's sent me about five hundred photos and videos. It's ridiculous.'

'Getting married is a pretty big thing,' I said, thinking that Hayley's behaviour towards her sister was really telling. I had thought her workaholic ways were something to aspire to, but although she had achieved a lot in her career, it made me determined not to be so one-track minded. Yes, work was important to me. Yes, I was ambitious. But my family and friends were important to me too. I knew if and when Liv married Aiden, I would be almost as excited as she was going to be. I didn't understand how Hayley could be so dismissive about her own sister's wedding. It was no wonder she didn't care about how she'd treated me.

'So she keeps telling me.' Hayley folded her arms on her desk. 'I thought we weren't meeting until lunchtime? I'm waiting for Jake to come in and discuss the offer we had in from Craig.'

I tried not to think about how I left Jake outside the office after being so honest about my feelings for him. He was probably still standing there, stunned.

I took a deep breath as Hayley was clearly impatient for me to speak or get out. 'I have been offered another job,' I blurted out quickly.

Her eyes instantly narrowed.

'When we talked about New York, you indicated that I could start to take on work that would lead to me becoming an agent,' I carried on even though the look she was now giving me bordered on murderous. 'But then you said it would be another six months before I could do anything outside of being your assistant. This new job will start me on track to becoming an agent straight away. And so, uh, I think for my career, I should take it.'

'Oh, do you?' she asked icily.

'I am so grateful for the past six months here,' I added quickly. 'I have learnt so much from you, Hayley. But New York was a huge challenge and I felt like you didn't exactly support me out there and when I came up with an idea that turned things around...' I had to summon every bit of confidence to keep going as she stared me down. No wonder she was such a good negotiator. I was almost ready to tell her I was talking nonsense but I knew in my gut, I was right. I was scared but there was relief now I had told her my feelings too. 'You then took all the credit for it. That was disappointing, if I'm honest.'

'It was disappointing that I had to come out there after you were messing things up.'

That felt unfair. 'Jake blurted out that article was true; that wasn't my fault. I did my best to make things better after that, encouraging him to be honest... In the end, that was what worked. Wasn't it?' I was confused why she wouldn't say that had been the right thing for Jake to do.

'I am your boss and Jake's agent. You are merely my assistant. But you think in an important meeting, I should give you credit for something that was a fluke in the first place?'

I immediately knew I had done the right thing. We both knew that had been no fluke. She really was incapable of praising someone and didn't want to admit she had been wrong. That didn't feel like a good mentor to me.

'I worked hard out there. I did everything I could to help Jake. And it worked. He's had a great offer from his publisher. But you refuse to even consider me taking on more responsibility. Simon Langley—'

'You're leaving me for Simon Langley?' she said with bitterness. Then she stood up and I took a step backwards on instinct. 'That dinosaur? He thinks more about caring for his authors than making money,' she said with a dismissive wave of her hand. 'He might molly-coddle you but he won't teach you to get the best deals, Freya. This was your opportunity here. But you're now wasting it. You know what? Any thoughts I had about helping your career are definitely over now.'

I raised an eyebrow. 'You didn't give me any indication when we spoke about it the other day of wanting to help me at all.'

Her cheeks turned red. 'You're throwing everything I've done for you in my face,' Hayley spat out now. 'Maybe Simon "Grandad" Langley might be willing to give you a job but good luck being an agent who can't get in to see any publisher!'

'What do you mean?' I asked, uneasy about the now triumphant expression on her face.

'I'll make sure no publisher deals with you,' Hayley replied, her red lips curving into a smile.

'Don't you dare,' came a voice from behind me.

I jumped and turned to see Jake in the doorway of Hayley's

office. I had no idea how long he'd been standing there but with the door open, he'd clearly heard Hayley's threat.

Jake stepped fully into the room as Hayley's smile vanished from her face. 'Freya helped my career so much in New York. I sat back in our meeting and let you ignore what she did and take all the credit for it but I won't stand back and allow you to ruin her reputation in our industry,' Jake continued, sounding like his usual calm self but I could hear the edge in his tone, and I was sure Hayley did too. 'She deserves this new job and a break in her career. And if you try to stop her, I will tell everyone you took the credit for what she did for me. Whose reputation will suffer then?'

Hayley's mouth fell open. 'Jake, you don't understand—'

'Actually, I understand perfectly,' he cut in. 'You don't like the fact Freya wants to leave but you have no say in it. You like to get your own way but that isn't what this job should be about. Freya understands that being an agent is about listening to and supporting your clients, and doing the best for them, and not yourself. That's why I wanted to come in and talk to you about my deal offer. You didn't listen to me on the phone about what I wanted. All you cared about was the money they're offering.' Jake turned to me. 'You should take the job, Freya. And Hayley will let you leave immediately but you'll be paid for the rest of the month. And she won't say anything negative about your time here.' He immediately turned back to Hayley, our eye contact kept brief. 'Right, Hayley?'

46

I was stunned. Jake protecting me like this... a little voice whispered that he must care about me a tiny bit to speak up for me to Hayley. But I knew he was a good man and he knew what she was threatening wasn't right. So, maybe it wasn't about me at all.

I wished it was, though.

Hayley sighed. 'Whatever. Get out of my sight, Freya, and stay out of my way if we ever see each other again. I thought you had the makings of an excellent agent but I bet you'll sink without a trace now.' She sat back down behind her desk. 'Let's talk then, Jake. Freya, take all your things when you leave.' With that dismissive ending to our six months together, she waited for us to do what she'd said.

Jake glanced back at me, gave me one nod then went to sit down opposite her. I longed for him to give me more than that but when he turned away, it felt like this was the ending for us too.

'Okay then,' I said awkwardly as they both looked away from

me. I edged out, exhaling hard that I'd made it out of that alive. Jake had rescued what could have been a disastrous meeting and I was so grateful to him. But I was also confused about how he felt about me. I was so stunned, I forgot to close Hayley's office door behind me when I left and it was too awkward to go back so I just hurried to my desk.

I was shocked at what had happened. I had done it, though. I had quit working for Hayley and now I could start my new job as soon as I liked, and was even going to be paid for the rest of the month. It was the best outcome possible. Jake had really stood up for me in a way no man ever had done before. And it had been pretty swoony.

Grabbing my things, I stuffed everything that belonged to me in my bag and then headed for reception. I glanced back at Hayley's office one last time as I walked away. I couldn't see Jake's face through the open door but Hayley was listening to him and from their body language, things seemed tense in there. I was desperate to know what Jake was saying to her but I guessed now I'd never know.

'Are you okay?' Ellen called over anxiously when I walked out of the office. 'I could hear raised voices and Jake Richards looked more furious than he usually does!'

I paused by the reception desk. 'I've actually just handed in my notice. Hayley wanted me to leave immediately,' I told her. I wasn't sure how my dream job had ended as such a nightmare but I knew I was moving on to bigger and better things.

Ellen looked shocked.

'I know, it's sudden. I was kind of head-hunted, I guess. And Jake actually really helped. Hayley was... pissed off.' That was an understatement.

'I bet she was.' Ellen whistled. 'Wow, Freya, well done on getting a new job. I'll miss you here, though.'

'I'll miss you too. I'm off to work with Simon Langley, and hopefully be an agent myself one day.'

'Well, of course you will do it. We have to keep in touch.' She leaned past me to try to see Hayley's office. 'I'll keep my head down for the rest of the day.'

'Might be a good idea. I'll message you once I've settled into my new job and we can meet for a drink.'

Ellen jumped up to give me a hug and wish me good luck; her reaction helped to make Hayley's contrasting one fade away a little bit. I left her and went back down in the lift and then outside into the morning sunshine.

The tension left my body as soon as the sun beamed down onto my bare arms. I set off not really knowing which direction I wanted to go in and found myself start to smile. That was not the way I had wanted my job with Hayley to go but how she had been with me made it clear I was doing the right thing in moving on. I didn't want to be an agent like her any more.

I wanted to do it my way.

* * *

Just two days later, I went into my new office. Simon had wanted me to start as soon as possible and now I'd left Hayley, I could. The first thing I did when I got there and had claimed a window desk in the open-plan office, was to meet with Simon and Davis again to discuss how we could get his book out into the world.

'When I first spoke to Jake, it didn't go well,' Davis said once we were back in the sofa area of Simon's office, the sun streaming in through his windows, each of us holding a coffee. 'He was annoyed as soon as I mentioned your name, Freya; I think he was jealous. I mean, I can understand why he thought you would like me more than him—'

'Davis,' I interrupted as he grinned at me. 'The point?' I prompted, not needing to hear his little digs about me and Jake. I saw Simon smile behind his coffee cup.

'You never want me to have any fun.' Davis pouted. He sighed but then carried on more sensibly. 'As I was saying, he didn't seem very keen on ending our feud or saying anything publicly about me being inspired by his work so I thought we were at a dead end but he rung me back yesterday and said he'd changed his mind and now wanted to help.'

'Oh, great,' I said, immediately thinking back to how I had told him off about Davis. Jake had clearly realised there was nothing at all romantic, nor would there ever be, between me and Davis so there was no need to keep their feud going. It did make me feel good that not only had Jake stepped in to help me with Hayley but he was doing the same with Davis. 'So, what's the plan?'

'I'll do a post on all my social media with a sample of one of the romance scenes and say how Jake inspired me, how hard it was to write and how I can't wait for readers to tell me what they think about it,' Davis said. 'Jake said he would share it on his accounts and say something supportive back, and he also agreed to read a proof so I've sent that over. Hopefully, he'll give us an endorsement quote but obviously, it's not guaranteed.' There was a hint of nerves in his voice and expression. His arrogance was a front, I was learning.

'It's a great book; I'm sure Jake will enjoy reading it,' I reassured him.

Simon nodded. 'Exactly. I'll email your publishers now to tell them what is happening and ask them to share your posts too. Once we get some good reader feedback through, and the boost from Jake, surely they will go ahead with the planned publication.'

'Let's hope so,' Davis said. 'I've also drafted an apology to the organisers of the romance conference; can you check it over, Freya?'

'Sure. That's a great idea. Maybe they can share it on their website; I'll talk to them.'

My phone was on silent on the table between us and I could see it start to light up with notifications. I wondered what was going on. I tried to concentrate on this meeting, though. 'So, let's get all that done today and see how it goes, and fingers crossed, we hear from Jake too. We could also get proof copies sent out to a few more romance authors. I bet my cousin, Liv Jones, would read it if I asked her.' I wrote down a reminder in my notebook.

'I also emailed my editor and told him to add in a dedication to my girlfriend,' Davis said. 'He was cagey about the book, saying they would be having a meeting sometime this week about it, but he would include it.' He shrugged. 'All we can do now is wait and see.'

'I think you'll get a good response and public opinion should go a long way,' I told him.

'Great,' Simon said. 'Davis, head off and get started on those social media posts. We'll share them from the agency account too and let's catch up on a phone call before close of business. Freya, I have to go out to a meeting but you're okay getting settled in, aren't you?'

I nodded. 'Yes. I'm going to email any contacts I made when working with Hayley to tell them I'm here now, and I'll look at your apology, Davis.' We all headed off and I looked at my phone as I walked back to my new desk. Most of the messages were from Liv, in capitals with exclamation marks, demanding to know why I wasn't responding to the big news. There was also one from Tessa. And Ellen at my old workplace. I frowned and scrolled back to Liv's first message to work out why everyone was messaging me.

> JAKE HAS MOVED PUBLISHERS!! TO MINE!!
> HE WILL NOW BE WITH TURN THE PAGES!
> DID YOU KNOW? THIS IS HUGE! OMG!

47

I sank into my new chair, ignoring the great view of the Thames I now had, and stared at my phone and re-read Liv's message about Jake three more times until it had properly sunk in.

So, Jake had turned down the offer from his current publishers. The huge deal Hayley had secured him. No wonder he went in to see her for a meeting. And it explained the tension in her office after I left. I assumed he had told her he wanted to move somewhere new as they hadn't supported him during the article debacle. And Hayley couldn't refuse with him able to destroy her reputation. My fingers hovered over my phone. I wanted to ask him what she had said. How he felt about leaving where his books had always been published.

But I put my phone down and logged onto my work laptop. I found the industry website and the news had been announced that he'd secured a 'huge' three-book deal with Turn the Pages and how 'excited' Jake was for the next chapter of his career. *When I Met You* would be published early next year. There also was a quote from Hayley Harper who the article said had secured the deal for him. I guessed though that Jake had reached out to them first himself. I remembered him asking Liv at the conference what she thought about her publishers. He had obviously listened carefully and thought they would be a good change for him. It said Hayley thought:

> This will be a great move for Jake and his books, and I know his readers will be delighted with this new novel, which in my opinion is the best he's written so far.

So, she was still full of bullshit. But I was glad Jake had done what he wanted, not what she thought he should do. I wanted to let my clients follow their hearts based on my advice, not boss them about and do what I thought was the best thing. It was their career as much as it was mine. Hayley had unwittingly taught me a lot about the kind of agent I wanted to be.

I pushed thoughts of Jake aside and got on with my work.

It was a busy day. Davis did all he promised and the early reaction on social media was overwhelmingly positive. Everyone loved the snippet from his new book and the fact that he was being so positive about romance. Jake, as he had promised, shared the posts, saying he had a copy and was 'looking forward to reading it'. Requests came in for proofs both to me and his publisher. His editor even emailed me and Simon towards the end of the day to say the team were 'impressed' with the response and they'd be in touch ASAP. Davis also sent his apology to the conference organisers who graciously accepted and added his open letter to their website. Davis thanked me and Simon when we spoke to him on the phone and sounded relieved that he was starting to repair the damage to his reputation. Like Jake, once he had been honest, people seemed open to giving him a second chance.

'This has been a brilliant first day,' Simon said to me. 'Thank you for everything you're doing for Davis. I know the two of you didn't exactly hit it off in New York. He told me he showed you the worst aspects of his character over there. I do think he is trying to turn over a new leaf. Or going back to the old Davis anyway.'

'Yeah, I didn't think I'd end up working with him for sure,' I replied ruefully. I wasn't going to tell Simon that he also caused issues in what I hoped had been a burgeoning relationship. But not just because I wanted to be professional here, even if I'd learnt to be honest and follow my gut. I didn't want to blurt out anything about my sex life like I had done in front of Jake! I also knew that yes, Davis had been annoying and clearly trying to push Jake's buttons, but Jake had let him. And I had let Davis get in my head too. We'd both been unsure about trusting one another in different ways. Jake, after his dad had let him down, and me because of past dating failures. We couldn't blame Davis for that.

'Honestly though...' I continued. 'I loved Davis's book, and I think it will be a huge hit so I'm glad I'm helping it get out into the world. I know now some of his attitude is a front, and I hope now he's had this shock with his career, he will calm the arrogance down a bit.'

'You're a breath of fresh air for the team here, Freya,' Simon said with a smile. 'You'll be good for all of us, I think.'

I smiled back, pleased. The atmosphere here already was so clearly different from working with Hayley. I knew I had made the right move.

We planned out what we would be doing tomorrow and then I left Simon so he could make a call and I went back to my desk. There was a large, padded envelope waiting for me on there. Intrigued, I sat down and opened it up, curious who was sending me things so early on in my new job. I had only just told people in the industry I was now working here. There was clearly a book inside it and I pulled it out, always eager to read an early copy.

It was a proof copy of a book with a Post-it stuck to the cover. Written on the small, yellow square in neat handwriting was a simple message:

I feel the same – J

I stared at the message for a while and then peeled the Post-it away to reveal that the book was a copy of *When I Met You*. It was now no longer an early copy on my Kindle like the one I'd read on the train but a bound copy sent out by Turn the Pages, clearly eager to make the most of the publicity surrounding the news of his book deal with them. I transferred the Post-it to the cover of my Kindle. I didn't want to lose it.

Those four words stared up at me, making my heart do a funny little skippy thing. He had listened to what I had told him outside Hayley's office about how I had felt about him, about us, when we had been in New York.

But not only had he said he felt the same way, he had used present tense. He *feels* the same way. My lips curved into a smile.

I picked up the proof copy and opened it up, excited to see it taking shape into a published book. Flicking to the first page, I saw the dedication. Then I did a double take and re-read it.

'Oh my God,' I said out loud.

One of my new colleagues asked if I was okay and, embarrassed at talking to myself, I told him I was fine, then bent my head and looked at the page again.

For Freya. It was a meet-cute.

I closed the proof and leaned back in my desk chair, my pulse picking up. I couldn't believe it. Not only had Jake sent me the book with a cute note; he had dedicated it to me!! I closed my eyes briefly and thought back to embarrassing myself when we'd gone to Heathrow airport. Jake had remembered it too and was telling both me, and everyone who read this book, that that *had* been a meet-cute. It had been the moment he saw me as something more than Hayley's assistant. He had been attracted to me. Drawn to me like I was to him. He'd noticed me and not in a bad way. I thought he had looked down on me and I had been intimidated by him.

But we clearly both had been attracted to one another from the start of our trip.

I still thought of our kiss outside my hotel room as the best of my life so far. I still missed being in his arms. And the way he looked at me. Yes, we were different. Yes, he was older and richer. Yes, we both had trust issues. We weren't sure we believed in love or happy ever afters. But we had still taken a chance in New York and had an amazing, romantic and passionate time there together. We'd run away from the risk of a relationship. Jake wasn't running away now, though. Like my speech to him outside Hayley's office, he was being honest about his feelings.

If we both felt the same, what then?

I looked at the time. It was the end of the day. I grabbed my things, including the proof of Jake's book, and threw them into my bag. I then pulled out my phone, waving to Simon as I passed by his door. He was still on his phone and gave me a thumbs-up.

Once I got outside the building, I called Hayley's office and was relieved when Ellen on reception picked up.

'Ellen, I know this is kind of unorthodox but can I ask a huge favour?' I pleaded down the phone.

48

I stood on the pavement and looked up at the building in front of me. It was an Edwardian apartment building in Knightsbridge and the contrast to my shared flat in Clapham couldn't have been starker. I wavered about what to do. I had obtained Jake's home address from Ellen after seeing how he'd dedicated his book to me. Now, I felt like I should have text or called him instead of just showing up. Maybe a neutral ground would have been easier in hindsight. This displayed once again how different the two of our lives were. And yet, I didn't want to walk away. Did it matter that our lives were different? Clearly opposites attracted when it came to us. New York had proved that. And we both still thought about it. I told Jake as much and now he had said he felt the same.

Pulling out the proof copy of *When I Met You* he'd sent me, I re-read the dedication and that spurred me on.

I walked inside and was greeted by a concierge. I asked for Jake's flat and had to give my name so there was an awkward couple of minutes while I waited for him to call Jake. But the concierge waved me up, and I hurried into the lift, relieved Jake hadn't refused to see me. Nerves settled in the pit of my stomach as the lift climbed to the top floor to Jake's penthouse apartment. My heart was pounding inside my chest.

The lift doors slid open so I stepped out and the door ahead, the only one on the top floor, opened up and there stood Jake.

'Freya, this is a nice surprise,' he said, breaking into a smile as I walked up to him. His smile eased my nerves a bit. He looked the way he had outside Hayley's office the other day: his facial hair unkempt, circles under his eyes, pale skin and his hair was tousled. He wore jeans and a white t-shirt, the most casual I had seen him since we first met. The style suited him but I didn't like the fact he seemed unlike himself.

'Are you okay?' I blurted out before I could phrase it more tactfully. 'You look tired.' I bit my lip immediately, hoping he wouldn't take offence.

Jake stared at me for a moment, those piercing eyes of his looking deep into mine. Then he started laughing. 'Like I said, you're not like anyone else I know. Are you coming in?'

I smiled, relieved I hadn't pissed him off. 'Yes, please.'

Jake stood back while I walked inside, and he closed the door behind us. I looked around his large flat, drinking in everything eagerly. The flat had high ceilings and sash windows that let the summer sun stream inside and pool on the shiny floorboards. The walls were also light and there was a stunning fireplace in the living area. There was a wall of bookshelves and I immediately wanted to look at all the books he had. There was a big sofa and an armchair with a reading light. A record player and stack of vinyl. In the corner was an antique desk with Jake's laptop on it. And next to the living area was a large, navy kitchen with an island and bar stools. The flat was stunning and Jake had made it cosy. The place also smelled like him, deep and musky, and it was neat, tidy and clean. I remembered he said that whenever he was procrastinating with work, he cleaned.

'What can I get you? Tea, coffee, soft drink... It's after 5 p.m. so I'll add wine to the list too,' Jake interrupted my thoughts as he wandered into the kitchen.

'Um, you know what? Wine sounds good if you'll have one too?' I said, turning to follow him over there.

'I think I could be persuaded,' he replied, giving me another smile.

I still clutched the proof copy of his book so I put it down on the island as he went to the fridge to get us a drink. 'I got a special delivery at work.'

Jake came back over with two glasses of wine and saw his book. 'That explains your surprise visit.' He passed me a glass. 'Cheers, Freya.'

'Cheers,' I echoed and we smiled at each other as we both took a sip. 'That was a big surprise for me,' I said, feeling a little bit shy now we were alone. 'And your Post-it note.'

'Why was it a surprise?'

I raised an eyebrow. 'Because I thought you were happy that we'd stopped anything between us, so for you to say you felt like I had in New York and to dedicate your book to me...' I swallowed, trailing off because he was giving me a smouldering look and it was making it tricky for me to concentrate on what I was saying.

'How could you think I was happy?' Jake said, shaking his head. 'I've been miserable since we came back. Especially dealing with all this book stuff and not being able to ask your opinion about it. I wanted to call you so many times, and get your advice. I've wanted to see you so much.'

'But when we spoke outside Hayley's office, I told you how I felt and you didn't say anything...' I found myself blurting out then wondering if I'd said too much again.

'I was stunned. I thought you had decided there was no hope for us. Then suddenly, you were telling me you'd felt the same way that I had. So, I wondered if there was a reason to hope but I didn't have time to respond before you walked away. Once I'd come to my senses, I followed you but then of course I walked in on you and Hayley...' Jake ran a hand through his hair. 'I was worried I'd overstepped during that meeting, butting in and making demands; I thought maybe you were annoyed with me. But I still couldn't stop thinking about you, and us, and hoping there still was a chance. So, when it came to writing a dedication to my book, I had to use it, and the note, to tell you how I feel.'

Jake came around the island so it wasn't in between us any more and put his glass of wine down. I copied him. He reached out and touched my arm. The touch was gentle and only lasted a second but my body instantly craved more. 'I know we met long before the airport but I told you, I wasn't myself in those few months. I felt like I saw you properly for the first time that day. I was shocked when you mentioned it had been like a meet-cute because I thought there was no way you'd be interested in me. Then we got closer and you did seem interested. When I saw you and Davis at the end of conference party, I let all my trust issues take over. I thought you didn't feel the same, that again, I had put my trust in the wrong person...'

I stepped closer and Jake's words died on his lips. 'Jake, I did the same thing. I was scared that I was starting to think what we had was something out of a romance novel. That maybe the happy ever after I had always wanted but never thought might happen could actually be possible. So, when I thought you didn't feel the same, I shut down. I didn't want to get hurt. I got hurt anyway, though.' I sighed. 'You said that we were too different and I thought that we were. I had always been intimidated by you, and it just made me think that you'd never want to be with someone like me so I shut you out.'

'I thought the same. Why would you want to be with me?'

'Um... why would you want to be with me?' I countered.

49

We both stared at one another.

Then Jake chuckled and wrapped his arm around my waist, pulling me towards him. My breath hitched as I looked up at him and reached up to hook my arms around his neck. My body felt better for being able to touch him again.

'I already told you, Freya, you're a breath of fresh air. You're honest and clever and ambitious; it's like you brighten up every room. You told me truths about myself that no one ever has. It made me want you so much. You drive me crazy and I was desperate for you to be in my life in whatever way you'd allow. And, my God, you're gorgeous. Look at you.'

He reached out to touch my lips. I shivered at the contact, my eyes dropping to his lips, wanting to taste them again. Jake gave me a sexy smile.

'Hmm, and your body... I'm not sure I've thought about much else since I first touched you. That time in your hotel room, it was so hot; we were so perfect together.' Jake leaned in towards my ear, moving my hair away so he could whisper, 'My good girl.'

Those words lit up a fire inside me. I didn't want to talk any more. I wanted to lose myself in him. 'Kiss me, please,' I pleaded, arching into him desperately. Jake cupped my face with his hands, leaning in to me, giving me what I wanted so much. When our lips met, we both murmured contently and the passion that had been between us in New York reignited instantly.

Then I pulled back sharply.

'What's wrong?' Jake asked.

'I need to tell you...' I clung on to him but kept a couple of inches back from his lips, even though I needed them back on mine so much. 'I think I wanted you from the first time I read one of your books. Your words have always meant so much to me. And when I met you, I couldn't get over how handsome you were. But I didn't think you'd ever look twice at me. You're older, successful, wiser...'

Jake shook his head like he disagreed with how I'd described him, but I ignored that and kept on talking. 'And often, you pissed me off, frankly. But when I got to know you, I quickly found out that cool, calm demeanour was just a front and I liked getting to know the real you. I was so attracted to you but I thought I irritated you. When you kissed me, I'd never been kissed like that. The way we were in bed together...' I felt myself blush but made myself keep going. 'It was like the sex I'd read about but never experienced in real life. But it was also the way you held me in your arms...'

'It was a wrench to let you go,' Jake said softly.

I nodded. 'Same.'

'So, we both didn't think that the other one would be interested, then we were and it...' Jake seemed to struggle to find the words.

'Freaked us both out?' I suggested. 'I'm not as eloquent as you are.'

'Freaked us out is the perfect way to describe it,' he assured me. 'I should have told you how I felt, that I wanted us to carry on what we had started when we got back to London, but I got in my head when I saw you and Davis. I guess it made me think about my mum and dad. How she had trusted him, and how he'd hurt her. I thought maybe I was making the same mistake.'

I touched his lips with my fingertips this time. 'I never had any attraction towards Davis Mulberry. In fact, the opposite. He's probably the last man I'd ever want to kiss. I'm getting to see a slightly better side to him now I'm working with him but that's as far as it will ever go. You do believe me, right?'

'I do, baby. I think I knew deep down that was true but maybe I was scared and it was easy to blame that, to blame you two when it was me that wanted to run.'

'What about when you said you thought I'd been with you to help my career?'

'That was so wrong of me. I knew you'd never do that. As soon as I said it, and saw your face drop, I hated myself.' Jake reached out and brushed my hair back off my shoulder. 'Can you forgive me for that? And you don't believe what Davis said about me and relationships, do you?'

'It never made sense with how you were with me. And he admitted he said it to wind you up. I do trust you.'

'Even after what my father has done?' he asked me quietly.

'I told you, you're not your father, okay?'

'God, I want to hold you and never let you go.'

'Hmm, sounds good to me.'

I leaned in and our lips met eagerly. Jake's hands moved to my waist and he pulled me into his chest while I rubbed his shoulders with my hands, enjoying the way our tongues explored one another. I pulled back and Jake made a protesting sound. 'I haven't had the full flat tour. Can I see your room?' I asked boldly but I wanted to be back in his arms properly.

'You want to?' Jake asked me, his eyes dropping to my lips in a hungry way. I liked that look.

'How can I get a proper feel of the place otherwise?' I asked him playfully.

'You're right. It was very remiss of me not to give you the full tour.' Jake picked up our two wine glasses. 'Let me show you.'

I followed him across the living-room floor. He pointed out the doors to the spare bedroom and bathroom and then, at the end of the corridor, opened the door through to the primary bedroom. I walked in behind him and stood there, stunned. It was almost the size of my whole flat. It was a huge room with an en suite. There was a stunning window with an armchair underneath what looked like another cosy reading spot, a four-poster bed in the middle of the room and an ornate fireplace in the corner. The colours were deep greens and creams. It felt serene and calm and looked incredibly comfortable, like a luxury hotel. I wondered what the bed would feel like to lie down on. I couldn't help it.

Turning, I could see the en suite had a large shower and a free-standing bath. I suddenly longed to be there under bubbles with Jake, steaming up the bathroom together.

'What do you think?' he asked. I realised he had been watching me anxiously as I stayed silent.

'Trying to not feel intimidated all over again...' I joked.

'All that matters is how we feel about each other, okay? Nothing else.' He put our glasses of wine down on his bedside table then came over and picked up my hand, kissing the back of it. 'I will have to fight the urge to want to take care of you, and look after you, though I'll be honest. I'll try not to beg you to move in here with me and leave your flat share,' he added with a rueful smile.

'Well, I can't be angry about you wanting to do that,' I said with a laugh. 'One step at a time though, right?'

'Yeah, do you want to go out for dinner or I can take you home or—'

'Jake,' I broke in. 'I don't want to go anywhere right now. If you don't want me to?' I looked behind him. 'Is your bed comfy?'

Jake grinned and moved suddenly. I squealed as he scooped me up by the waist, carrying me in his arms and laying me gently down onto his bed. And God, it was comfy. I sunk into it like I had melted into a cloud.

He climbed onto the bed and leaned over me. 'I have thought about you on my bed, I have to admit. And you look really good on it.'

'Is that why you look tired?' I teased him.

Jake reached for my hair and pulled it together over my shoulder in his hand. 'Yes,' he replied easily, no hesitation. 'I've been wondering how I can repair things between us since we got back from New York. When we had that meeting with Hayley, I hated thinking that you felt like you needed to change yourself even one little bit.'

I smiled. 'Your pep talk helped me. You were right. I don't want to be anything like how Hayley is as an agent. How mad was she when you turned down the deal she got you?'

'Very,' Jake said. 'But do you want to talk about that now, or later?'

'Later,' I said quickly, earning me one of his smouldering smiles.

Jake gave my hair a little tug, pulling my lips closer to his. I smiled, liking his bedroom moves. 'Now I've got you on my bed,

what shall I do with you?' he asked, his tone gruff, his eyes darkening as they looked into mine.

50

'Anything you like,' I purred back to Jake's question, thinking about how horny I had been since New York. I wriggled on his bed. 'I want you to touch me like you did in the hotel.' Jake made me bolder in the bedroom than I ever thought I could be.

'I think I might have less control than I did in New York; I've missed you so much. I want to drive you as crazy as I know you'll drive me,' he replied, brushing his lips against mine. He tugged me again and kissed me harder, parting my lips with his tongue. The kiss turned hungry and I wrapped my arms around him, pulling him down on top of me.

'You do drive me crazy,' I whispered as he pulled the strap of my dress down and kissed my bare shoulder. He pulled it further down and kissed the base of my neck, his hand brushing over my chest. He was moving so slowly, my frustrated body protested under my clothes. I sighed. 'Just take my clothes off,' I begged him then. Jake lifted up his head, his eyes finding mine. I felt myself blush. 'Oops, I just...'

'Don't ever apologise for wanting me to get you naked. I was trying to be restrained when all I want to do is rip them off, quite frankly,' he said with a mischievous grin. 'Sit up,' he added huskily.

'I like it when you tell me what to do,' I admitted then. I sat up and he told me to lift my arms, which I did. He pulled my dress off easily in one move. 'In the bedroom,' I amended, because that was the only place I would allow it.

Jake winked at me. 'Noted, Freya. And it's the only place I'd want to tell you what to do...'

This man was swoony. There was no other word for it.

He climbed off the bed. 'Come here, baby, please,' he said to me. I scooted off the bed and stood up in my underwear. 'Undress me,' he begged.

I smiled and reached for his t-shirt, pulling it off him as eagerly as he had taken off my dress. I then grabbed his jeans and unbuttoned them, enjoying feeling how turned on he was already. He slipped out of them and then pulled me towards him, kissing me with the same desperation I felt. I curved against him, both of us in our underwear, pulling each other closer, making it clear how much we had missed touching one another. Jake reached for my bra and undid it, tossing it onto the floor, then he pulled down my underwear and I did the same to his. Once we were naked, we looked at one other with smiles on our faces.

'Missed this,' Jake said, reaching down to drop kisses down my chest onto my breasts, pulling a nipple into his mouth, teasing it to harden.

'Me too,' I gasped, holding on to his waist to keep steady. My knees already felt in danger of trembling at his touch.

Jake trailed kisses down my body again all the way to my stomach and then he knelt on the floor. He gave me a gentle push and I sat down on the edge of the bed. Jake murmured in approval and parted my legs with his hands so he could keep on kissing. I hooked one leg over his shoulder as his tongue found me, and I gasped at the contact. Jake was hungry for me and I cried out in pleasure as he tasted me, reaching out to grip his hair like he had gripped mine.

'Don't stop,' I cried as he slid a finger inside me too. Pleasure built suddenly as my desperation for his touch was rewarded with satisfaction. 'Yes, Jake,' I said as I shuddered on the bed, heat flooding through my body. 'Wow,' I breathed, shaking my head with a giggle as Jake stood up.

'Did you like that, baby?' he asked. I nodded furiously, breathing hard and fast as my body continued to throb with pleasure. 'Want more?'

'Yes,' I said eagerly.

'Scoot closer,' Jake said as he reached for his bedside table and pulled out a condom. He put it on as I moved right to the edge of the bed and he reached out and wrapped my legs around him, sliding inside me. I gasped as he filled me up. 'You feel amazing,' Jake said as our eyes locked together. I loved how we connected during sex. Jake never seemed to be anywhere else but right in this moment with me, and I felt the same. He rocked into me, and I felt it in every part of my body. 'Please tell me this is just as incredible for you as it is for me,' he said then.

'I never thought sex could be like this,' I replied with a moan.

He grinned. 'I need to kiss you.' He pulled out of me and told me to move back up the bed. I sank into his amazing pillows and Jake leaned over, brushing my hair through his fingertips. Smiling, he reached down to give me a passionate kiss. I held on to him as he slid inside me again, his lips not leaving mine. Our tongues danced as our bodies clung to each other. We gasped breathlessly as heat continued to build, our skin starting to glisten as we moved together, faster and harder.

Jake's lips left mine and he looked down at me. 'You're my girl, aren't you?'

'I'm yours,' I confirmed as I cried out with pleasure, amazed that he could make me come all over again so quickly.

'I love making you moan like that,' Jake cried, shuddering on top of me, crying out my name this time, over and over like it was mantra. He then leaned down to give me the softest kiss before he rolled off me and onto his back.

Jake lifted his arm, so I collapsed onto his chest and he held me tightly against him. We had laid like this back in my hotel room and I had really missed it, his chest heaving with ragged breaths and my heart racing in time with his. His arms felt strong and safe, and my body lay contently against his, exhausted and sated.

After a couple of seconds of silence, I let out an involuntary giggle.

Jake wriggled to see my face. I looked up at him. 'You okay, cutie?'

'Just can't quite believe what happened,' I confessed.

Jake chuckled along with me. 'I know what you mean. I thought I'd ruined any chance of us being together, to be honest. Having you here in my bed does feel a little bit like a dream.' He brushed his lips against mine. 'I love having you here.'

'I love being here,' I replied, snuggling in closer. 'I still can't believe you dedicated your book to me.'

'It's only going to be published because of you,' Jake said as he stroked my hair. 'You're the perfect person to dedicate it to.' He moved then, rolling onto his side. I did the same so we faced each other.

Jake wrapped his arms around me and I melted into him. He was not only good at sex but this man could snuggle really well. A perfect combination. I felt a little bit nervous about that, though. I knew already that it would be easy to fall for him and that was more than a little bit scary.

'Are you okay?' Jake seemed to notice I had gone a bit quiet.

'My mind is just trying to catch up with my body, I think,' I said as we looked at one another side by side.

Jake leaned in and kissed me gently then he cupped my face in his hands. 'Will it help if I tell you that I'm serious about us, Freya? I want to be with you. I want us to be a couple. I want everyone to know about us. I want you to be my girlfriend. But...' He hesitated then. 'I don't know if that's what you want.'

I smiled. 'It is,' I reassured him. 'I know that you might find it hard to trust me and us, and the same goes for me. But we can find our way together, can't we?'

Jake, I knew, was haunted by what had happened with his parents. And I had almost given up on finding love. But I also knew that we had a really strong connection and I didn't want to let that go.

'We can do anything together,' Jake promised me.

I leaned in to give him a long, lingering kiss. When I pulled back, I raised an eyebrow. 'Have you started reading Davis's book?'

'I'll try not to be upset you're talking to me about another man while in bed with me,' he joked. I gave him a playful nudge and he grinned. 'Actually, yeah, I did, and I'm kind of hooked. It pains me to say...'

'It's really good. I've been missing out by not reading outside of romance sometimes. Thank you for reading it. I know that things between you two have been tricky for a long time. And how he was in New York...' I shook my head at the trouble that man had caused.

'Yeah, he'll never be my favourite person but I appreciated him apologising and trying to make amends. And saying I'm an inspiration to him. That must have caused a big dent to his ego.'

'Definitely,' I agreed with a laugh. 'You're okay with me working with him, aren't you?'

'I know I wasn't thinking rationally when I saw you two at the conference,' Jake said softly. 'But I trusted my dad and all the secrets he kept...' He shook his head. I hated to see the sadness in his eyes. 'I know you're not like him. And nor am I. You believe that, don't you?'

'I know that,' I confirmed. 'Davis did get in my head a bit about you and relationships...'

'I want to be with you,' Jake said.

'I want to be with you too,' I told him. Our lips met again and Jake rolled me onto my back and started to kiss down my neck, making me shiver. 'Not done making up?' I teased as his lips trailed down to my breast.

'Nowhere near done,' Jake replied, giving me a naughty grin before he pulled my nipple into his mouth. I let out a happy sigh, worries fading as he touched me. Once again, it felt like we were the only two people together in the world. Our hotel bubble had gone but we were in another one in Jake's flat, and I hoped we could keep that bubble around us for a long time.

51

The next three weeks were a whirlwind. I threw myself into working with Simon Langley, focusing mostly on Davis Mulberry as his publishers confirmed they would still bring out his book as planned, and the buzz around it kept on building. Everyone reacted well to him including romance in the thriller, and Jake endorsed it with a quote, along with a few other high-profile authors too. It got great press reviews and from book bloggers, and people on social media kept talking about it. His publishers threw themselves into publicity and retailers started to order even more copies than they had originally.

Davis found it hard to keep his arrogance in check as the buzz built but Simon and I tried to keep his feet on the ground and remind him how close he had come to losing everything. He kept to his word by going sober and I saw a different side to him, one that made me understand why Simon and his girlfriend had stayed in his life.

My relationship with Jake was easier than I could have expected. Now we had told each other how we felt, we were able to be open with one another and enjoy ourselves without being insecure. I loved going to his flat after work to cook dinner together or we'd have a takeaway or go out for a drink then tumble into his bed. We had amazing sex, yes, but we also talked and held each other for hours sometimes. His encouragement of me being honest made me feel like I could tell him everything. And Jake was more vulnerable than any man had been with me before. I knew so much about him already and he didn't hold back now we were together. So, we seemed to grow closer every day.

Publication day for *He's Behind You* came around so quickly, and we were all a mixture of excitement and nerves for it. Davis threw a lavish launch party then did a couple of bookshop events. After that, we had a few days to wait to find out where it had placed on the bestseller lists.

I arranged to meet Liv for lunch on the day we were due to hear. I needed a distraction and Liv was having a day at home writing so came along to keep me company. Davis kept messaging me on the hour every hour asking if I'd heard about the charts yet so I felt like I deserved lunch out.

'I'm so nervous,' I admitted to Liv as we sat in the café's comfy chairs with our food and drink. Soft music played in the background and the midday sun streamed in through the long, glass windows that displayed my office building opposite. 'I feel like I'm even more nervous than Davis!'

Liv laughed. 'That's why you're such a good agent. Hayley probably doesn't even know what the word "nervous" means.' She sighed. 'I feel like she hasn't had much time for me lately.'

'Oh no, why?'

'She's been bringing in lots of new authors. I think she felt she had to sign new people after Jake left her...' Liv bit her lip.

'She did take the news badly,' I agreed.

When Jake told her that he and I were an official couple,

Hayley was not happy. She seemed to think we had been conspiring against her the whole time, and after she said some really nasty things about me, Jake decided to leave the agency. He'd found a new agent since and was much happier with her, along with his new publisher. So much change but it had all been positive. He said he had realised how different his view of his career had been to Hayley's so everything had worked out. I did feel a bit guilty though at seeing their professional relationship end.

'Could you talk to her about how you feel?' I asked Liv.

'Maybe. There is something I wanted to talk to you about first, though...' She squirmed uncomfortably in her chair.

'What's wrong?' I asked, worried.

'I don't know if it would be like a conflict of interest or anything, and I know Hayley would be pissed off, but I need to think about myself and what's best for my career, and I've seen what you've done for Davis,' Liv said, pausing to clear her throat. 'Is there any way you would consider becoming my agent?'

I stared at my cousin in shock. Then my phone started ringing on the table. 'It's Simon,' I said, unsure what to say or do.

'Take it; he'll have the chart!' Liv cried excitedly.

Stunned, I picked up the phone. 'Simon...' I listened and broke into a huge grin. 'I'll be back at one! No, you tell him... Okay, we'll call him together when I come back into the office. Great. Bye!' I hung up and looked at Liv. 'Number one.'

'What?'

'Davis is number one on the bestseller list!' I let out a little scream, and so did she. Liv jumped up and held out her arms so I got out of my chair and collapsed into them, returning her tight hug. 'I can't believe it.'

'I can!' she said, letting out a little sob into my hair. 'I'm so proud of you, Freya!'

I pulled back, my own eyes welling up. 'And yes. As long as Simon says it's okay, I'll be your agent! We'll make it work. I'd love to help your career in any way I can, as you've helped me! And we'll work out how to tell Hayley together.'

'Oh, thanks Freya, it's going to be so much fun! I need to tell Aiden; he's been encouraging me to ask you for weeks. He's probably sick of me talking about it,' she said as we let each other go and sat back down.

'He's not sick of you talking about anything,' I assured her. I'd seen them together and they were head over heels. I looked at the sparking diamond band on her ring finger. 'I still can't believe you two eloped, though,' I said for maybe the hundredth time. Soon after Jake and I got together, Liv and Aiden went away to Scotland for a few days. They shocked all their family and friends by coming back married. Liv said Aiden had proposed on holiday and they had been so happy and excited that when they realised how close they were to Gretna Green, they had just gone to look around but there had been a cancellation so on the spur of the moment, they'd decided to jump straight into it.

'We'll throw a huge wedding party soon,' Liv promised, her eyes sparkling. She was even more of a hopeless romantic than me and she and Aiden had definitely got carried away in Scotland. I was so happy for them. They'd been together for a while and were a perfect match. 'God, we have lots to celebrate, don't we?'

'The past few weeks have been crazy,' I said, shaking my head in wonder. So much had happened since the day Hayley had asked me to accompany Jake to New York. I had been so close to refusing to go. Thank goodness I hadn't done that.

After lunch, I gave Liv a huge hug and told her I'd speak to Simon about us signing her to the agency and then I went back into the office to find Simon so we could call Davis with the good news.

He answered instantly when we called him from Simon's desk. 'What's happening?' he said in lieu of 'hello'.

'I'm really sorry, Davis,' Simon said dully, throwing me a wink.

I let out a melodramatic sigh. 'It's such a shame...'

'How bad is it?' Davis asked tightly.

'Look, we all tried our best,' Simon said. 'We should be proud of ourselves.'

I bit my lip to stop myself from giggling.

'I'm sitting down. Just tell me. I'm a big boy. I can handle it,' Davis said.

We left a long pause. I could practically hear Davis's rapid heartbeat down the phone line. Simon and I grinned across at each other, thoroughly enjoying winding Davis up a little bit. I don't think anyone would have blamed us for having a little bit of fun with him.

'Guys!' Davis cried then, his patience evaporating.

Simon nodded then and I nodded back. We had to put him out of his misery. 'Number one,' Simon said.

'It's gone straight to the top,' I added.

There was another silence.

'I'm sorry, what?' Davis asked, his voice quiet like he was far away. He sounded dazed. I understood the feeling perfectly.

'You're number one on the *Sunday Times* Bestseller List,' I repeated.

'This isn't a wind up, is it, Freya?' Davis asked suspiciously. 'Are you getting me back for everything that happened in New York? I won't blame you if you are...'

I giggled. 'No, Davis. Your editor should be emailing you the list right now so you'll see it in black and white.'

'Your first book to go straight to the top,' Simon added. 'Well done, mate. We all worked so hard on this; it's a great result.'

Davis went quiet. I could hear a tapping sound. 'He has just emailed... Oh my God. You aren't winding me up. There I am.' Davis whistled. 'Who would have thought adding in some romance would have this effect?'

'You take back everything you said about romance books then, Davis?' I asked, raising an eyebrow.

He sighed. 'I think I might have to. Jake's just sent me his book to read and I'm kind of getting into it.'

'Wonders never cease,' I replied.

'You two make a weirdly good team,' Simon said then. 'I know this agency will be in good hands when I retire,' he added.

Pride swelled inside my chest. I knew I had a long way to go before I was anywhere close to Simon's capabilities as an agent, he had decades of experience after all, but I was so keen and enjoying everything about my new job so far.

'I wouldn't be here without either of you,' Davis said then. He coughed a little uncomfortably. 'Now, I need to go and gloat on social media!'

'There's the Davis we know and love,' Simon said as Davis hung up. 'Well done, Freya.'

'It was a team effort,' I said but I smiled, pleased. My phone lit up with a message from Jake.

> Just saw Davis say his book is number one.
> Congratulations baby!

My smile broadened. I loved how Jake supported me and my career, how we supported each other. I could never have guessed what a big part of my life he would become this year.

But like a good book, life was better when you had no idea what the next chapter might bring.

EPILOGUE
ONE YEAR LATER...

'I can't wait to tell Liv the good news,' I said down the phone. I hung up and leaned back in my desk chair, swivelling it around to look out at the London skyline. I would never get tired of the view from up here. After a year working for Simon, I now had my own office opposite his and I loved it. I had signed Liv a year ago, the first author to my own client list, and her book contract with her previous publisher had now ended so I had been working the last few weeks on finding her the best deal I could elsewhere. I had grown to know the team at Turn the Pages really well – not only did they publish Jake but also Tessa, and Liv was best friends with Stevie, who worked as a publicist there so we all had hoped they might want to take her on. And now the official offer had come in from Gita, who was hopefully going to be her editor there. I knew Liv would be over the moon. They wanted four romance novels from her and had a great plan for making her a big success.

I sent Liv a message to ask her to come into the office tomorrow as I wanted to tell her face to face and go over the deal with her, ensuring it was exactly what she wanted. Then I turned off my laptop, grabbed my things and left work. Evening had fallen over the city and it had been a long, busy day so I was looking forward to going home. I took the Tube to Knightsbridge and walked to the Edwardian apartment block that I had fallen head over heels for. I had held out for as long as possible but Jake and I had spent so much time together here that it became crazy not to officially move in. I let myself into the flat and smiled when the smell of something delicious hit me.

'I'm home!' I called out, taking off my cowboy boots and putting my bag down on the console table. I let out a breath like I always did when the city was shut out, the work day was over, and I could come into this sanctuary.

I walked into the kitchen where Jake was stirring something on the cooker. Jazz music was playing softly in the background and he was bopping along as he stirred. Two glasses of wine were poured and ready on the island, and a Jo Malone candle flickered next to them, its fruity scent mingling with the smell of what Jake was cooking.

'A woman could get used to this,' I said as I paused to take in the scene. Jake looked as edible as what he was cooking in his dark jeans and shirt, glancing over his shoulder at my entrance, a slow and sexy smile appearing on his face. He was working hard on his next novel and was letting me read each chapter as he went along, and it was clear we were inspiring the characters and the setting too – he was writing a Christmas love story set in New York, and I knew it was going to melt every romance reader's heart when it was finished. Just like he had melted mine.

'Good. I want you to get used to it,' Jake replied. He left the cooker and came over to drop me a kiss on the lips. 'Mmm, you look lovely and smell good,' he murmured, wrapping his arms around my waist and pulling me into his chest. This time, he gave me a longer kiss as I hooked my arms around his neck. 'I missed you,' he added, leaning back to look into my eyes.

'You saw me this morning,' I replied, laughing a little bit.

Jake shrugged. 'I was thinking about you a lot today; my characters kissed and I really wanted to kiss you.' He brushed his lips with mine. 'And then my mind wandered even further...'

'Oh, did it?' I said playfully back. I raised an eyebrow. 'How long until dinner is ready?'

'It can simmer for twenty minutes or so...'

'Good. So can I.' I took his hand and pulled him towards the bedroom with me.

Jake laughed. 'I love it when you're naughty.'

'No,' I said, looking over my shoulder at him as we walked into our room. 'I'm a good girl, remember?'

We stopped and Jake took my face in his hands. 'You're my good girl,' he said huskily. His lips found mine, hungry and eager to taste. Then he pulled back suddenly, leaving me breathless. He stepped back and raised an eyebrow. 'I want to see you in nothing but your ring.'

I started to pull my sundress up and over my head, but I paused and looked at him. 'Ring?' I wasn't wearing any.

'Turn around,' he said gruffly.

I slowly spun around to look at the bed and I gasped. I'd been so suddenly horny for Jake, I hadn't even looked at the bed. It was scattered with red rose petals and in the centre was a red box that made my eyes widen. 'Cartier?' I managed to gasp out. I had always dreamt of owning a piece of jewellery from there.

'You didn't remember what today was?' Jake asked, walking over to the bed to pick the box up.

'Um... no...' I said, my heart starting to pound.

Jake shook his head. 'I'm glad one of us is romantic in this relationship.'

I rolled my eyes. 'Shut up! What's today then?' I asked as Jake held the box in his hands in front of me. My mind had gone completely blank. I couldn't think about anything else but the fact that the man of my dreams was holding what looked like a ring box.

'Today is the date we went to New York together last year. What I count as our actual first meeting because before then, I don't think we really saw each other. But when you sprawled on the floor in the airport in front of me, I definitely saw you, Freya.'

I chuckled. 'Yeah, you couldn't miss me! God, I was so embarrassed that you had to help me up. And that bloody penis pencil!' I shook my head at the memory.

Jake grinned. 'I was hooked from that moment. And when you said that was our meet-cute, you were right. I fell for you in New York. I almost lost you...' He bent down on one knee and I inhaled sharply. He looked up at me, his eyes locked on mine. As always, the world faded into a blur and all I saw was him. In our bedroom. In our bubble. 'But thank God, you came back to me. I've wanted to ask you this for a while but it felt right to wait for today to mark that meet-cute. I don't want to meet anyone else. You are it for me, Freya.' He opened the box and I gasped again because inside was the biggest, brightest diamond ring. 'Am I it for you too? Will you marry me? Will you give me the happy ever after I've always wanted? Will you let me give you the happy ever after you've always wanted?'

My throat threatened to close up with the lump that had appeared in it. My eyes threatened to spill over into hot tears. But I managed to smile and nod and choke out a, 'Hell, yes!' I crouched down and pressed my lips against his. 'You are my happy ever after,' I said as Jake slid the ring onto the finger on my left hand. 'I can't believe I was thinking about sex, and you were planning this!'

Jake laughed. 'Yeah, I thought we'd have dinner and I'd tell you romantic things but no, you're insatiable and wanted me naked in here,' he replied teasingly.

I nudged him as I stared at the sparkling ring. 'I had no idea. But those rose petals look like they might be comfortable...' I said, standing up.

Jake stood up and scooped me up off the floor. I squealed as he carried me to the bed. 'Now, be a good girl and take your clothes off for me...' he said, laying me down on top of the rose buds.

I giggled. 'I love it when you tell me what to do.'

Jake leaned over me and gave me a soft kiss. 'I love you, Freya.'

I reached up to touch his cheek. 'I love you too, Jake.'

'Every love story I write from now on will be inspired by you,' he said.

'Ours is the best love story I've ever read,' I replied, pulling him down on top of me, our lips finding each other like they should have never been apart.

* * *

MORE FROM HELEN ROLFE

Another book from Victoria Walters, *The Paris Chapter*, is available to order now here:

www.mybook.to/ParisChapterBackAd

ACKNOWLEDGEMENTS

A huge thank you to my editor Emily Yau for all your brilliant insights on this book and helping me make it the best it could be, you believed in this story and in me, which was hugely appreciated! And thank you to my fabulous agent Hannah Ferguson for also being so supportive and encouraging.

I love working with the teams at Boldwood Books and Hardman and Swainson – thank you all for your support and hard work on my books. I appreciate you all so much! Special thanks also to my copy editor Emily Reader, my proofreader Jacqueline Beard MBE, and Alexandra Allden for the gorgeous cover. And Geri Allen for reading my audiobooks so brilliantly.

Finally, sending lots of love to my family and friends for all your support. And to anyone who is reading this book – I'm so grateful you picked it up to travel to New York with me. I love receiving messages or seeing your posts on social media about how much you enjoy my stories – it makes my day every time! Thank you all so much. Hopefully, I'll see you for the next one soon!

ABOUT THE AUTHOR

Victoria Walters is the author of both cosy crime and romantic novels, including the bestselling Glendale Hall series. She has been chosen for WHSmith Fresh Talent, shortlisted for two RNA novels and was picked as an Amazon Rising Star.

Sign up to Victoria Walters' mailing list for news, competitions and updates on future books.

Visit Victoria's website: www.victoria-writes.com

Follow Victoria on social media:

- instagram.com/vickyjwalters
- facebook.com/VictoriaWaltersAuthor
- x.com/Vicky_Walters
- bookbub.com/authors/victoria-walters
- youtube.com/@vickyjwalters